CHRISTMAS MIRACLES
of MARBLE COVE

THE SOUNDING JOY

* * *

LOVE'S PURE LIGHT

SUNNI JEFFERS

* * *

CAMY TANG

Guideposts

New York

Miracles of Marble Cove is a trademark of Guideposts.

Published by Guideposts Books & Inspirational Media
110 William Street
New York, NY 10038
Guideposts.org

Acknowledgments

Every attempt has been made to credit the sources of copyrighted material used in this book. If any such acknowledgment has been inadvertently omitted or miscredited, receipt of such information would be appreciated.

Cover and interior design by Müllerhaus
Cover illustration by Bob Kayganich, represented by Deborah Wolfe, Ltd.
Typeset by Aptara

Printed and bound in the United States of America
10 9 8 7 6 5 4 3 2 1

THE SOUNDING JOY

SUNNI JEFFERS

CHAPTER ONE

Margaret Hoskins stood next to her husband, Allan, on the platform at Our Savior's Sanctuary, looking out at the congregation. The scene before her would make a great Christmas painting for one of her greeting cards. This third Sunday of Advent, the church was packed with Marble Cove townspeople in a sea of reds, greens, and gold. Margaret fit right in. She had on red slacks and a red sweater with embroidered holly and berries.

She suddenly felt like a fake. She'd dressed up for the occasion, but she didn't feel festive. She'd found the Christmas outfit at the back of her closet. She'd had it forever, and she couldn't even remember the last time she'd worn it. She much preferred her usual gray skirt and sweater, but it didn't seem right to wear something so ordinary while lighting an Advent candle.

She liked the red and gold bows on the ends of the blond wooden pews, and the evergreen boughs draped from the open beams overhead. Someone had gone to a lot of work to decorate the sanctuary.

Reverend Greene's resonant voice interrupted her thoughts. "As Allan and Margaret light today's Advent candle, let us contemplate the joy that comes to us because of the birth of our Savior. In Luke 2:8–12, we read, 'And there were shepherds living out in the fields nearby, keeping watch over their flocks at night. An angel of the Lord appeared to them, and the glory of the Lord shone around them, and they were terrified. But the angel said to them, "Do not be afraid. I bring you good news that will cause great joy for all the people. Today in the town of David a Savior has been born to you; he is the Messiah, the Lord. This will be a sign to you: You will find a baby wrapped in cloths and lying in a manger.""""

All the people? Not really. Not this one anyway. Margaret leaned forward toward the ring of candles, held out the propane stick lighter, and clicked the trigger. Nothing happened. She clicked it again and again. Still no flame. She could hear giggles from the congregation. Allan reached out and she handed it to him. Embarrassment warred with frustration. Those things never worked right for her. Allan clicked, and the flame burst forth. He lit the candle.

"Thank you, Margaret and Allan." Reverend Greene smiled at them, then turned back to address the congregation.

Margaret's hands were shaking as she sat down on a pew near the front. She folded them together in her lap. Allan reached over and patted her hands. What was wrong with her? Lighting the Advent candle was not a big deal. They'd done it before, several times over the past few years, since they'd become members of Our Savior's Sanctuary. The ceremony was a tradition at the church—one that included families. And that was the rub.

Adelaide wasn't there to stand up with them. Their daughter had lit the candle the last time they were part of the Advent ceremony. Adelaide was part of so many things. Decorating the house and the tree. Baking, mostly with Allan. They were the bakers in the family, and oh, the laughter and the sweet smells that came from the kitchen when they started making holiday cookies and Allan's favorite date bread. And Adelaide's favorite no-bake peanut butter cookies and cut-out sugar cookies that she helped decorate. This year, Margaret would have to be the one to get everything ready for Christmas.

Oh, how she missed Adelaide. Ever since their daughter had moved into the group home with several other young women with Down syndrome, Margaret felt like part of her life, her joy, was missing. Her friend Diane understood. She called it empty-nest syndrome. That certainly described their home. Their nest without their sweet, bubbly, loving daughter was empty indeed. Margaret didn't feel like decorating at home. Besides, she was extra busy at her Shearwater Gallery, and Allan was so busy with Christmas orders for his handmade wood furniture that there wasn't time to decorate or bake at home. Margaret didn't even miss it. Except at night, when they watched television in the evening and all the ads had Christmas songs and family holiday scenes.

Their Christmas tree was usually up by now, but perhaps they could wait and decorate it Christmas Eve when Adelaide came home. Maybe she would even come home on the Sunday before Christmas. Margaret would suggest it the next time Adelaide called. She could call Adelaide, but she was doing her best to let her daughter be independent. That took effort and restraint.

Then there was her friend Diane and her new project. Diane Spencer, best of friends and author extraordinaire, had convinced her friends to help her resurrect the traditional Marble Cove living Nativity. And it was Margaret's own fault. She had opened her big mouth and told Diane about the old custom that had ended years ago when Emma Nicol died.

In a week, the churches in town would put on the living Nativity, and they had no set. When the old costumes refused to turn up, Shelley had managed to get help making new ones from her family, including her mother-in-law, Frances.

But no one knew where the old set pieces were, and guess who had volunteered to be in charge of them? Or rather, she'd *been* volunteered. None other than yours truly. So now she had to come up with something new. But what? A sketched background, perhaps. At this late date, it would have to be simple.

*   *   *

After church, as Margaret got out of the car at home, Diane flagged her down from next door.

"Margaret, I've got good news!"

It was freezing cold, with a nippy north wind blowing in off the ocean, cutting through her clothes. She just wanted to get inside and warm up, but Diane was already halfway between their two yards. Margaret pulled the hood of her coat up over her short gray hair.

"Would you like to come inside? It's cold out here," Margaret said.

"No—we need to go out! We found the Nativity set pieces! Can you come now? Can we take your van? We can go get them."

"That's wonderful! Now I won't have to twist Allan's arm to make new ones." Allan had already gone into the house. "Where are they?"

"They're out in Arvid Pierson's shed. The couple who bought his place were at church this morning, and the wife told me about them. They found them while they were cleaning out the shed. She said they're life-size, so they're probably part of a living Nativity scene."

"Wonderful. I'll get Allan. He'll want something to eat first, but then we can go."

"All right. I need to change out of my church clothes, and I want to let Shelley and Beverly know too. So let's say in a half hour?"

"Sounds good. I'll see you then."

Margaret started to climb the steps to the front door. Something white and square leaned askew against the bottom step, as if it had blown there. She bent down and picked it up, thinking it was trash. It appeared to be a handmade envelope, worn and smudged. It felt thick and stiff. She turned it over. In neat but faded blue ink, it was addressed to Mr. and Mrs. Hoskins, and had their address.

She carried it inside, hung up her coat, and went into the kitchen, where Allan was taking food out of the refrigerator. He looked up.

"What do you have there? A Christmas card?"

"I don't know. I found it on the steps." She turned it over and held it up so he could see it. "It's addressed to us. If there was a return address, it's come off."

Allan set cold cuts on the counter, next to a loaf of bread. "Well, open it."

She laughed. "I guess that's the best way to find out who it's from." She used a kitchen knife to slit open the top and pulled out a square of white construction paper. A star made of Popsicle sticks was glued to the front, and on it were bright-colored buttons. "JOy" was written on the card in green crayon. On the back, also in green crayon, it said "ThANK yOu fOr COminG." The formative lettering revealed the untrained hand of a child. Beneath the lettering was a green smudge. A signature? Hard to tell. It was illegible.

She held it out to Allan. "I can't imagine who sent this. It looks like something Adelaide might have made when she was younger, but she does her letters better than this. And the address was written by an adult."

Allan glanced at the card. "I have no idea," he said. "I suppose it could be from Adelaide. Perhaps Elsa Kling at Adelaide's group home helped the girls make Christmas cards."

"Maybe. I'll have to ask Adelaide about it. I wish she were here."

"I know. So do I. I don't feel like baking Christmas cookies without her help. But I'm too busy to bake, so I suppose it's for the best."

"I don't need to eat Christmas cookies," Margaret said. "We can get our sweets from the Cove. I like the idea of supporting our local coffee shop—well, really supporting Shelley. Her cookies are the best. Not that yours aren't," she hastened to add.

Allan's eyebrows went up, but his eyes twinkled. He understood. Allan was a wonderful baker. But neither of them needed the extra sugar these days. Since their young neighbor Shelley Bauer had become a professional baker, Margaret indulged more often than she should anyway. The Cove was right next door to her gallery, so it was too easy to run over for a treat.

"Next time you're in the Cove, get a dozen to bring home." He finished constructing the sandwiches and put them on plates.

"I will. I was just talking to Diane before I came in. She found the living Nativity set. It's out at the old Pierson place. Can we take the van and go get it after lunch?"

Allan set the plates on the table. "I'd hoped to work on my furniture orders all afternoon, but we can take the time. If we don't have to cut out new pieces, it will save a lot of time in the long run. Better take some work gloves. Those pieces have been stored for quite a few years, so they'll be dusty. And take a whisk broom. I hope they aren't too deteriorated."

"Good idea. I hope they're usable." They sat down to eat, and Allan offered thanks to the Lord.

Margaret propped the handmade card against the napkin holder on the table. "A lot of attention went into that star. The buttons are so colorful and placed evenly around the star. I wonder who made it."

"I can't imagine." Allan took a bite of his sandwich.

"What if it was meant for someone else? A teacher or a parent?"

"It has our name and address on the envelope."

"Yes. Very curious. And how did it get on our step? Maybe it's from Shelley's kids. Aiden might have made it at school. I'll have to ask her."

A short time later, Allan, Margaret, and Diane got out of the van at the old Pierson farm. The old farmhouse had a new coat of yellow paint and new windows with dark-green trim. Colored Christmas lights framed the roof and porch, giving the house a cheerful look. A tall blond man came out to greet them. After introductions, Chuck Johnston, the new owner of the Pierson farm, led them to a large wooden shed that leaned slightly to the left. The oversize door scraped against the ground as he opened it. He pulled a string overhead, and a lightbulb flicked on, barely illuminating the room.

"This shed was filled with old junk," Chuck said. "We've cleared out about half of it. I hauled several loads of old plywood to the dump, and would have removed these pieces too, but Cathy, my wife, thought they looked like some kind of artwork. When she heard you were looking for set pieces for a living Nativity, she thought these might be the ones. If they're what you're looking for, you're welcome to take them."

"Thank you," Diane said.

Margaret squinted, trying to make out the painting on a large piece of wood. Chuck turned on a flashlight and shone it on the wood. The colors were faint and obscured by dirt, but it looked like a wall with a cow painted on it. "This might be the back of the stable," Margaret said.

"There are more in back of it, but in shapes," Chuck said. "Allan, would you help me move this out of the way?" He handed Diane the flashlight.

Diane held the flashlight while the two men pulled the plywood sheet out of the way, revealing a stack of shapes leaning against the wall. Diane shone the light on them. "Look, Margaret. I think that's a sheep," she said, excitement in her voice.

"Yes, and up there's a camel, if I'm not mistaken."

"Great! I'm still hoping to get some live animals. Leo thinks he has some leads, but nothing has panned out yet," Diane said. Leo was the local veterinarian, and Diane's close friend. If he couldn't get animals for the Nativity, no one could.

Margaret pulled out the lamb. Another lamb stood behind it, and a goat. The cutouts of animals got larger. An ox. A camel. "This is great. I can refresh the paint on these." She couldn't tell what condition they were in, but the shapes looked good. "I wonder how they ended up here."

"Mrs. Peabody told me that Delia Pierson and Emma Nicol were good friends," Diane said. "They were both active with the historical society. Emma didn't have much room at her place for storage, so maybe

Delia offered to keep them here. Since they've all passed away, we'll never know for sure, but thank goodness we found them!"

"Let's put the big ones in first," Allan said, grabbing hold of a full-sized piece of plywood. Chuck picked up the other end. It was so grimy that Margaret couldn't make out the scene on it, but there was something painted beneath the dirt.

Allan and Chuck carried the largest pieces out to the van, while Margaret and Diane carried the smaller animals. The wood was damp, crumbly along the edges, and very heavy. Margaret brushed off cobwebs and dead bugs before they picked them up. As they loaded the animals into the van, the camel's head broke off.

"Oh no! We need that camel," Diane said.

"Maybe we can fix it," Margaret said. She began to have doubts about their great find, but she didn't want to dampen Diane's enthusiasm, so she kept her thoughts to herself. She'd examine the rest of them later.

"Let's take them to the gallery. I can put them in the back, where I can work on them," Margaret said as they drove out of the farmyard.

"I hope you can use them," Allan said. "The wood is damp and soft."

"I noticed that too," Diane said. "Do you think they'll dry out in time?"

"I hope so," Margaret said, giving her friend a smile, but not at all sure they were any better off than before they found the old set pieces. "I'll turn up the heat at the gallery overnight to dry them out faster. We might have to reinforce some of the pieces, but I'm sure it will be all right. Are we still meeting for coffee in the morning?"

"Yes, we'll meet at the Cove. Beverly and Shelley will be there. We need to compare notes on the living Nativity. We're nearly down to the wire."

"Honestly, Diane, I don't know how you're going to pull this off. I'm glad you're the one in charge, not me!"

Diane chuckled, but then her brows furrowed. "There are a lot more problems than I anticipated, but I'm not doing it alone. And look at the progress we've made! We will get it done. We must. Thanks to Beverly's promotions, the townspeople are looking forward to it now. I'd hate to disappoint them." Beverly was the town's mayor, but she also ran a successful consulting business.

Margaret just nodded. What could she say? She didn't want to discourage Diane or dash her hopes, but she had doubts. She hoped, for her friend's sake, and for the town, that they could resurrect this wonderful old tradition. But how in the world was she going to be able to fulfill her part? The set pieces didn't look promising—they needed a lot of work.

And worse yet, she had just one week to refurbish them.

CHAPTER TWO

After they had unloaded the set pieces and Allan had returned home, Margaret inspected the wood carefully. They'd leaned the various plywood pieces against the walls in the gallery's work area. With all the lights turned on, she was finally able to get a good look at them, and it wasn't encouraging. The wood was damp and caked with dirt from being stored in the old shed. Much of the paint had worn off or faded. A cow's leg had broken off. Half of a lamb's head was missing.

Even the manger was broken. She picked up the pieces, thinking she could use glue and screws to fix it, but the wood crumbled in her hand. Maybe Allan could make a new one, but he was so busy with Christmas orders for furniture, she hated to even ask him.

Margaret set a couple of fans in the workroom. She turned up the thermostat for the gallery. She couldn't do anything to the pieces until they dried out. She hated leaving the heat turned up all night, but she didn't have any other option. She just hoped one night would do it. She made a list of the various paint colors she would need to refurbish the set pieces, then shut off the lights and locked up before the walk home.

Allan was sanding a piece of maple when she entered his workroom. A fine cloud of sawdust hung in the air and covered every surface. She sneezed, and he looked up. He shut off the sander, lowered his dust mask, and lifted his safety goggles. She went to stand beside him and looked down at the satin-smooth tabletop. The grain had the lovely swirl pattern of cross-cut wood. "That's a beautiful piece."

"Thank you. I love the way the grain is showing. So how are the Nativity pieces?"

"Not very good, I'm afraid. I hope they look better when they dry out. Unfortunately the wood has completely rotted on the manger and it can't be fixed. Is there a chance you could make a manger for the set?"

"By next weekend?" His mouth scrunched into a frown. He looked around the workroom. "I have enough scrap lumber. It'll have to be rough. I won't have time to finish it properly."

"It needs to be rough. The other pieces will look rough at best."

"All right, I'll see what I can do."

"Thank you, Allan." She leaned over to kiss his cheek, but reached up and dusted off the fine grit on his skin first. Then she gave him a light kiss.

"Don't thank me until you see if I can do it. I've got a stack of orders yet to get ready before Christmas."

"I know. Thank goodness I've gotten my special orders finished. All right then, I'll get out of here so you can get back to work."

The sander buzzed to life before she had closed the shop door. She felt bad asking him to take on one more project before Christmas. His Scandinavian modern furniture pieces had become so popular that he had orders to ship out of state, and they needed to go out in the next two days to arrive before Christmas.

Margaret changed out of her grubby work clothes and put on comfortable pants and a warm sweater. She made a cup of tea, then looked around for a sweet treat. Allan and Adelaide usually turned the kitchen into a gourmet bake shop in the weeks before Christmas, but Adelaide wasn't at home and Allan didn't have time, so there weren't any cookbooks, cookie cutters, or baking ingredients sitting out, and the spicy sweet scents of vanilla and gingerbread were missing. No doubt Allan felt Adelaide's absence as much as she did. The holidays weren't fun without their daughter laughing and giggling and begging them to decorate or make baked goods.

Margaret opened a fruitcake tin that they'd received as a gift, and cut off a slice. She slathered on butter, then took her tea and fruitcake into the living room. A stack of hand-painted Christmas cards sat on the table next to the couch. She liked to send out a few original cards to friends and family. Good thing she'd painted too many last year. In truth, she had no enthusiasm for filling out and mailing cards this year.

She sighed and picked up her lap desk. She took a bite of fruitcake and a sip of tea, then picked up a card and a pen.

Dear Sam and June, she wrote. They were friends from years ago who had moved out of state. Now what to write? Something cheery. She couldn't think of anything. *Hope you are well. Merry Christmas and happy New Year. Fondly, Allan and Margaret.*

She stuffed the card into an envelope and addressed it, then picked up another. She simply signed their names on the rest of the cards. She hated being so impersonal, but she couldn't think of a thing to say.

The phone rang. Adelaide's name appeared on the ID. Margaret grabbed it.

"Hello, sweetheart." Her heart did a little dance in anticipation, as if she hadn't heard from her daughter in a month. It had been almost a week, which was unusual for Adelaide.

"Hi, Mom. I had to go to a new Sunday school class today, because they didn't need me in the nursery. It made me sad. I miss the children."

"I'm sorry, Adelaide. I know how you love working with the children. Did you enjoy the Sunday school class?"

"It was okay. I know Mrs. Burnett, the teacher, and my friends go to her class too."

"That's nice. Sometimes it's good to be with people your own age."

"Yes, it was all right. But I told her I want to go back to the nursery next week."

"Next week?" Margaret's heart fell. "But that's Christmas Sunday. We were looking forward to seeing you."

"Oh, that's right. I forgot. I can't do the nursery next week. Mom, guess what? I'm going to Cassie's house in Boston for Christmas! The other girls too. We're going to see *The Nutcracker*. It's a ballet."

"Boston! Oh no! Adelaide, we always spend Christmas together. It won't be Christmas without you here." Margaret's eyes filled with tears. What would they do without their daughter home with them? It was unthinkable.

"But Mom, I thought you'd be happy. You know I love dancing. And they're going to take us ice-skating. Don't you want me to have fun?"

"Of course I want you to have fun. It's just . . . just that I miss you so much. We miss you."

"I miss you too, but I can see you anytime."

Margaret could hear a note of petulance in Adelaide's voice. Her sweet, usually cheerful daughter wanted her mother to be excited about her plans, but how could she? It had been hard enough for her and Allan to let their daughter move into the group home with other young Down syndrome women. She had to admit Adelaide had bloomed with taking college classes and becoming independent. She wanted Adelaide to have her own life and to succeed, but her abilities and the options opening to her had taken them by surprise. Margaret had expected Adelaide to live with them forever. Now they wouldn't even have her home for Christmas. Maybe they would just skip Christmas this year.

After she hung up, Margaret noticed the card with the Popsicle stick star propped up on the mantel where she'd placed it. She'd forgotten to ask Adelaide if she'd made it. Then she realized that was unlikely. Adelaide was too busy with her schooling and her new social life and friends to make the card.

*   *   *

Margaret eyed the pastries at the Cove Monday morning. Shelley Bauer had outdone herself with an amazing array of holiday goodies. Shelley was a petite young woman who lived across the street from Margaret and had small children. She'd begun her passion for baking out of her home, which had evolved into a busy bakery service. She'd been supplying the Cove coffee shop for a couple of years, and now had the opportunity to buy the business when Rusty, the owner, retired after the first of the year. Shelley was spending more and more of her time working in the Cove kitchen and managing it for Rusty on his days off.

"What do you recommend, Brenna?" Margaret asked the pretty raven-haired twenty-something woman behind the counter. "I can't decide between the Christmas scones, the eggnog buns, or the gingerbread cookies."

"They-ah all good, you know." Brenna's charming Maine accent, smile, and cheerfulness were infectious. She was one of the reasons the Cove was so popular. A little cheer from her, plus the good coffee and sweets, got the day off to a positive start. Today, Margaret needed an extra dose of cheer and positivity. "I love the scones. They have candied walnuts and cherries, with eggnog frosting."

"I had a Christmas scone yesterday," Diane said, coming up behind Margaret. "They're delicious."

"All right, I'll have one of those," Margaret said. She put on a smile for Brenna and her friend. "And I'll take a gingerbread cookie for later." She paid for her coffee and sweets and stepped aside for Diane. Beverly joined them in line.

While they ordered, Margaret carried her coffee and goodies to their usual table back against the wall. Shelley came out of the kitchen wearing an apron with gingerbread men and candy canes all over it.

"You look festive," Beverly said as they all sat down.

"I love Christmas." Shelley said. Their petite friend looked like one of Santa's elves, with a twinkle in her blue eyes and a dusting of flour on her nose. "It gives me a chance to make all kinds of fabulous recipes and to decorate." Her smile had joy written all over it, Margaret thought. But she had little ones at home, plus her dream of her own bakery was coming to life. And a stressful and contentious surprise visit from her divorced parents and their spouses had ended on a peaceful and happy note for her. No wonder she was joyous.

"And we love all of your Christmas goodies," Beverly said.

"I have your cookie order ready, so be sure you get them to take with you," Shelley told Beverly.

"Wonderful." She turned to the others. "I'm going to have cookies and coffee set out at town hall for anyone who comes in this week."

"Then I may have to visit town hall," Diane said with a grin. "Now we need to get down to business. Thanks to Shelley, we're set for costumes. We have most of our cast lined up, except—Beverly, would you be a wise man? You'd be perfect for the part."

"Me?" Beverly's eyes widened in surprise. "But the wise men were . . . *men*. I mean, traditionally . . ."

"I think you'd be perfect," Shelley said, her admiration of their friend clear. "You'd have on a head cover, so no one would know."

"I need someone regal," Diane said. "You have the posture and height we need. Please?"

"I agree," Margaret said. "You'd be great for the part."

"Well, all right. If you think so."

"Great!" Diane made a note on her schedule. "And Rita Candleford agreed to play the angel! I'm working on getting the other parts cast. Margaret and Allan and I picked up the set pieces yesterday. How are they looking, Margaret?"

"I don't know. I checked them this morning, and a couple of the smaller ones have dried out, but the big ones are still damp. The main backdrop has mold growing on it. I'll try to scrape it down and hope it dries out."

"I hope you can make it work," Beverly said. "It won't be much of a Nativity scene without the set."

"I'll do my best." Margaret mentally crossed her fingers. Based on her first impression of the old sets, she doubted her best would be enough.

"You'll do great. You're a miracle worker with a paint brush. Give them a fresh coat of paint, and they'll be fine. It will be dark at the Nativity, and the lights focused on the players, so the set pieces don't have to be perfect." Beverly's smile was filled with encouragement, but Margaret couldn't do shoddy work. No set at all would be better than a bad set.

As they gathered up their coats and purses to leave, Margaret thought about the handmade card on her mantel.

"Shelley, I received a darling handmade Christmas card with a Popsicle stick star on it. Did your children make it?"

"No. Aiden made a handprint card for me at school, but nothing with Popsicle sticks. Sounds like a cool idea though. Why?"

"I found a card on my front steps Sunday when I got home from church. It looked like it had blown there, but it was addressed to Allan and me. There was no return address and I can't read the signature, which is in crayon. It looks like the work of a child, except for the address."

"Could Adelaide have made it and left it there?" Shelley asked.

"I considered that, but it isn't like her. She is too forthright about the things she does. And she has been very busy with school and her friends. Besides, she is very careful with her writing." Margaret pictured the crayon lettering in her mind. "No, I don't think it was Adelaide."

"Margaret, that is such a coincidence," Diane said. "It's like the anonymous ornament I got."

"You're right. Isn't that strange?"

"And don't forget *my* little wingless angel," Shelley said.

"True! How could I forget? It is odd that we've each received something in an unexplainable way."

"I haven't gotten anything," Beverly said. She sounded slightly envious.

"As Diane said, these might be coincidences," Margaret said. "This card is handmade, with a Popsicle stick star and bright-colored buttons glued to it. The word *joy* is written on it in crayon. That's something I certainly haven't felt lately." Margaret hadn't meant to blurt that out. It was the first time she had admitted her lack of Christmas spirit. Saying it out loud made her feel guilty and sad.

Diane put an arm around her shoulders. "I remember my first Christmas without my kids. All the traditions and preparations leading up to Christmas are part of what makes Christmas so special. I remember that it seemed like everyone around me was doing Christmas activities with their children, and I felt alone. Maybe being part of the living Nativity will help. Adelaide will be home for Christmas Day, won't she?"

A hard fist grabbed Margaret's heart. "No, she won't." The words stuck in her throat. "She's going to Boston with her friends from the group home."

"Oh no, Margaret!" Shelley cried, concern on her face. "No wonder you're depressed. I can't imagine Christmas without my kids."

Beverly reached over and put her hand on Margaret's arm. "I'm so sorry, Margaret."

"That's a blow. I didn't know," Diane said, her eyes narrowed with concern.

Her friends were so sympathetic that Margaret had to choke back tears. "We'll live through it." She forced a smile for her friends. "Honestly, we're both so busy that the time will go fast." She heaved a sigh. "We'll be fine. And it's a great opportunity for Adelaide. They are going to *The Nutcracker* ballet."

"The ballet in Boston is wonderful," Beverly said. "Mother and I went there one year. Adelaide will love it."

"Boston at Christmas would be fun to see," Shelley said.

"It's amazing how Adelaide has blossomed in the last couple of years," Diane said. "She's become a very independent adult. I know you are proud of her."

"Yes, and I am excited for her," Margaret said. She wanted to mean it—ought to mean it—but she didn't. She didn't want to dampen her friends' enjoyment of the holidays, but her situation was different. Other parents expected their children to grow up and become independent. But neither she nor Allan had dreamed Adelaide would be able to become as independent as she had. They had believed their daughter would live with them all her life. Besides, Adelaide had just recently moved out, and they'd expected her to join them for Christmas. The wound of separation was fresh and painful.

Still, no need to burden her friends with such things. She might not feel joy, but she could pretend, for their sakes.

*   *   *

Twenty minutes later, as Margaret stood in front of the set pieces leaning against her workroom walls, she pursed her lips together and wondered how she could salvage the Nativity animals and why she'd been crazy enough to let Diane talk her into this project in the first place. Miracle worker indeed! Michelangelo himself couldn't resurrect these decrepit plywood pieces.

A glance at the clock told her it was 9 a.m. She unlocked the front door of the Shearwater Gallery, turned over the Open sign, and switched on the sound system. Christmas music filled the air. She didn't expect many customers this early on a Monday morning, even though it was the week before Christmas. A quiet morning would be a blessing today.

The bell on the front door chimed, and Margaret peeked out front. Bernadette Lassiter sailed into the store as if swept in on a stiff breeze, her bright red, purple, green, and yellow cape flowing around her, and her long curly hair covering her face. She shook her head to throw it back. Her hands were full, as she carried a bright-green basket.

"Good morning!" she called out.

"Boy, am I glad to see you! I'm back here in the back." Without Adelaide to help in the gallery, she'd called on Bernadette, who displayed her jewelry in the gallery.

Bernadette set the flat, square basket on the workroom table. "I brought some new jewelry."

"Good. We've sold most of your pieces."

"I thought they'd sell fast. I'm doing well online too. I'll arrange these around the basket with some white velvet." She held up a wire-wrapped fused glass star pendant that shimmered with gold, blue, and purple, with earrings to match.

"Those are beautiful," Margaret said, and she meant it. She wasn't always crazy about Bernadette's jewelry, but they were beautifully made and unique. Her work sold well.

Bernadette beamed. "Thanks. It's called dichroic glass. I'm having fun experimenting with different glass fragments and metal shavings to make fused glass pendants and forms. I can stay until two to help out." Bernadette then looked around. "What are those?"

"They are set pieces for the living Nativity that we're putting on next weekend. I have to clean them up and repaint them."

"Looks like it'd be easier to throw them away and make new ones."

"You're probably right, but there isn't enough time or money."

"I'll let you get to it then. I'll handle the front."

"I really appreciate your help."

"Oh, that's all right. I needed an excuse to get out of the house. Mother is decorating. She wants things a certain way, and she asks me to help, but I can't do anything right. It's better if I'm not there. Besides, I get cabin fever, especially during the holidays, when everyone is out shopping and having fun."

"I know how you feel. All the things that lead up to Christmas are so much fun. Without Adelaide at home, I'm missing that this year too."

"Yeah, I bet. She's always happy, and you get along so well. I wish my mom and I could have fun together, but, well, I don't know if that'll ever happen." Bernadette rolled her eyes. "Oh well. Such is life, I guess." The bells on the front door jingled. "I'll get that so you can get to work." Bernadette went out into the gallery.

Bernadette and her mother were such different personalities. It was a shame they couldn't get past their differences and just enjoy each other. It wasn't just a case of different styles and likes. Bernadette was a free spirit. She would have fit right in with the hippies in the sixties, and her mother did not approve of her likes, her friends, her styles, or her activities.

Margaret turned on the gallery's sound system as she did every morning. The lilting melody of "Christmastime Is Here," from *A Charlie Brown Christmas*, came over the speakers.

Good music to work to. She rolled up the sleeves of her painting smock, put on a dust mask, and picked up a stiff brush. First task—get rid of the layers of dirt and mold that had accumulated over the years. The plywood animals looked drab and pathetic—certainly not part of any celebration. Kind of the way she felt.

Hours later, chips of wood flew as Margaret brushed and scraped the surface of the stable backdrop in rhythm to the jazzy holiday music piped through the gallery's sound system, and the jingling of the front door bells. The gallery was busier than she'd expected. She was grateful for Bernadette's help. Without it, she'd never be able to repair the Nativity set. However, it wasn't going well. One of the lambs had crumbled under her hands as she cleaned it. The backdrop was splintering.

"Margaret, I have to leave now," Bernadette said, breaking through her concentration. She wrapped her cape around her shoulders and slung one end across her chest and over the other shoulder. "It's quiet right now, but it's been busy. I sold one of Allan's tables and a painting of the wharf in the snow. Oh, and several pieces of my jewelry."

"Goodness, is it that late already?" Margaret took off her smock. "Thank you so much for helping. I didn't expect to be that busy today."

Bernadette laughed, a cheery sound. "It's Christmas." She picked up her colorful hand-woven tote bag. She looked around at the set pieces and the dust and wood chips covering the floor and every surface in the workroom. "I can come in for several hours tomorrow if you want."

"That would be wonderful. I don't know how I'm going to get these done in time."

Bernadette shook her head, her long, curly hair cascading around her shoulders. "I don't see how either. Well, Merry Christmas." With that, she sailed out the back door.

CHAPTER THREE

Merry Christmas indeed," Margaret muttered after the door closed behind Bernadette.

Her workroom was a mess. She cleaned up a bit and made a cup of tea. Her stomach rumbled, reminding her she hadn't eaten since the scone she'd had at the Cove early that morning. She took a bite of the gingerbread cookie she'd bought. The bell jingled as someone entered the gallery. She swallowed the bite, barely tasting it, which was a shame. Shelley's cookies were always delicious, but today it tasted like the old wood dust that covered everything. Including her hair. She put the half-eaten cookie back in its plastic bag, then shook her head, ruffling her hair with her hands to get rid of the dust.

"Hello?" a deep voice called from the gallery.

Margaret smoothed her hair and went out front. "Good afternoon." She smiled up at the tall man. He wore a charcoal-gray, full-length coat that looked like cashmere wool, dress slacks, and black dress shoes. His black shiny hair and dark complexion and eyes made him an imposing figure. She'd never seen him before and wondered what brought him to Marble Cove. "May I help you?"

He smiled, showing very white, slightly crooked teeth. "You have a nice gallery. Are you the artist?"

"I am. Many of the paintings are mine, but there are several other artists on display too. Are you looking for something specific?"

"Yes. My wife loves lighthouses. I thought I might find something here, since you have an old lighthouse."

"I have one lighthouse painting left. They sell well this time of year."

She led him around to the other side of the gallery. One small oil painting of the Orlean Point Light rested on a small easel on one of Allan's tables. A soft coral sky at twilight outlined the white tower, and the intense light shone a path out on the darkened sea. Though small, the painting held a lot of detail. A small brass plate at the bottom of the frame held one word.

"Hope," he said. "It's well named."

"Thank you."

"But I was thinking of something larger."

"I'm sorry. I do take commissions, but it would be February before I could deliver a painting. I have limited edition and giclée prints, if you'd like to see them."

"No, thank you. I need something for Christmas, and I want an original."

"I'm very sorry. I can't help you. My lighthouses are my most popular paintings."

"I can see why." He gave her a polite smile. "I shouldn't have waited until the last minute. I do that too often these days." He ran his hand along the top of the small table that held the painting. "Nice table. Is it for sale?"

"Yes. All of the tables and furniture are for sale. My husband makes them."

He nodded and glanced around. "How about toys? Is there a toy store in town? I'm looking for an Erector Set."

"There's the Crow's Nest bookstore. She carries a few toys. You might also find something at the Cannery. It has some eclectic shops." She started to mention the Walmart over by Tussacusset, but he didn't look like he shopped at discount stores, and she liked to support her fellow Marble Cove business owners.

"I've been to the Cannery. I saw your magnificent mural of the lighthouse there, and I was hoping you'd have a painting like that in here. I'll check out the bookstore. Could you recommend a place to stay in town?"

Margaret was pleased by his compliment. The large mural on one wall of the converted old cannery showed the Orlean Point Light in all its glory and splendor, shining its beacon of light out through a dark sky with clouds rolling in, and a misty layer of fog over a rough, wild sea, to a clipper ship in distress. She and Bernadette had worked together to create the mural, and they had become friends, in spite of their differences.

Margaret had poured her talent and emotions into the project. The lighthouse held a personal, special place in her heart. Many others felt the same way, making it a very popular and loved landmark. She could believe this man wanted to see the lighthouse, but she couldn't help wondering why he wanted to stay.

"Well, I can recommend the Landmark Inn up the hill. It's very nice and has a good restaurant. Do you have friends here, or business in the area?" she asked.

"No. Just passing through. I've never been to this part of the coast. Your lobster trap Christmas tree caught my eye. Very unique," he said, smiling.

"Yes, it's a long-standing tradition here. It draws a lot of visitors this time of year."

"I can see why. Thank you for the recommendation. I'll go find the Landmark. And you are"—he peered down at the painting—"Margaret Hoskins?"

"Yes."

"Shane Smith," he said, holding out his hand. Margaret accepted his handshake. He had a firm yet gentle grip. "I'll be back. I'm interested in your husband's tables. And maybe I'll find a painting I like."

Margaret watched him leave. Confident. Obviously well enough off to dress nicely and to appreciate and even purchase original art. But he had an air of mystery about him. What in the world would attract such a man, traveling alone, to come to Marble Cove, and to even stay overnight in the middle of the winter?

*   *   *

Margaret had rubber gloves on and was scraping splattered dirt off the ox when her cell phone rang. She ignored it for several rings, then went to the coffee stand to see who was calling. Adelaide.

She grabbed the phone and tried to answer, but the ringing stopped. She removed her gloves and tapped in Adelaide's number.

"Mom? Oh, good. I was afraid I wouldn't get you. I need some money."

"What's wrong, honey?"

"Wrong? Nothing is wrong, Mom. I have to buy a dress and new shoes to wear to *The Nutcracker*. Cassie says we have to dress up to go to the theater. She looked in my closet and says I don't have anything nice enough."

Margaret took a deep breath. "What about the dress we bought you last spring for Easter?" It was a lovely dress. Margaret wondered just how dressy Cassie wanted Adelaide to look. The theater was in Boston. Margaret knew people dressed up to go, but was it really necessary? She hated to spend money on a dress Adelaide would never wear again.

"No, Mom. I have to look nice. Cassie showed me pictures of what she and her mother wore last year. They had on long dresses and fur coats. Not real fur, 'cause no one wears those. She said it was fake fur."

Margaret had been to the theater, and knew some people dressed in formal clothing, but she also knew a simple outfit was acceptable. But she didn't want to argue with Adelaide or disappoint her either. "How much money do you need?"

"Cassie's mother said I can find something on sale for a hundred dollars. And I need shoes too."

That could be another hundred, Margaret thought. But she could take Adelaide to Augusta to find something at reasonable prices. She could ask Beverly. She'd know where to shop since she used to live there and moved in elite circles. But when could she take time to go? She'd just have to make time. After all, this was her daughter, who rarely asked for anything. "I can come get you this evening or tomorrow afternoon and we can go to Augusta to go shopping."

"No, Mom. I'm going to go with Cassie and her friend. She knows what to buy. You don't know what I need."

Adelaide's words stabbed into Margaret like a dagger. She couldn't know how her simple statement hurt. Margaret swallowed a retort. It was true—she dressed in casual, practical clothing. She didn't spend a lot of money on clothing and accessories, and she'd never dressed Adelaide in fancy, frilly dresses. They didn't live that kind of lifestyle, and Margaret considered it unnecessary and frivolous. But this was special. Adelaide had been invited to go to the big city, wear a formal outfit, go to the theater, and experience a fairy-tale type of holiday. How could she deny her daughter that opportunity?

"I will put money into your bank account, so you can use your debit card. Adelaide, you have a limit. I'll put one hundred and fifty dollars in your account, so you'll have to find everything you need within that amount. Can you do that?"

"Yes, Mom. Mrs. Kling is going to take us all shopping tomorrow. She'll help me if I need help."

Margaret was relieved that Elsa Kling, who operated the group home where Adelaide and Cassie and a few other young women with Down syndrome lived, was taking them shopping. Elsa was practical and really cared about her charges. She would keep Adelaide from going overboard.

"Adelaide, I have a lovely faux-fur jacket that belonged to my mother. I'd love to have you wear it to see *The Nutcracker*. When do you leave to go to Cassie's home?"

"We go on Thursday night. Cassie's parents are coming to get us. It's going to be so fun!"

"Can you come by the house, or I can take it to the gallery, so you can pick it up?"

"I don't know. Let me ask."

Margaret could hear Adelaide talking to someone in the background. Then she came back on the phone.

"I can come get it at four o'clock Thursday at the gallery."

"Oh, good. I want to send your Christmas present with you too." She didn't have a gift for Adelaide yet—hadn't thought of what to get her—but Bernadette's jewelry popped into her mind. Adelaide would love it. "Maybe your father can be there too, so you can say good-bye to him."

"Oh." There was a long pause. Margaret wondered if she had hung up. "Mom, I love you. Tell Daddy I love him too."

"I will. We love you, Adelaide. We'll see you Thursday afternoon."

"Bye." The phone went dead.

With a sigh, Margaret ended the call. How did it all happen so fast? Adelaide had become a young woman who no longer needed her parents.

Once upon a time, people with Down syndrome lived at home with their parents their entire lives and rarely lived past their teenage years. But Adelaide was healthy and independent, able to attend college and live away from home. She still needed a caretaker, like Elsa Kling, but Adelaide and her friends were able to make their own decisions and have meaningful jobs. Someday, when her schooling was completed, Adelaide would work in the child care field and contribute to the love and care of other children. What a blessing for her and for those children. Shelley's children adored Adelaide.

And what a hole that left in Margaret's life. She knew it was a natural part of life. Children grew up and left home every day. She would adjust, but she didn't like it one bit.

Chapter Four

As she dished Crock-Pot chicken stew into bowls, Margaret thought how blessed she was to have a husband who loved to cook. Even though he was busy with his own woodworking business, he did most of their cooking, and his creations were always good. She'd made cornbread from a mix to round out their dinner.

As she set the bowls on the table, Allan washed up and joined her. He asked a blessing on their meal and asked the Lord to watch over Adelaide, finishing with a heartfelt *amen*.

"Adelaide called this afternoon," Margaret said before she took a bite. "She needed money to buy a new dress."

"Oh? Ran out of her allowance? Do we need to increase it? I have no idea how much it costs a young person to live these days."

"She hasn't asked before. We cover her room and board and schooling, plus her allowance, so she seems to have enough. But this is a special occasion. She needs a formal dress and shoes for *The Nutcracker* ballet."

Allan took a bite and looked up at Margaret. "Oh? I didn't realize this was a high-society event."

"Evidently Cassie's parents go all out for this. She's leaving on Thursday evening, so she's coming by the gallery to pick up my mother's faux-fur jacket at around four. This will be our only chance to see her before Christmas. Can you come down to the gallery then?"

"I'll make it a point to be there. I'm making her an inlaid jewelry box for Christmas. I hope I can finish it by then. I've put it off to work on all the orders I have. I expected to have until Christmas Eve to finish it."

"That's perfect! I was thinking about giving her some jewelry. Bernadette makes some nice pieces, so I'll pick out something she can wear to *The Nutcracker* with her new dress."

Allan raised his eyebrows. "What about my mother's jewelry? She had some nice pieces."

"I never thought of those. They were too fancy for my tastes. I could lend her my pearls, but I think they're out of vogue. There might be something she'd like in your mother's jewelry. I'll look after dinner."

"Hard to believe our little girl is so grown up," Allan said, shaking his head.

"I know. I can't quite wrap my mind around it."

Allan nodded. "Just the two of us, like when we met, only we're that much older."

Margaret laughed. "And I feel every day of it sometimes. Like now." A lump in her throat made it hard to swallow. She coughed. "Oh my." She dabbed at the corner of her eye. "I guess I'm going to have to adjust to this new normal. I don't like it."

"Neither do I, but we'll manage." Allan's understanding smile made her feel a little better. She was not alone in her loneliness, missing their daughter. Allan and Adelaide had always shared a special relationship. She loved doing things with her father, and he'd been protective, yet encouraged her to broaden her abilities. He must miss her as much as Margaret did.

After they cleaned up the dishes, Allan went back out to his workshop. Margaret went looking for his mother's jewelry. If she remembered right, much of it dated back to his grandmother, who had been somewhat of a society matron. Antique jewelry was back in style. People often asked about it in the gallery, but Margaret didn't carry any antiques. She vaguely remembered Allan's grandmother—an imposing woman who wore pillbox hats and gloves whenever she left the house.

Margaret found the box of jewelry in her cedar chest, beneath the faux-fur jacket, a hand-crocheted tablecloth, several lace doilies, and a box with Adelaide's baby things. She took out the jacket and hung it up to air it out. It smelled like cedar, but looked in good condition. She set aside the other items and took out the jewelry and the baby things.

The jewelry box held gaudy costume jewelry of aurora borealis crystal clip-on earrings, strands of crystal necklaces, and bracelets that changed color as the light hit them. The pieces were heavy, and the silver settings had turned black. Not appropriate for a young woman. Bernadette might be interested in the crystal beads, though, to use in her jewelry. There were several heavy rings and pearls that needed to be restrung. She took out a small-hinged box that dated back to the 1930s. Inside was an exquisite diamond-cluster pendant on a white-gold chain. The pendant had several tiny pale-blue aquamarine stones in the center, surrounded by a square formed with small diamonds. Margaret guessed the necklace was worth hundreds of dollars, if not more, but it just wasn't her style. It would look gorgeous on Adelaide. She took the box out to wrap it up, set aside the junk jewelry for Bernadette, and put everything else back into the cedar chest except for the baby things. She carried that box out to the living room.

She sat on the couch and opened the box. One by one, she took out the contents. They smelled of cedar and baby powder. A small pair of black patent-leather shoes. Tiny socks with lace edging. She remembered pulling them on over Adelaide's tiny toes and pudgy little baby feet.

She held up a dress—white with pink and yellow flowers and ruffled sleeves. Adelaide's first dress. She had been a tiny baby, and the dress would barely fit a baby doll.

There was a small round green rattle that Adelaide would shake and then squeal with delight. A hand-knit blue sweater. A nightie. Margaret fingered the soft fabric and blinked back tears. So many years ago, and yet it seemed like yesterday that she'd dressed Adelaide for her first outing, not in the dress, but in the soft yellow one-piece nightie that was long and tied at the bottom to keep her little feet covered. She'd wrapped her in a flannel receiving blanket, and then in a warmer fleece blanket to keep her protected for the trip to the doctor's office. Adelaide had been premature, and Margaret had kept her in, away from people and germs and the nippy, damp spring weather for many weeks after they'd taken her home from the hospital. That first outing to the doctor had been a momentous occasion. They'd known from the moment she was born that she had Down syndrome. Those first years held many challenges, but Adelaide had thrived in spite of the issues associated with her condition.

Now look at her. Hard to believe that tiny baby had become a healthy, spirited, independent woman.

Thinking back, Margaret realized that the dreams she'd hardly dared to dream for her daughter were coming true. Like every parent, she'd wanted to raise her daughter to become a strong, loving, compassionate, generous adult. Instead of grieving Adelaide's new independence, she should be rejoicing that her daughter, despite her challenges, was becoming everything a mother could want for her daughter.

Margaret was so proud of Adelaide. What a blessing she was!

And how hard it was to let her go.

*   *   *

Margaret was determined not to bother Allan on Tuesday morning. He had enough work without the added burden of the Nativity pieces. The lamb with the broken head looked repairable. She had scrap wood that she'd brought from home, but she needed wood glue and putty and screws. If she'd asked Allan, he would have insisted on helping her. Surely she could handle this problem by herself! So Margaret made her list and headed to the hardware store by the wharf before she opened the gallery.

She found the paint primer and the wood putty, and she picked out some wood screws that looked long enough, but not too long, to attach to the back of the lamb to hold the head on to the body. Then she found the glue display. There must have been a dozen different types and brands of glue. Which one? She read the backs of several. That just confused her more. She went looking for a clerk. The only store clerk was behind the checkout stand. At the counter, talking to the clerk, was the man who'd visited the gallery. What was his name? Something with an S. Shawn—no—Shane. Smith. That was it. Was he looking for toys in the hardware store? She doubted he'd find any. She stood back, waiting for him to finish.

She couldn't make out his words. He had something in his hand that he was showing to the clerk. It looked like a small piece of wood. The clerk shook his head. Shane put the object in his pocket and turned around. When he saw her, he smiled.

"Good morning, Mrs. Hoskins." His smile was more than polite. Welcoming, as if they were old friends. She returned his smile.

"Good morning, Mr. Smith. I hope you enjoyed your evening here in Marble Cove."

"Very much so. In fact, I plan to stick around another day or two."

"Really?" Margaret couldn't imagine what would attract someone like Shane Smith to visit Marble Cove, let alone to stay more than a day. She loved the town, but it was . . . homey. A few stores. A few places to eat that had above-average food. A few historical sites. It was a fishing town. A nice place to settle down, with people who were friendly enough, but a bit reserved. Tourists came in the summer but not so much in the winter. So why was Shane Smith here? What did he want? She was puzzled, but she had little time to think about a stranger. She had work waiting and a gallery to run.

"It's nice seeing you again. Enjoy your day." She smiled, then took a step toward the counter.

"Thank you." He nodded and smiled back. "Have a great day, Mrs. Hoskins. Perhaps I'll see you later." He went out the front door.

The clerk raised his eyebrows as Margaret stepped up to the counter. "Friend of yours?"

"No. I just met him yesterday when he came into the gallery."

The clerk shook his head. "Not from around he-ah, that's for sure. City fellow. I can tell." He looked out in the direction the man had gone, then back at Margaret. "So what can I do for you, eh?"

"I need some kind of wood glue that can bond two pieces of plywood together on the ends."

"Are the cuts clean?"

"Sadly, no. The edges are worn and crumbly."

He rubbed his chin and frowned. "You've got a problem. I can help you though."

He walked back to a different aisle than the glue display. "You'll be needing liquid wood and a good wood epoxy." He picked up a plastic bottle and a small plastic tub and put them in her cart. "You'll need rubber gloves, sand paper, a scraper, and a wood rasp." He loaded items into her cart.

"I don't need all these things," she said. "I have most of them." Or Allan does, she thought. She didn't have unlimited funds to repair the Nativity set—if it could be repaired. Diane and Beverly and Shelley were donating their time and energies, and there had been a few donations of materials, but they didn't have a sponsor. "I'm operating on a shoestring here," she said. "I'm restoring the set pieces for the living Nativity."

"You don't say. I remem-bah when Emma Nicol ran the Nativity for the town. She'd come in he-ah looking for us to donate materials."

"If you'd care to donate this wood epoxy, I'll be happy to tell folks how you support the Nativity. I think the mayor is doing some promotions. Maybe we could add your name on there."

"It's not up to me. Since we became part of a franchise, I can't just give things away, but I can ask my boss. He won't be in until noon."

"I can't wait until noon. But you ask him. I believe my husband has an account here. I'll put it on Allan's account, and you can take it back off if your boss wants to make a donation."

"Fay-uh enough. I'll ask him."

Margaret signed an invoice and left. She didn't expect the manager to donate the materials. He wasn't from Marble Cove; the company had hired him from the city. But it didn't hurt to ask.

She had walked from the gallery. The earlier fog had frozen as it hung in the air, covering everything with hoarfrost. The traditional two-story-tall lobster trap Christmas tree out in front of the wharf was covered in long white spiny ice crystals that shone like glass, reflecting the red, blue, green, and yellow Christmas lights and sparkling in the rays of sun beginning to peek through the lifting fog. She stopped for a moment, envisioning a painting, capturing the scene in her mind. The frost bit into her cheeks, so she hurried along.

Bernadette arrived just as Margaret opened the front door of the gallery.

"*Brr!* I'm glad you opened up. It's freezing out here," Bernadette said, following her inside. She stomped her feet on the welcome mat, then followed Margaret through to the back.

"I'm glad you're here," Margaret said. "I bought supplies to repair some of these set pieces. How long can you stay?"

"Until two," Bernadette said. "Will that be long enough?"

"That will be a big help. I really appreciate it. I can get a start on these if you can handle the front."

"Happy to. My mother is still on her Christmas-decorating marathon, so I was glad to escape. I brought a new Celtic Christmas CD. I'm dying to hear it. Is it okay if I play it?"

"Why, yes, if you'd like." Margaret liked Celtic music—not as much as jazz, but variety was good once in a while. She'd forgotten to turn on the sound system, which wasn't like her. She usually did it out of habit, as part of her opening routine.

The sounds of jaunty fiddle and Irish flute music blared loudly, jarring her. She waited until Bernadette went out front, then she turned the sound down but left it on the Celtic music. Toned down, it was nice, though still not her favorite. Celtic music fit her young artist friend, who leaned toward a bohemian style.

The song changed to a slow, mournful sound of a bass, a fiddle, and a penny whistle playing a piece that sounded more like a lament than holiday music. It was almost depressing.

Oh well. She'd ignore it. After all, it was a perfect fit for her mood.

Chapter Five

Margaret spread newspaper over the table and put the body and head of the lamb on top of it. She set out the supplies she needed, then got out the liquid wood and epoxy and read the directions. Following each step carefully, she reinforced the wood and set it aside to dry. She worked on the edges of several other pieces, then set each of them aside to dry. A goat and a donkey were in reasonable shape, but needed cleaning and paint. She started on the goat.

Several times, she heard the jingle of the bell out front, but she ignored it. Bernadette would let her know if she was needed. She took pictures of the cleaned animals and the backdrop so she could recreate the pieces as much like the originals as possible. Whoever had made the set had taken great care to make them lifelike. Then she applied a coat of white primer to the set pieces that were cleaned and leaned them against the walls to dry. As she finished the last one, Diane came through the doorway to the back room.

"Good morning." She removed her gloves and rubbed her hands together, then blew on them.

"Is it still morning?" Margaret put down her paintbrush.

"For the next five minutes. Looks like you could use a break. Did you bring your lunch to work, or would you like to go get a bite?" Diane looked around at the white figures. Her eyebrows peaked. "Are they ghosts or clouds?"

Margaret would have laughed, but the humor evaded her. They did look more like clouds than animals. "That's the primer coat. I'll paint them to look like animals when this dries."

"Oh, good. That's a relief."

"I brought my lunch," Margaret said. "I have enough to share if you like egg salad sandwiches."

"Are you sure? I could get something and bring it over here."

"No, really. I have plenty. Just let me clear a space." She wadded up the newspapers that covered the table and threw them in the trash. "I can't do any more until everything dries."

Diane took off her coat and hung it up on a hook.

"There's a pot of hot spiced cider out front if you'd like some," Margaret said. "Or I can make tea back here."

"Cider sounds wonderful. Do you want one? I'll get cups for both of us."

"Yes, I believe I'd like a cup." Margaret washed up, then set out paper plates and napkins. She got out her sandwich, chips, carrot and celery sticks, and hummus. The sandwich was on wide rye bread, cut in half. She put half on each plate. Diane came back, carrying two cups of steaming cider.

"Bernadette is waiting on a couple who are buying your large painting of the harbor decorated for Christmas. I love that painting. It looks cold, and yet the colored lights on the boats and the chestnuts roasting over the fire in the big iron kettle on the dock look so inviting."

"Oh, good. I didn't know if that one would sell. It's so seasonal. That was my last Christmas picture. My other winter pictures are more general."

"I love your Christmas pictures. I would leave that picture up all year round."

"You're being kind. Come sit down."

They sat at the small table and began to eat.

"This is good," Diane said after she swallowed a bite. She took a sip of the hot cider.

"Allan's secret recipe," Margaret said. "So how is the writing going?"

Diane sighed. "Slow. This living Nativity has taken over my life. I can't concentrate on writing. I'm starting to panic. Are the set pieces going to work? I know you're swamped, and here you are working on those wooden animals and stable. I feel guilty asking you and Shelley and Beverly to take all this on when I know your lives are extra busy right now. And I'm wondering if we're going to be able to pull it off."

Margaret was surprised to see Diane's distress. She'd been so excited to revive the living Nativity tradition. Margaret hoped her own lack of joy wasn't spilling over on to her friend. "It's coming together. Didn't you say you have all the actors? Most, anyway? Maddie Bancroft is taking care of the choir. Shelley has the costumes under control. It sounds like we'll have lots of cookies and drinks. We found the sets. And Beverly's flyers around town have generated lots of interest. I've heard people talking about the event here and in the Cove, and almost everyone at church and at my tai chi class plans to come see it. Don't worry about it. We'll pull it off." Margaret conjured up a confident smile.

"I hope you're right." The worry lines on Diane's brow eased. She smiled. "Next year we'll start earlier."

Next year. Margaret held back a sigh. Next year they would have the costumes and the sets and the momentum of having experience under their belts. People would be looking forward to a second year. That is *if* this year was a success.

Please, Lord, for Diane's sake, for the town, for all of us, please help us make this work, Margaret silently prayed. She was surprised to realize she wanted the Nativity to be a blessing to the town almost as much as Diane did. She had to get the set pieces restored, and she only had four more days to finish them. She wished Adelaide was home. Before she'd started taking college classes, Adelaide had helped in the gallery. Bernadette was a big help, and she seemed happy for an excuse to be there, but her time was limited. Margaret missed her daughter and the fun and completeness she brought to their family, but more than that, Margaret needed her. But Adelaide wasn't coming home. Margaret would have to manage without her—somehow.

* * *

After Diane left, Margaret checked on the plywood animals. The primer coat had dried. She started on the donkey, applying a mixture of yellow and tan as a base coat. She'd covered the body and started on the legs, and one of the legs fell apart. She hadn't realized how badly it had deteriorated. She set it aside to look at repairing later.

She picked up a lamb and examined it. It seemed sturdy enough. She applied a base coat of light blue in swirling strokes over most of the figure. So far, so good. As it dried, she mixed colors in small containers to get the shades of green, blue, magenta, and sienna she needed to bring the lamb to life. It always amazed her how many colors it took to paint something that appeared to be white.

Working on a life-size animal required a lot more brushstrokes than her usual paintings. She worked for a while, then stepped back to view it with a critical eye. Satisfied, she jumped back in with her brush. It had been years since she'd tackled a life-size project. With the Trans-Siberian Orchestra's rendition of "Carol of the Bells" playing in the background, her painting became like a dance, swooping and twirling the paintbrush in broad strokes. It was fun. She hummed along and forgot everything but the lamb. As she put the final touches around the ears and the nose and mouth, she heard a sound behind her. She spun around and stopped, her brush in midair.

Bernadette and the tall, dark stranger were standing in the doorway, watching her. Bernadette's wide-eyed expression indicated they'd been standing there awhile. Shane Smith was grinning. Margaret wished the floor would open up and swallow her. She raised her eyebrows and smiled back. Had she been dancing? She hoped not!

"Good afternoon. Just a moment." She went through the motions of wrapping her brush in plastic wrap so it wouldn't dry out. Then she looked up, feeling a bit more composed. "How can I help you?"

"Margaret, this is Mr. Smith. He has a question about Allan's tables." She glanced up at the man, who was considerably taller than she was. "Oh, and I need to leave."

"Of course. I didn't realize what time it is. Thank you, Bernadette." She turned her attention to Shane Smith as Bernadette got her coat and bag and left.

"It's nice to see you again. You have a question about my husband's tables?"

"I'm sorry. I didn't mean to interrupt your work."

"Oh, no bother. I need to stop and mind the gallery now anyway."

"Your lamb is very lifelike. What are you making?"

"Thank you. It's part of an outdoor Nativity set. The churches in town used to hold a living Nativity every year, but it hasn't been done for quite a few years. This year we're reviving it. The lamb is part of the old set."

He looked around the room at the pieces leaning against the walls and whistled low. Some were white with the primer coat, but many others were still in various states of disrepair. "Looks like you've got a big job here."

Margaret sighed. "A bigger job than I expected. We just found these stored in an old shed. What you see is what was under many layers of dirt."

He put his hand on his chin and rocked back on his heels. "Wouldn't it be easier to make new ones?"

"It would be if we had the time. It's next weekend. And then there's a matter of money. This is a volunteer project started by one of my friends. I'm hoping to get this in passable condition for this year. If it goes over well, maybe we can raise funds to get new sets next year."

"Then this is a labor of love," he said.

"Love?" Margaret thought about it for a moment. "I suppose so." Love for Diane, who wanted the living Nativity to be a success. Love for Marble Cove, and all the townspeople. Margaret honestly hadn't thought about her own motivation. Why had she let Diane talk her into this? Because she cared about her friend.

"I remember when I was growing up, the church next door always had a large outdoor live Nativity," he said. "When I was eleven, I was taller than most of the older boys, so I got to be a wise man. It was pretty cool. I held the box of gold. It was just painted rocks, but I felt so important."

"Where did you grow up?"

"Down in Portland."

"That's a nice memory."

"Yeah. I'd forgotten all about it until now. I don't have much time for church these days." He let out a short laugh. "Or anything else, for that matter. My business keeps me busy." He looked directly at Margaret. "Too busy, according to my wife. She's in Canada with our son, visiting her family."

Something about the look in his eyes caught her attention. Pain? But then the look was gone. Could have been her imagination.

She and Allan had been fortunate to be in business together, running an accounting business until they retired. The gallery and his woodworking were second careers, and they hadn't really expected them to be so successful. Their only daughter Adelaide had come along later in their lives, and she'd always fit in well. Margaret had worked some at home or taken Adelaide to the office with them.

"Being in business can become all-consuming," she said. "I imagine that could be hard on family life."

He ran a hand through his thick, dark hair. "Yeah."

She hadn't meant to make personal observations to this stranger. A customer, no less. "But you didn't come in here to see my project or talk about work. What can I do for you?"

"Oh yes. I like your husband's woodwork. Does he take special orders?"

"Yes, he does. Is it something you want soon? He is completely booked through Christmas."

"I'm not in a hurry. I'm looking for something for my office."

"Will you still be in town tomorrow? I'm afraid he is out of town making a delivery this afternoon. You could talk to him tomorrow."

"Tomorrow will be fine. I'll make a sketch of what I want and bring it by. What time?"

"He usually works in the mornings, and brings in finished pieces in the afternoon. Do you have a card? I can have him call you."

Shane fished into his back pocket and took out a wallet. He took a business card out and handed it to her.

"I'll come by after lunch unless I hear from him before that. I look forward to meeting him." Shane stepped back and turned to leave. Then he looked back at Margaret. "Good luck with your animals. If they all turn out as good as your lamb, they'll be masterful."

Margaret beamed. She couldn't help it. "Thank you. I hope you're right." It meant a lot that this stranger thought her lamb was good. She'd completed one good piece. It was a start. Now if only the other pieces would prove solid enough to get through the next week.

CHAPTER SIX

Dinner was a simple affair. Neither Margaret nor Allan had the energy or even the appetite for cooking or eating, so grilled-cheese sandwiches and tomato soup filled the bill.

"How are the set pieces coming?" Allan asked as they did the dishes. He handed her a wet soup bowl.

"So-so," she said as she dried it. "A donkey fell apart on me when I went to paint it, but I finished a lamb today that came out better than I expected. A customer told me it looked lifelike, so I was pleased."

"Was that your first finished piece?"

"Yes. The others are primed. I hope they'll hold together. I glued and reinforced another lamb this morning. Tomorrow when I go to paint it, I'll know if my repair worked."

"What about the stable background? It looked dilapidated to me, but I didn't see it up close. If I have to make a new one, I need a couple of days to do it."

"I know. I haven't started on it yet. I scrubbed it and scraped off some mold. It was still damp, so I haven't primed it yet. I'll work on it in the morning, so I should know the status tomorrow."

"Good. I hope it's all right. I had a piece of wood split on me this afternoon. It has a hidden flaw, so I'll have to replace it."

"Oh dear, that puts a crimp in your time." All the more reason not to bother Allan with the Nativity set problems. He didn't need any more projects until after Christmas. Which reminded her . . . "A young man came in the gallery today looking at your tables. He's interested in having you make something for his office—after Christmas."

"Well, if he's willing to wait, I'll be happy to talk to him."

"Good. He'll still be in town tomorrow if you can spare a few minutes."

Allan handed her the last wet dish and pulled the plug in the sink. He looked at her and frowned. "I suppose I can talk to him. I need to bring several pieces to the gallery for pickup. Can you have him come by about one o'clock?"

"I got his card. I'll call him and tell him." She dried a pan and had started to put it away when the doorbell rang.

"I wonder who that is."

"Here, I'll put that away. Go answer the door," Allan said.

Margaret was surprised to find Shelley at the door, all bundled up and holding a white box the size of a bakery pie box.

"Shelley, come in."

"Hi, Margaret. I can't stay, but I brought you some goodies." She stepped inside the doorway. "The kids were helping me, and they decorated some cookies especially for you and Allan."

"That's so sweet." She took the box and opened it to look. A layer of brightly frosted sugar cookies in shapes of stars and Christmas trees and angels covered the top layer. Margaret got a lump in her throat as she viewed the colorful, unsophisticated decorating on the cookies. So artistic in such an innocent, uncomplicated way. "These are beautiful. Please tell the children thank you from us."

"There are some other goodies under the sugar cookies. I've been experimenting, so you're my guinea pig. Please let me know what you think, and be honest."

"I know we'll love them. Your recipes are always delicious. We'll try some tonight. Are you sure you can't stay for a cup of tea?"

"No, really, I can't. Dan and the kids are cleaning up our mess. We promised the kids we will watch *A Charlie Brown Christmas* tonight, and then I have more baking to do." She paused, then added, "How are the Nativity backdrops coming along?"

"It's a mixed bag, really. I have one finished, and it looks good. Others are partly painted, and some, well, let's just say they've seen better days. How about the costumes?"

"I have helpers. My mother-in-law has taken charge of the task, you know. She has a group of women sewing the costumes. Thank goodness they're coming along fine, because I sure don't have time to make them."

Margaret laughed. "I understand that! Well, tomorrow I hope to make real progress on the Nativity set pieces."

"Let me know if we can do anything. Dan said he'd be happy to help with setting up the Nativity."

"Tell him thank you. I'll keep that in mind. But I know he's really busy these days."

Shelley glanced over at the fireplace, and Margaret suddenly realized how bare her living room looked without a tree or any decorations. She felt a twinge of guilt that she wasn't participating in the Christmas spirit.

"Is that the card you told us about?"

"What? Oh, the mysterious Christmas card? Yes." Margaret got the card and showed it to Shelley.

"It's adorable. I hadn't thought of having the kids make ornaments out of Popsicle sticks. It doesn't look hard to make."

"No, it doesn't. I just can't figure out who sent it."

"Well, whoever did must have had you in mind. You said you weren't feeling very festive this year. I'm so sorry about that. I can't even imagine how much you're missing Adelaide."

"I really do. More than I anticipated. It kind of hit me out of the blue. Diane says it's empty-nest syndrome, and I'm sure she's right."

"My kids miss Adelaide too. They love it when she comes over to babysit. I don't mean to impose, but if you decide to put up a tree, I know Aiden and Hailey would love to help decorate, and Emma too, but I'd come along to supervise her."

Margaret couldn't help smiling at the thought. Aiden was almost six—old enough to be helpful. Emma was just three, and would certainly need a lot of supervision, but it might be fun. She remembered when Adelaide was barely walking, how she would reach up to try to hang an ornament on the tree, and Allan would lift her up so she could reach higher. Adelaide's eyes would sparkle at the pretty, glittery ornaments and the lights and she would giggle and squeal with delight.

Maybe they should put up the tree this year. If they could find the time.

*   *   *

After Shelley left, Margaret placed the handmade card back on the mantel. She stared at it for a moment, thinking about what Shelley said. Whoever made it and sent it to her must have had her in mind. To cheer her up? Could that be the reason she'd gotten the card? But who sent it?

Who thought she needed cheering up? It was obviously made by a child, but what child would send her a card? None that she could think of, if not Shelley's children.

For a moment, she was tempted to go over to Shelley's to watch the Christmas special with them. She and Adelaide always watched Charlie Brown and a bunch of other Christmas classics. They would have a marathon day of Christmas movies. But not this year.

She felt a little like Charlie Brown. She couldn't get excited about Christmas. Without Adelaide to share it with, it held no interest, no excitement, no meaning.

Sighing, she returned to the kitchen. Allan had finished the dishes and gone out to his workshop. Margaret glanced down at the box of goodies in her hand and decided they had to be tasted and shared. She made two cups of hot cocoa and hooked two small candy canes that were in the box of cookies over the rims, then made a plate of cookies and took it out to Allan's workshop.

He was sanding a cut board. He looked up. His hand stilled, and she could tell by the widening of his eyes that he was grinning beneath his dust mask.

"You must be a mind reader. I was just thinking a cup of cocoa would be nice right now."

"I got hit with the same inspiration. That, and Shelley brought us some homemade goodies." She placed the plate on the workbench as he removed his mask.

"This looks like the work of Hailey, Aiden, and Emma," he said, selecting a bright-green frosted Christmas tree with red hots and candy-pearl decorations.

"You're right. They wanted to cheer us up. Isn't that sweet of them?"

"Sure is. I was thinking it's sad that we haven't put up any decorations this year. I've been so busy, and I know you have too, with the gallery and this living Nativity that you're working on. We're the only house in the neighborhood with no Christmas lights or a tree showing through the window. I don't know when we'd find the time to decorate though. And then we'd just have to take it down again. Hardly seems worth it." Allan took a swig of hot chocolate. "This is just what I needed. Thanks."

"You're welcome. I've been thinking I might drag out the Christmas decorations. At least the tree. Shelley offered to have the kids come over and help us decorate it. I know that would be fun for them."

"Do you have time?"

Margaret chuckled. "Not really, but how long could it take? Just the tree with a couple of light strands and some decorations. We could do it in the evening."

"We?" Allan sighed. "I'd love to help, but I don't see how I'm going to get all my jobs finished now."

"I know. We'll see. It's a thought anyway."

*   *   *

As she let herself in through the back door of the gallery early Wednesday morning, Margaret's cell phone rang. She checked the caller ID, then answered. "Good morning, Diane."

"Hi. I saw you leave early. Can you meet us at the Cove this morning about eight thirty?"

It was seven now. Margaret wanted to get as much done on the Nativity set pieces as possible before the gallery opened. And Bernadette couldn't come in today to help her. "I really need to work on these animals if I'm going to get them done. Is it important?"

"I was just hoping to get a progress report and compare notes with everyone. Can we come by there?"

"Sure. I can put on a pot of coffee."

"Don't go to any trouble. I'll bring you a coffee."

"All right. Come through the back. It will be open."

"See you then."

Margaret said good-bye and hit the end button. She needed to make some progress before her friends arrived for coffee.

The lamb she'd glued and reinforced seemed solid. She examined the pieces of the donkey that had fallen apart yesterday. The pieces were too jagged and crumbled to reconstruct, so she set it aside. An ox was ready to paint.

She put on a Mannheim Steamroller Christmas CD. The upbeat instrumentals felt cheery and set a perfect background mood for painting. She quickly mixed her colors, took a large paintbrush, and began the short dabbing strokes to get the effect of a bristly hair coat. Brown, green, black, yellow, ochre, and red combined to create a very realistic coat on the ox. She decided he needed to be shaggy, so she added more gray and white around the muzzle and ears and along the fetlocks. The back door opened as she stepped back to examine her work.

"What a great ox!" Diane said. She came in carrying two tall cups of coffee and a sack clutched in her free fingers.

"Ah, it's warm in here," said Beverly, who was right on Diane's heels. She shut the door behind them as soon as Shelley too stepped inside.

"Is it eight thirty already?" Margaret asked. "I'd hoped to get more done before you got here."

"It looks like you've accomplished a lot," Diane said. "Those were all ghost figures when I was here yesterday."

"Counting this, I've painted three, but one fell apart on me before I finished it. I've barely made a dent," Margaret said. "I've got all those to do, plus the background." She pointed to the stack of plywood figures against the back wall.

"If I didn't know better, I'd think that was real," Shelley said, staring at the lamb she'd finished yesterday.

"Thank you."

"Here's your coffee. I got you the special gingerbread latte. I hope you like it." Diane handed her a cup.

"That's one of my favorites," Margaret said as she covered the newspapers spread on the table with a clean newspaper. "Don't mind my fancy tablecloth. I need to stash these brushes, if you'll just set the coffee on the table."

"Sure." Diane put both coffees and the sack on the table, then went over to inspect the unfinished set pieces.

"Margaret, this is a huge job," Beverly said, looking around the room. "I had no idea. How are you going to do all of this by this weekend? And how can we . . . how can I help you? I'm not good at painting, but there must be something I can do for you."

Margaret wrapped the paintbrushes and covered the mixed paints. "Want to run the gallery for me? That's my biggest problem. But I know you have a million things on your plate too. All of you do."

"I had no idea this would be such a monumental task when I asked you all to help me do the living Nativity," Diane said. "I'm sorry. I don't see how we're going to have it all done by the weekend. And you've done such a fabulous job of promoting it, Beverly, that I think we're going to have a crowd."

"Hold up there," Margaret said, waving her hands in the air. "It's always a chaotic rush before any production. It's all going to come together. You'll see."

Diane sighed. "Do you really think so? Looking at these sets, I don't see how that's possible."

Margaret didn't see how it was possible either, but somehow, they would make it work. They had to. If they failed, the living Nativity would never be revived. Margaret remembered the warm, loving feeling she'd experienced watching the Nativity years ago. Somehow, in the middle of the bustle and commercialism of Christmas, it brought clarity and meaning to the holiday celebration. Christmas was about a miraculous birth—a tiny baby who would bring eternal hope to the world. Just thinking about it brought a tear to her eyes. All this time, as she'd been bemoaning her loss of joy and excitement without Adelaide, she'd forgotten what Christmas was about. She was determined that this Nativity project would be a success.

"I don't honestly know," Margaret said, "but I believe it. I've really come to believe that we're *supposed* to present the living Nativity this year. And we will. And it will be beautiful."

"Shelley, how are the costumes coming?" Diane asked.

Shelley raised her shoulders in a shrug and smiled. "They're coming. Honestly, that's all I know. Francis told me she had a sewing bee at her house and in one afternoon, she and her friends got most of the costumes made. Of course, I have no idea what they look like."

"I bet they're wonderful," Beverly said.

"Well, that's a relief," Diane said. "So we have our costumes and our actors. And your publicity, Beverly. It's amazing." She sat down and took a drink of her coffee. "I've been worrying that perhaps we should scrap the whole thing, but I'm starting to think maybe it will work out. Worst case, we could hang sheets in back of the Nativity for the backdrop. The animals you've finished look wonderful, Margaret. If we don't have lots of animals, it will do, I'm sure."

"Has Leo had any luck getting some live animals?" Margaret asked.

"He's had a hard time getting people to commit. The other day he said he might be able to get a Shetland pony and an old ewe. Other than that, no luck. People don't want to transport their pregnant cows and sheep. Most of the males are too unruly to keep still for very long." Diane opened the bag and held it up. "Shelley's raspberry-and-cream cheese kolaches. Anyone want one?"

"I do," Margaret said, taking one out of the bag. "I didn't eat breakfast this morning."

"I'll have one too." Beverly took one. "Thanks, Shelley. Margaret, I don't know anything about retail, but I'll be happy to spend some time in the gallery so you can keep working on the Nativity set pieces. I have a meeting this morning, but I could come in this afternoon for a few hours. If I can bring my laptop, I can do some correspondence when it isn't busy."

"Oh, Beverly, that would be wonderful! Most people like to browse, so I just let them and answer any questions they have. I'll be here so you can ask me. Everything is marked for prices."

"All right. I'll be here about one. Diane, do you need me to do anything else to help get the Nativity ready?"

"I don't think so. Thank you for all you've done, all of you. I feel a lot better about the Nativity than when we came in this morning."

"Good."

"I've got to get back to the kitchen. I have cookies to bake," Shelley said.

"Oh, Shelley? Are the children busy tomorrow in the evening after dinner?" Margaret asked. "I think I'm going to set up the Christmas tree. I'd love to have their help decorating it."

Shelley smiled. "Tomorrow night will be perfect."

CHAPTER SEVEN

How could she paint animals and wait on customers at the same time? That question was taken out of her hands by the constant ringing of the bells on the front door of the gallery. With a week left until Christmas, the last-minute rush had begun.

Bernadette stopped in with a new display of bracelets. "I thought you might need some more pieces to sell. These are really popular online." She held up a bracelet for Margaret to see. It was five strands of colored glass beads in uneven shapes, like smooth pieces of sea glass, strung together with crocheted loops. There were other, similar pieces, and bracelets made of colored chording in nautical knots with metal clasps and bangles.

"They're very attractive," Margaret said.

"And fast to make. I made all these while I watched Christmas movies last night."

"I wish I could do two things at the same time," Margaret said with a chuckle.

Bernadette laughed. "I guess I'm just ambidextrous. Or is it multitasking?"

"Maybe both. Here, I have something to show you." Margaret got out the bag of costume jewelry she'd brought in. "These pieces are old, but the crystal beads are good. I thought they might be something you could use in your jewelry making."

Bernadette picked up a heavy, five-strand necklace and held it up to the light. Colored lights swirled around the room, like lights from a mirror ball. "These beads are amazing! They reflect colors."

"We used to call them aurora borealis crystals. My great-aunt had some, and I was fascinated with them as a child. I guess they were very popular."

"I can totally use these! Thank you. I can't wait to see how they come out."

"Me too. The way they are, they just look gaudy."

Bernadette laughed. "When I get done repurposing them, you'll love them."

"I'm sure I will." Margaret handed her the full bag.

"I'll put these new pieces out front. I put prices on them already. Do you want me to come help out tomorrow morning? I can stay until after lunchtime if you'd like." In a hushed voice, she said, "My mom is having a bunch of ladies over for tea. I need an excuse so I don't have to join them."

Margaret loved tea parties, and she'd give anything to have her daughter join her for tea right now, but she didn't mention that. Bernadette and her mother didn't enjoy the same activities, and a ladies' party might require proper etiquette. Definitely not Bernadette's idea of fun, she guessed.

Bernadette and Adelaide were close in age. Margaret wondered if Adelaide was discovering interests that differed from her mother's. Was that why she didn't want to come home for Christmas? That startling thought hadn't occurred to Margaret before. She hoped she and Allan would encourage Adelaide's interests, and not criticize them, the way

Bernadette's mother did with her clothing and activities. Margaret suspected Bernadette sometimes made choices that she knew her mother would disapprove of. She couldn't imagine Adelaide doing that, but perhaps, like Bernadette, she was looking for her own interests and styles.

After Bernadette left, Margaret's attention was drawn back to customers. Three bracelets, a blown-glass vase, two pottery pieces, an original painting, and several framed prints had sold by eleven. Margaret wondered if her walls would be bare by the end of the day. She pulled more framed prints out of the storeroom to hang. As she passed her workroom, she glanced at the primed white and tan animals resting against the walls, waiting for a painted coat of hair, and for eyes, ears, and noses. No time now. She would have to work late tonight.

At a lull, Margaret called her artists who sold on consignment to see if any of them had more pieces. Two of them promised to bring in more artwork the next day.

Margaret was wrapping a painting in brown paper when Shane came in. She'd left a message on his phone to come at one. She was startled to realize it was 12:45. Where had the time gone? He looked around while he waited for her to finish. He'd wandered into the second room, behind partitioned walls, so she went to find him. He was standing looking down where one of Allan's small tables had been.

"It's gone. Did you sell it, then?" he asked.

"Yes, I only have a couple of Allan's pieces left."

"Oh no, I meant the small lighthouse painting that was here the first day I came in."

Margaret remembered that he'd been looking for a large painting of the Orlean Point Light. "I had to move it. It's over here." She led him to a corner where she'd hung it on an ornate clothing tree that held several smaller artworks.

"Good. I've decided I want it for my office. I've been walking out to the lighthouse every day, and it fascinates me. I've been to the library and the museum and read up on your local history. I imagine Marble Cove would be a great place to grow up."

"It's a nice town with friendly people and good values," Margaret said, wondering again why Shane had come to Marble Cove. Was he thinking of moving here? "I can't attest to what it's like growing up here. We moved here about thirty years ago. But it's a kid-friendly town. I see youngsters and their parents on the beach all the time."

"My son would love it, I'm sure. Maybe I'll rent a place here this summer for him and his mother."

The way he said it made Margaret wonder about his family, but she didn't ask. It was none of her business. She felt sad for him that he was here alone though. "Would you like me to wrap the painting up for you?"

"Yes, please. I found a wonderful sailboat kit for my son, but I still need something for my wife. I noticed you have some art glass vases. She loves beautiful glass."

"There are a couple left, and I have more pieces coming in tomorrow, if you are still in town."

"I might be. I'll check back before I leave. How are your Nativity pieces coming?"

Margaret groaned. She hadn't meant to, but it just slipped out. She'd spent all morning working in the gallery, which was her business and her priority. But the clock was ticking away, and the sets weren't getting done. "I'm having a few problems. The wood is old and rotting from exposure and dampness."

"That's too bad." He wandered over and looked into her workroom. She wished she had shut the door. She usually kept it closed off to customers. Right now the room was a mess.

"Your ox looks great. Very realistic." He turned to look at her. "May I go in? I'd like to look at the stable walls."

What could she say? "Sure. But excuse the mess, please. It isn't usually such disorder."

"No need to apologize. It looks like a busy workroom." He disappeared inside the room. A moment later he came back out. "If you want a crumbling stable, you certainly have that. Looks like you need a replacement."

"Or a miracle," she said. "Here's your painting." She handed him the package.

"Thank you." He paid for the picture. Then he looked at his watch. "I have drawings of a table for your husband. Your message said to meet him here around one. I guess I'm a few minutes early."

"I can call to see when he's coming."

Just then, the back door opened and Allan came in, carrying two small tables, one in each hand. A blast of cold air came in with him.

"Here, let me help you," Shane said, stepping forward and taking the tables.

"Thank you. I've got one more." Allan went out again, then returned with a chair. He set it in the back.

"These are for customers. They'll be in to pick them up this afternoon." He put the tables with them, then turned to Shane and held out his hand. "Hi. I'm Allan. You must be Shane. Margaret told me you're interested in my tables."

They shook hands, then Shane took the large manila envelope he'd had tucked under his arm and opened it.

"I'm impressed with your tables. I've been looking for a drafting table for my office. I'm an architect, so a drafting table is essential to my work. I love your style. So here's what I need." He took out several drawings. The pencil sketches were done neatly and accurately, furnished with exact angles and measurements. He handed them to Allan. The top one was a sketch of a finished table. The next two drawings filled in the details.

"I've never made a drafting table before," Allan said. His brow furrowed as he looked at the drawings, but Margaret read his interest in the way he studied the pages. The drawings were exquisite. The lines, even in their precision, showed wonderful artistry. If he designed buildings the way he drew diagrams, his work must be wonderful.

"Judging by your workmanship that I've seen here," Shane said, "you'll have no problems."

Allan pointed to the round gears on the side of the tabletop. "What about the adjustable mechanism?"

"I have an antique cast-iron gear and axle that I got off an old table. I'd like you to incorporate it."

"*Hmm.* I'll have to see it, but the project intrigues me. I'd love to build it for you."

"Great. I'm thinking hardwood so it doesn't scratch easily. Maybe oak or maple?"

"I have those and some other good woods in my workshop. Do you have time this afternoon? You could take me to my workshop at home and I'll show you."

"Yes, I have time. I'll be happy to."

"Good. Margaret, I'll leave you the van, then."

She watched them leave together. Shane Smith puzzled her even more than before. He looked successful. His business card said he was an architect from Portland. Money seemed inconsequential when it came to art or furniture. The desk he wanted Allan to make would be expensive.

Why Marble Cove, and why the Shearwater Gallery and Allan's furniture? Portland had wonderful galleries and surely it had good wood craftsmen, and in his line of business, he probably knew all of them. He seemed in no hurry to leave town. It wasn't exactly the kind of town that attracted outsiders in the wintertime, and it wasn't a holiday type of town. Besides, he didn't seem like a holiday kind of man. He said his wife and son were in Canada visiting her parents, but didn't he need to work? Why didn't he go home? Was he hiding or running away from something?

She shook her head. Diane would laugh at her fanciful ideas. Or maybe she would turn them into a best-selling mystery.

*   *   *

Margaret went through every piece of jewelry in Bernadette's collection. She had the diamond pendant wrapped and ready to give Adelaide, but still wanted to get something bright and fun, something in style. She had to admit, she had no idea what young women were wearing these days. Bernadette had a bead in her nostril and several earrings in each ear, but Adelaide showed no interest in that kind of adornment, thank goodness.

The corded colored bracelets were bright and fun, and there were necklaces to match. Adelaide loved colorful things. Margaret picked up a bright-red necklace with cats dangling from the strands. She held it up to look at it just as Beverly came into the gallery.

"Hi. I'm reporting for duty," she said as she unwrapped a long woolen scarf from around her neck and took off her gloves. "Sorry I'm late. *Brr*, it's cold out there. I sure hope it isn't this cold for the Nativity."

"Beverly, am I glad to see you! Your timing is perfect. I've been busy, but it wouldn't have mattered if you'd gotten here earlier. I couldn't have worked on the Nativity set anyway."

"Well, I can stay all afternoon, so you can paint to your heart's content. What do you have there?" She stepped closer. "How pretty! Bernadette's work?"

"Yes. Do you think Adelaide would like it?"

"She'd love it! Those multistrand necklaces and bracelets are all the rage."

"Really? Good. Adelaide doesn't think I have any fashion sense." Margaret laughed. "And she's right. But I don't want her to think that."

"Oh boy. I bet Adelaide wants to pick out her own clothes now."

"How did you know? Have you talked to her?"

"No, but I was a teenage girl once. I probably rebelled about my clothing at an earlier age than Adelaide, but it's perfectly normal. She wants to be independent."

"And fashionable, which I am not. I admit it. I like practical and functional. And comfortable."

"And those words are anathema to a teenage girl. Adelaide isn't a teenager, but she's in that stage, isn't she?"

"With a vengeance. She is buying a formal outfit to wear to *The Nutcracker* in Boston. She informed me she was not going shopping with me."

Beverly chuckled. "I'm sorry, Margaret, but I remember telling my mother the same thing. And I meant it." Beverly's smile went away. "I suppose I hurt her feelings. And Adelaide has hurt yours, hasn't she?"

"I try not to be thin-skinned. It's just that it's hard having her gone. I miss her."

"I'm sure you do. I miss her too. She can light up a room with her cheerful smiles. Jeff and Dad and I would love to have you and Allan come over for Christmas dinner. Have you thought about it?"

"Honestly, I haven't, I've been so busy. I need to check with Allan, but that would be lovely."

"Good. All right, what do I need to do?" Beverly asked.

"My system is very simple. I write up receipts and ring up sales through the register. It has change in it." She showed Beverly how to run a credit card sale. "Any questions, I'll be right here to answer them."

"Got it. I'll take over now so you can work on the Nativity set."

Margaret went to the back and put on her painting smock. She hadn't made great progress on the set pieces. There were enough actors that perhaps people wouldn't notice the lack of animals and the stable. That was her biggest concern. Every time she touched the large plywood background, more pieces of wood flaked off. Even a heavy coat of paint wouldn't mask its crumbling condition. She tried to think of an alternative. A frame against the backdrop of the railroad station wall? It would be better than nothing. It would certainly be better than the old stable backdrop. If she had to, she would improvise. It was the best she could do without funds and lots of time.

As she worked on a goat, giving it a brownish-tan coat, she thought about things that would enhance the scene. She made a mental note to ask Diane about bales of straw or hay for the stable scene. That would help cover the ground and add to the stable atmosphere. There was an angel in the script, but what about the star? She needed to produce a star, and she hadn't seen a cutout for one. The card back home on her mantel gave her an idea. She could make a frame of one-by-four slats, like the Popsicle sticks, only large. She could paint it with glow-in-the-dark paint and attach a string of white Christmas lights.

The afternoon flew by. Beverly popped back several times with questions, or for a customer picking up a special order, or fetching more prints from the back. Margaret had to stop and fill out consignment sheets when two of her exhibitors brought new pieces of art-glass vases and pottery pieces and fused-glass trivets and wall hangings for sale.

Beverly left at four. By then, Margaret had completed the goat. She felt good about her progress. At least they had a few decent animals for the Nativity set. She looked at the headless camel. The Nativity needed a camel, but this one was too splintered and the neck too narrow to repair. She had three days left to come up with the stable and a few more animals. She hoped Allan had time to make the manger. He'd been so busy, she hated to even ask about it.

CHAPTER EIGHT

Margaret was surprised to find a black Lexus parked in front of her house when she got home. Shane must still be with Allan. She went inside. Marinara sauce and meatballs bubbled in the Crock-Pot. A loaf of french bread was cut, slathered with garlic butter, and ready for the oven. She would need to cook the pasta, but that could wait.

She hung up her coat, then headed for the basement.

Thinking about Beverly stepping up to help, and inviting them for Christmas dinner, made Margaret realize how blessed she was. Shelley and her precious children with cookies and offers to help her decorate, and Diane commiserating and confiding in her about her own doubts—how could she be so fortunate to have intimate friends who trusted her and who loved her? That was joy. She'd been investing all her feelings in her daughter, and that wasn't fair to Adelaide.

Just because Adelaide wouldn't be there for Christmas was no reason not to decorate. Maybe putting up some ornaments would help her feel some Christmas spirit. She didn't need decorations to find joy, but they might help.

She carried several boxes marked Christmas up the stairs to the living room and stacked them in a corner. She was tempted to dive right into them, but decided she'd better dust first. She wasn't much on housekeeping, but neither she nor Allan had had a minute to spare for the house. She really didn't have time now, but she knew she'd feel better when she finished. After dinner.

The Lexus was still out front, so Margaret ventured out to the workshop.

"Joy to the World" poured out from the radio. Allan was humming along as he rubbed a finishing coat on to a bench. On the opposite end of the room, Shane had his back to her, singing along with the carol in a deep baritone voice, his arm outstretched, a paintbrush in his hand. He was working on a large sheet of plywood, covering it in tan paint. Stacked to the side, against the wall, were two more sheets of plywood, already painted. There were lengths of two-by-fours and a long piece of board with rough fabric, like burlap, attached.

"What are you making?" Margaret asked, interrupting him.

Shane's hand stilled, and he looked over his shoulder at Margaret. His expression showed hesitance. He stepped back so she could see. "It won't look like much until it's put together, but it's a stable for your Nativity. I hope it will work out all right."

Margaret stared at Shane, then at the large plywood sheet, stunned. "What . . . why . . . how . . . ? I don't know what to say. This is amazing. You did all this this afternoon?"

"Is it all right? I didn't want to overstep my bounds, but what you had was hopeless, and you were trying to do it all yourself. When I got here with Allan, I could see he has a full plate too. I thought maybe I could help out."

Allan had turned from his work and was watching them. He had to have been involved in Shane's project. She wondered if he'd suggested it.

"This is fantastic! How does it go together?"

Shane showed her how the sides would attach to the center with heavy-duty Velcro hinges, and the roof would partially cover the stable, enough to steady the sides and make it freestanding. Though it only had a primer coat of paint on the walls, Margaret could envision the finished stable, with painted rock-and-plaster walls and a stable scene. For the first time since they'd found the old set pieces, she had hope that the set would be finished in time and would make the living Nativity come to life.

"I can't thank you enough! I just can't believe you did this for me—for the town."

"I like Marble Cove. But my motives are more selfish than you think. I remember that living Nativity from my childhood." He hesitated for a moment. "I didn't have a nice childhood. It was pretty rough. But the Nativity made an impression on me. It was something special that symbolized hope and a better life, and I got to be part of it. I guess I'm kind of trying to recapture that feeling."

"Wow." Margaret shook her head as she stared at the wood pieces. Did that have something to do with his reason for hanging around Marble Cove? Was he searching for something? "I never imagined all that would happen when I told my friend Diane about the living Nativity we used to have."

"When I showed Shane my workroom, he asked right off if he could use some of my tools," Allan said. "When he told me why, I couldn't say no."

That was significant. Allan had only ever shared his workroom with one other person. Dan—Shelley's husband—from across the street. He had encouraged Dan in his woodworking interests, and it had helped develop new skills for Dan. Margaret couldn't help wondering if Shane, for all his obvious success, needed an encourager. In his quiet way, Allan was perfect for the job.

"Whatever your reason, you're an absolute godsend to me and the Nativity. I didn't know how I was going to come up with a stable background. This is beyond anything I even dreamed of. Thank you so much!"

"You're welcome." Shane looked relieved, which puzzled Margaret. Did he imagine she wouldn't have been pleased? She was thrilled.

"I noticed a large pot of marinara sauce in the kitchen," Margaret said. "Allan is an amazing chef, you know." Of course he didn't know. "I do hope you will join us for dinner, Shane."

Shane looked at Allan, who nodded. "I don't know about the chef part, but I told him he was invited," Allan said. "Long as he doesn't mind plain fare."

"So when would you gentlemen like to eat? Shall I put the pasta on to boil?"

"What do you say, Shane? Are you about finished?" Allan said.

"I would love to have dinner with you. Maybe in, say, fifteen minutes? I need a little time to finish and clean up."

"Perfect. Margaret, we'll be in in twenty minutes. That will give us time to wash up too."

Margaret returned to the house and turned on the pot of water to boil. She just had time to set the table and throw together a salad while the pasta cooked and the garlic bread warmed up. As she worked, she realized she was humming a tune: "Joy to the World." That made her smile. A stranger was in Allan's workshop, helping her with the Nativity set. He was a real, live man, no doubt about that, but she couldn't help wondering if God had sent an angel to her at this moment, for this reason. It could be a coincidence, but, along with her friends, she'd experienced a few miracles in recent years—enough to make her wonder. She silently thanked the Lord for Shane. Whatever his reason for being in Marble Cove, it had blessed her for sure. She couldn't wait to show her friends the stable.

*   *   *

"That was delicious," Shane said as he folded his napkin and placed it on the table. "You are a man of many talents, Allan. And Margaret, a woman of many talents."

Margaret chuckled. "Allan is the cooking expert. It's a good thing, or we'd probably starve." She got up to remove the dirty plates. Shane started to rise to help her, but she motioned him to sit down.

"So have you decided on which wood you want for your drafting table, Shane?" Allan asked.

"I like the European walnut and the red oak for the richness of the grain. I'll go with the red oak, as you suggested. It will fit nicely with my other furniture."

"Excellent choice." Allan pulled a small notepad and a pencil out of his pocket and jotted down the wood. He started writing calculations on the pad.

"Allan, could I see that pencil?" Shane asked.

Margaret and Allan both looked at Shane. Allan held up the carpenter's pencil. "This?"

"Yes, please." Shane reached out and Allan handed it to him.

Allan glanced up at Margaret and shrugged. Shane held the pencil and turned it over to read the writing on it. "Keeley and Sons Hardware and Feed Store. I have one just like it."

He reached into his pocket and took out a stub of a carpenter's pencil. "You can't read all the writing anymore." He held it up for them to see. Margaret could just make out *Keeley and Sons Har* before the end where the wood had been shaved away.

"I've been carrying this pencil around for thirty years, hoping to find out where it came from," Shane said. "I'd forgotten about it, but I remembered it a couple of weeks ago and did an online search. I found a reference to Keeley's associated with Marble Cove, so I decided to come check it out."

"That's what brought you to Marble Cove? A pencil stub?" Margaret blurted out.

Shane gave her a sheepish look. "Yes. Curiosity. I know it sounds odd, but it's a link to my past."

"Keeley's used to be the hardware store in town," Allan said. "It was more of a general store. They sold everything, from nails and paint to seed and tack. The sons sold the store ten years ago, after their father died. The boys had moved down south and started their own business and they didn't want to keep the old store. A franchise offered them a good price for the store, then the new company changed the name to Marble Cove Hardware. Old Mr. Keeley always had a jar full of pencils at the front counter. He must have purchased a thousand of them for advertising. If you bought something at the store, you got a pencil with his name on it. Then, when times got tough, he sold them for a nickel. They're handy pencils. I've still got a few. Would you like a new one?"

"Thanks." He took the proffered pencil. "What did Mr. Keeley look like?"

"He was a big man. As tall as you. He had a limp and a hand that was missing two fingers from a construction accident, but it never hampered him. He was kind of bent over the last twenty years before he died," Margaret said. "Where did you get the pencil? Did he give it to you?"

Shane shook his head, his expression sad. "I don't remember anyone like that." He looked up and smiled. "At least I know it came from Marble Cove."

"So you got it from someone in Marble Cove?"

"I don't know. It was thirty years ago. I was living in a children's home in Portland, and there was a Christmas party. I remember the party because it was kind of a turning point in my life. Some people put on a party for us, and they gave us presents. That's what I remember the most. We played some games and ate a bunch of cookies and candy, I think. Santa Claus was there, and Mrs. Claus too. At least that's what I thought. The old lady had a big bun and glasses and a red sweater, just like you'd picture Mrs. Claus. We made ornaments and she told me I was talented."

"That's a nice memory. And you think it was someone from Marble Cove?" Margaret asked.

"Well, that's where the pencil came from. I suppose a batch of the pencils could have been donated to the children's home. I think everyone got a pencil that night. I liked the flat, wide shape of the pencil, but then Santa passed out presents. He handed me a present, and I expected it to be socks or shoes or a sweater, because that's what we always got at the children's home. When I opened it, I couldn't believe it. It was an Erector Set. That was the best present I ever got. Still to this day, I don't think I've ever gotten a better present. I still have the Erector Set, but it's in pretty bad shape." He chuckled. "I wore it out."

"Is that why you wanted an Erector Set for your son?" Margaret asked.

"Yes. My son Anthony is six. The same age I was when I got mine. I didn't find one, but I got the sailboat kit we can build together."

"Did that Erector Set have an influence on your career choice?" Allan asked.

"I believe it did. I discovered I love to design and build things, and I'm good at it. I enjoyed sports, but when I felt alone or inadequate, I'd get out the Erector Set and build something."

"That's a wonderful story. And to think, it might have been someone from Marble Cove who encouraged you. I wonder who it could have been," Margaret said. She tried to picture Shane as a little boy. An orphan. How sad it must have been not to have a family at Christmas. She hoped the children's home made Christmas special for the kids, but it couldn't have taken the place of a family. What older lady from Marble Cove could have been his Mrs. Claus? Maybe someone like old Mrs. Squires, or Coral Peabody, their neighbor. She was in her eighties. It could have been her thirty years ago, or her sister, Celia Patterson. Coral's husband could have been the Santa Claus.

"Would you like some coffee, Shane? I have some wonderful cookies made by our neighbor Shelley, who does the baking for the Cove."

"I can't pass that up. I've been in the Cove several times for her pastries. Probably gained a few pounds while I've been here," he said, patting his stomach. "I've tried walking it off on the beach."

"You've had some brisk walks then," Allan said. "It's been cold out there this week."

He chuckled. "Yes. Invigorating. Good for the circulation."

They went into the living room with their coffees, and Margaret carried in a plate of cookies. She must remember to thank Shelley again. Even though Adelaide wasn't there, they should have made an effort to do some holiday baking and decorating, just in case they had visitors. She was embarrassed that she hadn't put up any decorations. The boxes sat in the corner of the living room. Tomorrow she would do some decorating for sure.

CHAPTER NINE

Y ou said your family is in Canada visiting relatives?" Margaret asked, making it more a question than a statement. She understood Shane wanted to find out about a moment in his past, but it still seemed odd that he would spend several days hanging around Marble Cove alone.

"Yes. My wife's folks live in Edmonton, Canada. Marissa wanted to spend Christmas with them, so I took her and our son up there. I had a job in Bangor. I finished that up and was heading back to Portland. I'm in no hurry, so I took the scenic, coastal route. When I saw the turn for Marble Cove, I decided to stop and take a look. There's a small-town, friendly atmosphere here. I like it."

"So you'll be headed back up to Edmonton for Christmas?" Allan asked.

Shane frowned and folded his hands together in his lap. "I don't know. You see, Marissa and I are . . . struggling. She wanted time away from me." He pressed his lips together. Margaret could see Shane had his own inner struggles. "She thinks I spend too much time working and not enough time with her and our son."

"Balancing a business and a family isn't easy," Margaret said. He had mentioned his wife's dissatisfaction with his busyness to her before. She and Allan had run their own accounting business for years. And most of the time, the amount of time spent working hadn't been an issue, because they worked together. She couldn't imagine the struggles they would have had if they'd worked separately. Add a child on top of the mix, and it got more complicated. They were fortunate that Adelaide had been an easy child, happy to sit quietly at the office with a coloring book, picture books, or her dolls. Lunchtimes had been more like indoor picnics as they'd eaten together.

"Balance is the key," Shane said. "At least that's what Marissa says, and I suspect she is right. I came to Marble Cove to find out where the pencil came from, but I was really looking for answers to my own problems."

"And have you found the answers?" Margaret asked.

"I know I don't want to lose my family. I never had a family growing up, so I'm not sure what one looks like, but I'm willing to learn."

"That's the first step in the right direction," Allan said. "What we all have every day is time. And it's like money. Once you spend it, you can't get it back, but you can invest it. Look at you. Someone invested a small fraction of time in you, and it probably seemed insignificant, and yet you remember it. It encouraged you to do something with your life. That's what families do for each other every day."

Margaret stared at her husband. His words sounded just like the accountant that he'd been. Investments and fractions. But he was right. She and Allan had invested time in Adelaide's life, and now Adelaide was doing something with her life. And that was reason to rejoice.

"I hadn't thought about it that way, but it sounds good. It's worth a try," Shane said. Then he looked embarrassed. "It's not that I don't want to spend time with my family. I love my son and my wife. I just thought it was more important to provide for them, to make sure they have security, you know?"

"Security isn't always tangible," Margaret said. She felt sorry for this man who wanted to do the best for his family, but with no experience to understand what they really needed. "They need you, and they need you to need them too."

Whoa. Her own words hit her square between the eyes. Was that why she felt so depressed? Did she need Adelaide to need her? That was a startling thought. Her little girl didn't need her anymore. But that was a good thing. Wasn't it? Oh, how complicated life could get.

Shane stared at her, as if her words stunned him. "I . . . that never occurred to me. I've spent my entire life working hard to be self-sufficient, so I don't need anyone. But I do. I need them."

Margaret took a sip of coffee and nearly choked as she swallowed it around the knot in her throat. She had to let go of Adelaide and stop needing her daughter to depend on her. That didn't mean Adelaide didn't care anymore. But she needed to stretch and become her own person. It was like the opposite end of Shane's problem.

Shane stood. "Seeing you and Allan interacting and helping each other, and watching you work on the Nativity, Margaret, has made me long for something I'm missing. I'm not sure what it looks like, but I want to do something special with my wife and my son, something meaningful. Not just a one-time thing, but a new focus."

He looked around their living room, as if taking in his surroundings. "I can't even tell you what's in my living room at home. I know it's attractive and comfortable. That's my wife's doing."

He stopped and looked at the mantel. He stared at it, until Margaret began to wonder what he saw. Dust? Probably. The lack of Christmas decorations? He walked over to the mantel and picked up the handmade Popsicle stick–star card. He held it, studied it, turned it over, then gasped.

"This." He held it up. "I made this. I . . ." He looked at Allan, then at her. "Could you be . . . ?"

"You made it? But that's not possible. I just got . . . "

"I made this card. I'm positive." He showed her the back. "There. That is my name. Shane. I signed it and gave it to the lady in the office at the children's home. Every kid made one. It was an assignment, that we had to make thank-you cards for the people who put on the party for us. And you've kept it all these years." He shook his head. "I can't believe it."

"But it just arrived."

"But I made it thirty years ago."

Margaret felt like she'd stepped into another dimension. If Shane was right, where had the card been for thirty years? Besides, she couldn't have been Mrs. Claus. She wasn't old enough.

"Did you go to Portland thirty years ago to put on a party for a children's home?"

Margaret shook her head, but then a memory unfolded. They had just moved to Marble Cove, and the friend who sang with a church choir made a trip to sing at a church in Portland and invited her and Allan along. Afterward there was a party for underprivileged kids. She looked at Allan. He was remembering too.

"Was it at a church?" Allan asked. "I remember we put on a program and then had refreshments. There were children from the neighborhood, and the choir director made me wear a Santa suit. The choir brought presents that the church had collected."

"I bet I wore that red sweater that I still have. In fact, I wore it at church on Sunday, Allan. I've had that sweater for as long as I can remember. And my hair was long in those days. I might have put it up in a bun." Margaret began to laugh. "I was only about forty years old, but I must have looked old to a six-year-old. That was a long time ago."

"Yes, but I've never forgotten it. That gift brought me so much joy for so many years."

Joy. They had helped bring joy into a lonely boy's life, and they didn't even know it. A Bible verse, Matthew 25:40, popped into her mind: "Truly I tell you, whatever you did for one of the least of these brothers and sisters of mine, you did for me."

"Shane, I don't pretend to understand how you found us, or how your card arrived on our doorstep after thirty years, but I'm so glad it happened. I can't tell you how much you have encouraged me. I've been stressing over getting the Nativity set done, and you came along and made the stable for us. And I've been feeling sorry for myself because our daughter Adelaide recently moved out on her own, and I miss her so much. But you've reminded me that joy doesn't depend on our circumstances. You found joy in creating things with that Erector Set. I guess joy isn't something that happens to us. We need to look for it. I think I need to start looking."

Shane's smile was a little sad around the edges. "Me too, Margaret. Me too."

*　　*　　*

Margaret was still trying to process Shane's revelation as she opened the top box of Christmas decorations. It was nine o'clock, and Shane had just left. He'd promised to come back in the morning to finish up prepping the stable for her before he left town.

What an amazing gift to see the results of a small act of kindness thirty years ago. None of it had been her doing. She and Allan had gone along with the choir that night. But God had used them to bless Shane and perhaps some other children too.

Inside the box was another box. She opened it and took out the first piece, carefully unwrapping the tissue paper around it to reveal the figurine of a wise man. She placed it on the mantel that she'd just dusted. One by one, she unwrapped the other pieces to a crèche scene.

The Nativity set was a classical Italian Fontanini set that Allan had given her on their fifth Christmas. She'd loved it for its beauty, though she hadn't really believed in God all those years ago. Now the artistic figurines held a special meaning, reminding her of the miraculous birth of the baby Jesus. Adelaide loved arranging the set on the mantel, and they always placed it first, before any of the other Christmas decorations. Margaret almost felt guilty putting up the Nativity without Adelaide, but she wasn't going to be there to help.

Margaret set out a few other favorite decorations. She put battery-operated candles in the windows and turned them on. The soft lights gave the room a lovely glow, but the best part was that the neighbors—Shelley, Diane, Beverly, Mr. Wheeland, and Mrs. Peabody—would see the Christmas spirit shining out from her house. She knew her friends had been concerned about her sorrow since Adelaide moved out. They would be happy to see the decorations, and that made her smile.

*   *   *

Margaret had just opened the gallery Thursday morning when the door opened and Bernadette rushed in.

"Good morning, Margaret. I'm here, ready to go to work. I brought some more jewelry. Wait until you see the new pieces I made with those crystal beads you gave me!" She opened her bag and held up a long necklace with clusters of the beads between lengths of braided chains. They were delicate and sparkly. "Here. I made this one for you." She held out a simple necklace that would look lovely on a sweater.

"Oh, goodness, I didn't expect you to make one for me. It's beautiful." Touched by Bernadette's gift, Margaret accepted it and looped it around her neck. It sparkled against her forest-green mock-turtleneck sweater. She leaned forward and hugged the young woman. "Thank you!"

Bernadette beamed. "You're welcome. It looks good on you. I thought it would."

Margaret rarely wore jewelry, but it wouldn't hurt to look festive. After all, it was the Christmas season. She touched the delicate necklace and felt pretty.

"I didn't expect you so early," Margaret said.

"I know. I wanted to get out of the house before mother started in on her tea party. She gets so obsessive about everything. And my sister-in-law Angela is there. She came down from Bangor yesterday. She's almost as old-fashioned as my mother." Bernadette made a face showing her distaste.

"Oh dear." Margaret knew about the friction between Bernadette and her mother. It had taken Margaret quite a while to warm up to Bernadette. Her free-spirited ways were old-fashioned in their own way, like a hippy or a gypsy, but Margaret wasn't going to point that out. It fit with her artistic style, but Margaret wondered if it was partly a rebellion against her mother's traditional lifestyle. It had been somewhat of a shock to Margaret to realize her own daughter thought she was old-fashioned.

"You know, I really appreciate your help. But I wonder if you might consider going to your mother's tea. I know it isn't something you want to do, and I suppose you might feel a little uncomfortable, but this sounds like it means something special to your mother."

Bernadette sighed. "I guess it does. She makes a big deal about it. I feel awkward around her friends. They act so proper and stilted. I can't do that. It just isn't me, you know?"

Margaret couldn't help smiling at Bernadette's assessment and her pursed lips, as if she'd eaten a sour lemon.

"I bet, if you tried, you could smile and be congenial for an hour."

Bernadette raised her eyebrows. Then she laughed. "Yeah, maybe."

"I'm thinking it would mean a lot to your mother. I know it would to me. Adelaide has decided to go to her friend's house for Christmas, and I realized for the first time how much it means to me to have her around."

"Yeah, well, Adelaide is a sweet girl and she never complains. But I can't be quiet like that. I say what I think. Mother hates that."

Margaret stifled a sigh. "Think about it as a Christmas present. An hour of smiling and being sweet to her friends and actually listening to their conversations. It might surprise you. They might be interesting."

"I doubt it. They're exchanging gifts."

"That's perfect. You have the prettiest bracelets and you admitted to me that they didn't take long to make. I'm thinking about the colorful beaded ones that are crocheted together."

Bernadette got a pensive look on her face. "Do you think they'd like them?"

"I think they're beautiful, and I am terribly old-fashioned too, you know."

Bernadette laughed. "Okay, I'll give it a try, but if it's a disaster, I'll tell my mother it was your idea."

Margaret had no idea how Bernadette would act around her mother's friends. Her mother might not thank her, but then again, it might work out well. "You can do that."

"What shall I wear?"

"What you are wearing now is fine." It was one of Bernadette's more conservative outfits, with a silky, calf-length skirt in a rainbow of pastel colors, black high-heeled boots, and a soft teal turtleneck sweater with layers of beads around her neck. Her long dark hair was pulled back in a loose French braid, with a few wisps of hair hanging loose and curly around her face. She looked as lovely as Margaret had ever seen her.

"Okay. I've got a new batch of bracelets and little bags for them. You really think they'll like them?"

"I do. How many will be there?"

"Mother said ten. Plus her and my sister-in-law."

"Take a few extra, just in case."

"Are you sure you'll be all right without me? You've been really busy this week."

"I'll manage." It meant she couldn't work on the Nativity set, but this was more important.

"I'll be back as soon as it's over. And if it goes the way things have gone before, I'll be back sooner."

"All right. I'll want to hear all about it."

Bernadette gathered her oversize bag and her jewelry. "Off to the guillotine." She gave Margaret a wink, then sailed out the door.

Chapter Ten

Without Bernadette's help at the gallery, Margaret was stuck. She needed to find some craft materials before Shelley's children came over that night to help her decorate the Christmas tree. She wanted to give them a special treat, but since she couldn't compete with their mother's baking, she wanted to do something artistic. Shane's Popsicle stick star had given her inspiration.

Fortunately, Margaret remembered the craft supplies she'd stashed away at the gallery ages ago. She dug out the plastic bin (slightly dusty) from a cupboard in her workroom and found most of what she needed. Card stock. Glue. Assorted buttons, beads, and ribbon left over from an art day she'd held at the community center for a group of children. Glitter. Red and green gel pens.

Standing at the checkout counter, she put together small kits for the children. The only thing missing were Popsicle sticks. She'd seen some craft sticks at the hardware store. She'd have to wait until Bernadette returned to get those.

She wondered how the tea party was going, and chuckled at the image of Bernadette with her mother's very proper friends. What an interesting painting it would make. She could imagine an entire line of pictures with a free-spirited young woman in plain, old-fashioned settings, a contrast of bold colors and flowing styles in dull, staid backgrounds. The images were total departures from Margaret's usual landscape paintings, but what fun it would be. Something to explore after the holidays. The idea brought a bubble of joy to her thoughts. Like her young artist friend, the drawings would be a blast of fresh air barging into a stuffy room.

The front door bell jangled as Beverly came in.

"Good morning, and Merry Christmas!" Margaret called out.

Beverly stared at her, then smiled. "Merry Christmas to you. What's happened?"

"I'm just happy and feeling the Christmas spirit today," Margaret said, which was true, but she wasn't ready to share the reason yet. She wanted to tell all of her friends at the same time about Shane and the Popsicle stick star. It was beyond amazing.

"That's wonderful. Have you heard from Adelaide?"

"No, but she's coming by this afternoon to get her Christmas presents and my mother's faux-fur coat for her trip."

"That will be quite an experience for her. I hope she has a wonderful time."

"So do I. We'll miss her, but it's a great opportunity for her. Oh, and Allan said he'd love to come to your house for Christmas dinner. Thank you so much for thinking of us."

"My pleasure. I just thought I'd stop in and see if you need some help today. I have a couple of free hours this afternoon."

"Bless you for offering, but Bernadette is coming in as soon as her mother's tea party is over."

"Bernadette is attending her mother's tea party? That's interesting. I'd love to be a mouse in the corner to see how that's going."

Margaret grinned. "Me too. She wasn't going to attend and I talked her into it."

"I hope it doesn't backfire. She's a sweet girl, for all her flamboyant ways. What made you do it?"

"I was thinking about Adelaide and how I miss her, and how she's spreading her wings, looking for her own style and place in life. Suddenly I'm old-fashioned. It stung at first, but then I remembered feeling the same way about my mother when I was about Adelaide and Bernadette's age. I'm sure Bernadette's mother wants to be part of her daughter's life, even though they have different tastes."

"I hope you're right. Her mother is a bit, uh, stilted."

"Yes, she is." Margaret hoped she hadn't made a mistake, encouraging Bernadette. She didn't want her young friend to be hurt. She suspected her boldness and bohemian style hid a tender heart.

"Well, I'd better get to town hall. I have an appointment with a couple of people from Augusta who don't like us holding our Nativity at the train station." She sighed. "These people have nothing to do with Marble Cove."

"I'm glad I don't have to deal with them. I never realized how much a mayor has to put up with."

"Yes, well, it's good problems most of the time. I'll see you later."

*   *   *

Diane came into the gallery as Beverly was leaving. "Good morning," she said.

"Good morning. Gotta run," Beverly said. "Margaret can fill you in."

Diane watched the door shut behind Beverly, then turned to Margaret. "What was all that about?"

"She has to go deal with some out-of-town people about the Nativity being at the train station."

"Honestly. If it's not one problem, it's another. Well, if anyone can handle that, it's Beverly." Then she smiled at Margaret. "How are you doing?"

"Wonderful. Couldn't be better."

"Really?" Diane raised her eyebrows. "What happened?"

Margaret hadn't realized her depression had been so obvious to all her friends that they were surprised to see her smiling. "I'm just catching the Christmas spirit," she said. "I must have been miserable to be around. I'm sorry. I didn't mean for my sadness in missing Adelaide to rub off on you and Beverly and Shelley. I'm so lucky to have understanding friends."

"Hey, you've been my friend through thick and thin, my best and my worst. I should be thanking you. It's what friends do."

"Yes, it is." Margaret was tempted to share with Diane about Shane and the Popsicle stick–star mystery, but she still wanted to tell her friends together. It could wait. "So what brings you out this fine, cold morning?"

Diane's face lit up with a smile. "Exciting news! I couldn't wait to tell you! We have animals, after all!"

"Animals, as in sheep and cows for the Nativity?"

"Yes. A few. Not too many." Her face brightened. "But guess what! We have a camel and some sheep. Leo had just about given up on finding one, but then he did! I'm so excited. A camel for us, and its owner is coming with it, dressed as a shepherd, so he can help keep an eye on it."

"Really? That's amazing. Where in the world did Leo find a camel?"

"There's a rescue farm not far from here. He got called out to pull a bad tooth on one of their animals. They have an old camel that came from the Desert of Maine near Freeport."

"Really? I may have seen that camel before. It's been years ago when we took Adelaide to visit the desert."

"I need to go see it. I thought Leo was kidding. I'd never heard of it. I guess it's an actual, naturally formed desert."

"Yes, it was formed by glacier action, then was covered for eons by a build-up of dirt and the forest. When the Tuttle family bought the land in the late 1700s, they cleared the land for farming and overgrazed with sheep. Eventually the topsoil eroded and the sand took back over. Sad for them. They had to give up farming. Someone bought it and turned it into a desert attraction."

"Thanks to them we get a camel, though it isn't coming directly from them. We have to provide a place to keep it overnight and during the daytime. Chuck and Cathy Johnston have offered their place—you know, Arvid Pierson's old farm. The owner is bringing a donkey too, and Leo has a Shetland pony lined up. It isn't a lot of animals, but it will be enough to make it seem more real."

"That's wonderful!" And a huge relief. They would have enough for a good Nativity, and she didn't need to keep trying to fix the crumbling old pieces. "We can use the few that I've managed to repair to fill in."

"What about the stable? Have you been able to fix it?"

"Nope. Better."

"What? Did you find something else?"

"Let's just say, it found me."

"What do you mean?"

"You'll have to wait and see." Margaret grinned. "I think I'll be able to show it tomorrow. It's going to be a great living Nativity!"

Diane's eyes sparkled with anticipation. "Now you have me excited. You are so mysterious. I can't wait to find out what you've done!"

"Yes, I have a lot to reveal. Tomorrow morning, when we all meet for coffee—I'll tell you then."

*   *   *

"I'm back," Bernadette said as she came through the back door of the gallery. "And I brought you some lunch, so I hope you haven't eaten."

"Lunch! Is it that time already? I am hungry, now that you mention it."

"Leftover goodies from my mother's tea. The cucumber and arugula sandwiches with herb cream cheese are really good. And there are also sandwiches stuffed with chicken with orange and cranberry. The only thing wrong with them is they're too small." Bernadette giggled as she took the little triangles of sandwiches out of a bag. Each was neatly wrapped in plastic wrap.

"So the food was good?" Since Bernadette was smiling and upbeat, it couldn't have gone too poorly.

"Really good. And that's not all. There's handmade chocolate truffles and a pecan tassie tart, and cheesecake and cherry squares, and bacon and cheddar scones with pepper jelly."

"Your mother must be quite a cook."

Bernadette shrugged. "She does all right. This was special. She's been cooking all week."

"I'm glad you enjoyed it. Was it hard to sit still and visit with a bunch of ladies?"

"No. They were actually really nice and one of them brought her daughter, who was dressed like me. She was a lot younger, like eighteen. One of the older ladies said she liked our old-fashioned clothes. She said she wore clothes like us fifty years ago. Can you imagine?" Bernadette shook her head. "I can't believe that."

Margaret chuckled. "Have you checked out what the hippies wore in the sixties and seventies? You would have fit right in."

"Really? You're not kidding me?"

"Honest. Look it up on your computer. You might get some new ideas."

"I will."

"Did they like your bracelets?"

"Mixed reactions. Some really liked them. One lady held hers up and said, "In-ter-esting," in such a drawn-out way, it was like she was trying to figure out what it was. The lady next to her said hers was beautiful and she put it right on her wrist. It had lavender and orange beads, and she was wearing a red blouse. I thought it was nice together, but Angela said it clashed and offered to trade. The lady said no. She liked it."

She hoped Bernadette's sister-in-law's comment hadn't hurt Bernadette. The colors did clash, but somehow Bernadette made wild combinations work.

"Well, thank you for bringing me leftovers. They look delicious. I'm going to make a cup of tea to go with it. Would you like one?"

"No, thank you! I've had enough tea to last me a year!"

Margaret laughed. "I bet you have."

"But it was good tea. Mango. I liked it. I'm glad you talked me into going. And I think I made enough points that I don't have to go to the library event they were all talking about. Someone is doing a dramatic reading of *A Christmas Carol*."

"I think I would like that. It might be good."

"If they do a reading of *How the Grinch Stole Christmas*, I might just consider it. Now I'm going to get to work while you eat. Oh, and thanks for suggesting I take extra bracelets. I had just enough."

"Good. I'm glad."

Bernadette changed the Christmas music to a modern station. She looked back at Margaret. "I hope you don't mind. I can't take that jazz stuff."

"It's a small price to pay for free help," Margaret said. Bernadette was volunteering her time, but Margaret intended to pay her something for her help. She would add a nice bonus to the check for Bernadette's jewelry sales. She didn't care for Bernadette's taste in music, but she would turn it way down or change it back to her jazz if it got too raucous.

Bernadette went out front, humming to the music. Margaret made tea and cleared a spot to eat at the table. The leftovers from the tea were delicious. Margaret remembered all the tea parties she and Adelaide and Allan had had over the years. Maybe she would get the recipes from Bernadette's mother. She would fix them for Adelaide next time she was home. The thought made her heart hurt from missing her daughter.

She was getting the table ready to paint a baby lamb when the phone rang. She picked it up.

"Shearwater Gallery. Margaret speaking."

"Margaret, this is Eugenia Lassiter, Bernadette's mother. I want to thank you for sending her home to my tea party. I know she didn't want to come, and I know you need the help at the gallery this time of year, but it meant so much to me."

"Goodness, you are so welcome. I'm glad she went. We don't have that many special moments with our daughters. They grow up so fast."

"Yes, they do. Bernadette told me your Adelaide has moved out on her own. You were always so close. That must be hard for you."

"Yes, it is. I miss her. But I just realized that we've raised them to become independent, so it's a blessing when they do make their own lives, isn't it?"

"Yes, I suppose it is. Even when we don't always see eye to eye with them."

"I know. That's the hard part. Bernadette is a lovely young woman," Margaret said, and she meant it.

"Thank you. My friends loved seeing her. So did I, and that was a rare treat these days."

"I really enjoyed the leftovers Bernadette brought me. I'd love to have your recipes."

"Really? You're welcome. It was her idea. I'll send the recipes in with her next time she goes in. Oh, and Bernadette said you're working on the set for the living Nativity! I'm so excited that you and your friends are reviving that tradition. I'm looking forward to going."

"Wonderful! Thanks so much for calling," Margaret said, and started to hang up.

"Wait. One more thing. Could you, maybe, suggest to Bernadette that her mother would love to get a piece of her jewelry for Christmas? I think she doesn't believe I like it. I usually wear pearls, you know. But I think her jewelry is lovely."

"I will be happy to drop a hint," Margaret said. More than a hint, because she was right. Bernadette would never believe it.

Chapter Eleven

Margaret hummed along to "White Christmas" as she painted curly hair on the baby lamb. She was surprised by her excitement about the living Nativity. Something had changed inside of her in the past few days, and the gloom she'd felt had lifted. Looking backward, she realized she'd been grieving for Adelaide, which seemed odd. Adelaide was alive and doing very well. But she wasn't in Margaret's world anymore, and that hurt.

She didn't miss her daughter any less, and Christmas was going to be tough without her, but she had Allan—they had each other. That's how they started out, before Adelaide was born. It was as if they'd stepped back in time, and yet not. They had almost twenty-six years of memories stored up of all the joyful times and even the struggles with their precious daughter.

Adelaide would love the lamb. She loved animals. Especially baby animals. Perhaps, in honor of Adelaide, she would paint a cat or two, or three. After all, every stable should have barn cats. Wouldn't Adelaide love that? Too bad she wouldn't be there to see it.

There was a knock on the back door. She went to see who it was. Shane was standing there, propping up the largest piece of the stable background. She held the door for him while he lugged it inside.

"Where shall I put it?" he asked.

"Against the wall. Oh dear. I should have moved the old pieces out to make room."

"They're heavy and crumbly. Let me do it. I'll put them outside, and Allan can move them later. They need to go to the dump."

Margaret helped maneuver the old pieces out. They disintegrated into large chunks as they moved them.

"What a mess," Shane said as they finally got all the pieces outside. He brushed his hands together to shake off the grime.

"Worse than I realized." Margaret got a broom and swept up the debris. Then Shane set the new pieces against the wall and stepped back so she could see.

"This is perfect." Her voice cracked from the lump in her throat. "You cannot imagine what a gift this is to me and to Marble Cove. How can I thank you?" She looked up at Shane. He towered above her and was so strong, and yet she thought she detected a tear in his eye.

"It's nothing, Margaret. I'm glad I was able to help. Coming here and meeting you and Allan means a lot to me."

He swallowed, then went on. "I had hoped to recapture something here, some passion like I felt when I first started designing buildings, and like when I first got married, and like when my son was born. But I realize there was something lacking even then. My motivations were all about gaining something I never had before. They were never about giving. But that's going to change. I'm not going back to Portland. At least not yet. I'm going to go to Canada and get my wife and son and bring them home where they belong."

"Shane, I'm so glad. You enjoy that precious family while you can. That boy is going to grow up so fast. You won't believe how fast it's going to happen."

"I hope not too fast. I have a lot of making up to do."

Margaret opened her arms, and Shane reached down and gave her a big hug. She held on for a moment, and so did he. A tear leaked out of her eye. How strange. She was not the sentimental type, but this big man brought out all of her maternal instincts. In a few days, he had become a special part of her life.

"Next time you are near Marble Cove, please come visit us," she said. "And bring your family. I'd love to meet your wife and son."

"I will do that. I promise. I think they will like it here as much as I do. I've already talked to your Realtor, Patricia Finley, about finding a place to rent this summer."

"Wonderful!"

"Now before I go, did you get those vases in? I still need a gift for my wife."

"Yes. There's an especially nice one I think you might like. I set it aside for you, but there are others if you don't like this one."

Margaret led Shane to a vase on her desk. She turned on the overhead light and held it up. It was a rounded vase, shaped like a fish bowl, with gentle ripples in shades of blues and greens and streaks of clear and hints of golden light, like the ocean. A sea turtle and a school of small silver fish swam through the shimmery current, almost real enough to see them move.

"Yes. I see the ocean and light and life. I think Marissa will love it," he said.

"I hope so. And if she still wants a large lighthouse painting, I'll be doing more pictures of the Orlean Point Light after the holidays are over."

"I'm sure she will. I hope . . . I pray she'll give me a chance to show her what I've found here."

Margaret wrapped his gift in brown paper, and then in some red Christmas wrap that she kept in case someone requested gift wrap. She made a bow out of wide silver ribbon. It looked elegant. She hoped Marissa would love the gift, and she added a prayer that she and Shane would have a great future together.

"Stay in touch, won't you?" Margaret asked as she handed the wrapped vase to Shane. "Let us know how things go for you."

"I will," he said. "Merry Christmas, Margaret!"

As he left, she felt another pang of sadness. Shane had entered her life as a total stranger just a few days ago, but in that short time, he had blessed her. She would miss him.

*   *   *

Margaret prepared the paints she needed to finish the stable. She stood, staring at the large plywood background. Two sheets of plywood mounted on a two-by-four frame formed the back wall. Two more pieces of plywood formed each side. Strips of Velcro made hinges to keep them attached to the back wall. An overhang was a separate piece that would attach at the top to all sides as a roof, holding the back and side pieces in place and giving a small amount of shelter. If the weather was bad, at least the actors could huddle under the roof. Shane had done an amazing job. She couldn't wait to show Diane, Shelley, and Beverly, but first she had to finish it.

Shane had primed the walls of the stable with a background wash the color of dried mud. Margaret envisioned the scene. Her research indicated the stable would be an enclosure open on the outside, and attached to the domicile, where the animals could be brought close to the family at night. There might be a variety of domesticated animals such as a donkey, an ox, sheep, and goats. She imagined there would be dogs and cats.

As she began to paint a scene on the walls, she noticed the music had changed. One of her favorites, "Christmas Is Coming" from *A Charlie Brown Christmas*, filled the gallery. She glanced over and saw Bernadette smiling from the doorway.

"Thought you might be tired of my music," she said. "So I put on your favorite CD."

"Thank you, Bernadette. That's very thoughtful of you. I can use the inspiration."

"I like Charlie Brown, but I always thought it was just a kid's show. I haven't watched it in years. I think my mom has it in her collection. Maybe I'll get it out tonight."

"Maybe your mother would like to watch it with you."

"Yeah. I'll ask her. So how's it going?" She stepped into the workroom. "Wow, that's cool. It's new, isn't it?"

"Yes. The man who was just here made it for us."

"I saw him. He isn't from around here, is he?"

"No, he was just visiting the area. He remembered being part of a Nativity when he was younger."

"That's cool! I remember the living Nativity we used to have here. My mom took us every year. I can't wait to see it. Especially after seeing you do all this work on it."

Margaret was surprised by Bernadette's enthusiasm, though she didn't know why. Something about Christmas often brought out sentimentality and childlike delight in people. "I think you'll enjoy it."

"I know I will." The front door bells jingled. "Oh, a customer. I'll let you get back to painting."

Margaret hummed to the Christmas tune and went to work. Square clay blocks and stucco and mortar took shape on the walls. She painted in the appearance of antiquity, with chunks of stucco falling off, revealing the hardened clay beneath. In one corner, they could set the ox, looking over the scene where Mary and Joseph and the baby Jesus would be. She painted a rafter, and on it, looking down upon the scene, the first of the cats. An orange cat was licking her paw, ignoring what was going on. Behind her, a striped tabby, watched with half-opened eyes, as if curious, but not wanting to show too much interest.

She was standing back, surveying her work, when the back door opened and Allan came in. He had a red-and-green package with curly ribbon in his hands, his gift of the jewelry box for Adelaide. The reality of his reason for being there dropped a sour pill into her stomach. Adelaide would be there any minute to collect the fur coat hanging on the coat hook and to get her Christmas gifts. Then she would be off on a grand adventure. Without them.

CHAPTER TWELVE

Allan set his package on her desk, then came over to look at the stable background she'd been working on.

"That's really taking shape. I like it." Then he chuckled. "That looks like Lizzy and Butterscotch up on the beam."

"It is. I suspect they needed cats back in Jesus's day to keep the mice away, just like today."

"And your cats had to be Adelaide's cats. But where is Oreo?"

"I haven't figured out where to put him yet."

"He could go up on that ledge. It would be the perfect place for him," he said, pointing up toward the corner. "Too bad Adelaide won't be here to see it."

"I know." Margaret sighed. Her idea to add their cats had backfired on her. Seeing them in the scene made her sad. "I was just thinking about that."

"This stable set should last for many years. She can see it next year."

Margaret straightened her shoulders. "Of course. She'll be back. She won't go off somewhere every year." This was a one-time trip for Adelaide, Margaret reminded herself. At least she hoped so. Not that she didn't want her daughter experiencing new places and people. Just not without them. And not on the holidays.

The sound of jingling bells and laughter announced Adelaide's arrival. Her laughter was unmistakable. A little loud. Giggly, like a little girl with a grown-up voice. Allan went out first, and Margaret's feet felt like lead as she followed him into the front of the gallery.

"Daddy! Mom!" Adelaide gave Allan a stiff hug, then turned to Margaret and gave her an awkward hug too. They had never been a hugging family. Adelaide hadn't been a cuddler since she learned to walk.

Behind Adelaide were her friends from the group home and a man and a woman. Margaret recognized Cassie, Chloe, Tina, and Elsa's daughter Maryann. The man extended his hand to Allan.

"Hello. We're Cassie's parents. Adelaide will be with us the entire time she's in Boston."

Allan and Margaret exchanged greetings with Cassie's parents. Her father had on jeans and a wool sweater. Her mother was dressed in wool slacks and a sweater. They looked like average people—not the social elite Margaret expected. Their clothing looked like something she and Allan might wear.

Adelaide had on a brown wool skirt and a green sweater-and-cardigan set. Her friends were dressed in jeans and warm tops. All of them had on ordinary, practical clothing for a Maine winter day. Adelaide looked impatient.

"It's so good to meet you all. Thank you for inviting Adelaide to your home for the holidays. I'm sure you will have a wonderful time," Margaret said, though the words cost her dearly. With a twinge of guilt, she knew what she really felt was anything but gratitude. These people were taking her daughter away for the holidays. She should be at home.

But then she'd gotten over her disappointment because this was a grand opportunity for Adelaide. So why did she want to grab Adelaide and drag her home?

"Thank you. Cassie didn't want to be away from her friends—not even for two weeks. We have some wonderful activities planned for them. And we'll make sure they are well taken care of," Cassie's mother said.

"I'm sure you will. Adelaide, the fur coat is in the back, and we have your Christmas presents too. You can take them with you to open on Christmas Day."

"Oh." Adelaide frowned and her eyes clouded. "Your present is in my suitcase. I have to get it." She turned toward the door.

"I'll get it for you," Cassie's father said. He went out the front door.

"Come back here, Adelaide." Margaret led her daughter to the back. Allan followed her.

"I want to say good-bye in private," Margaret said. "Do you have everything you need?"

"Yes, Mom."

"Here's some money, in case you see something in Boston that you want to buy," Allan said, handing Adelaide a wad of bills.

"Cassie said I don't need money."

"That's all right. Take it. Just for emergencies."

Adelaide gave her father a confused look. "What kind of emergencies?"

"Oh, I don't know. I'm sure there won't be any, but it doesn't hurt to have a little extra. You can spend it on yourself."

"Sweetheart, it's all right. Your father wants you to have some spending money so you can have a good time and not have to be concerned about what things cost. Take it. If you don't use it, you can save it for later."

"All right." She still looked doubtful.

"Here are your Christmas presents," Allan said.

Adelaide looked at the two gifts in her father's hands: the square red-and-green package with curly ribbon and the smaller red package with a fancy silver bow.

"You can save them and open them at Cassie's on Christmas Eve or whenever they open their gifts," Margaret said. Adelaide seemed hesitant to take them, so Margaret put them in a handled bag and handed it to her.

"Here is the faux-fur coat for your night at *The Nutcracker*." Margaret took the soft, beautiful fake-mink jacket off the coat hook and handed it to Adelaide.

"Oh, it's soft."

"Yes, and it's nice and warm. Now be sure you stay with Cassie's parents all the time, and don't wander off," Margaret said.

"I will. I won't."

"And remember your manners," she added. "Tell them thank you for meals and when they take you places or give you anything."

Adelaide nodded her head. "I will." Her expression grew more troubled.

"You are going to have a good time," Allan said, smiling at Adelaide. She nodded.

They went back out to the front where the others were waiting.

"You have a lovely gallery," Cassie's mother said. "I'll have to spend some time here when we bring Adelaide back."

"Thank you."

Adelaide put her bags on the floor, then squatted down and opened her suitcase. She pulled some of the clothes out and put them on the carpet.

She took a package out of the suitcase, then she sat down on the floor holding it.

"Do you need help getting up?" Allan asked, reaching out his hand.

Adelaide shook her head. She stared at her lap.

"Come on, get up, Adelaide," Cassie said. "We have to go now."

"Yes, Adelaide," Tina said. "Come on."

"Give her time, ladies," Cassie's father said. He looked down at Adelaide with a compassionate expression, which relieved Margaret. These people understood. Their daughter also had Down syndrome. Adelaide would be well cared for.

Margaret could see Adelaide's distress was growing. She knelt down on her knees beside her. "Can I help you repack your suitcase?"

"No," Adelaide said. "I'm not going."

"Not going?" Cassie cried. "You have to!"

"No, I don't."

"Mother, make her come," Cassie said to her mother.

"Adelaide, don't you want to come with us and be with your friends?" Cassie's mother asked.

Adelaide looked at her mother and father. "Do I have to go?"

"Well, no, but I thought you wanted to," Margaret said. "You're going to *The Nutcracker* and you bought a pretty new dress and shoes. You'll have a good time, sweetheart." What was she saying? She didn't really want Adelaide to go, and yet she didn't want her to throw away a chance for a wonderful trip and a special experience.

"It's up to you, Adelaide," Allan said in a calm voice. "You get to choose what you want to do."

Sitting on the floor, looking at the parents, her three girlfriends, plus Bernadette, Adelaide folded her hands across her chest. "I want to stay home with my mom and dad."

"You're certain?" Margaret asked.

"Yes. I'm staying."

Cassie looked like she was going to cry. The other girls looked confused and upset. Margaret wondered if they were about to have a fourfold meltdown in the middle of the gallery.

"Girls, it's all right," Cassie's father said. "We'll let Adelaide stay here with her parents, and we'll go on now." He tried to usher the others toward the door. His wife took Cassie's arm and tried to lead her away. Cassie shook off her mother's arm.

"I don't want to leave you," Cassie said, plunking down on the floor beside Adelaide.

"Me too," Chloe said, dropping down next to them.

"Me too," Tina said, joining her friends on the floor.

With such a crowd around Adelaide, Margaret stood and stepped back by Allan.

Four young women cried and hugged each other. Margaret and Allan stared at Cassie's parents. Cassie's father shrugged and grinned at them. "Girls," he said.

Cassie's mother laughed. "I have a feeling we're in for an eventful Christmas."

"I'm sorry," Margaret said, as if it were her fault the girls were having this emotional scene.

"Don't be. Just be happy Adelaide wants to stay at home. Cassie wouldn't come unless we promised to invite her friends. They've become so close, living together, that they are inseparable."

"I'm glad they are such good friends. I know it's been good for Adelaide," Margaret said. Her daughter had become an independent young woman since she'd moved into the group home.

"Okay, girls, the bus is leaving," Cassie's father boomed out in a deep voice. The young women pushed to their feet.

"Daddy, we don't have a bus," Cassie said.

"You're right. Okay, the van is leaving," he said. "All aboard that's going aboard."

After the friends shared a group hug, the other three girls headed for the door. Cassie's father held the door open as they trooped out.

"Are you sure, Adelaide?" Allan asked. "It's not too late to go with them."

She nodded. "I'm sure."

Cassie's father gave them an understanding nod, then closed the door behind him.

Adelaide turned to Allan. "Daddy, what are we making for dinner?"

Allan put his hands on his hips. "I don't know. What do you want for dinner?"

"Can we make pizza?"

"Yes, we can, but we'll have to go to the store." It was one of their favorite father-daughter dishes. The two of them worked well together in the kitchen.

"Okay."

"Let's put your suitcase in the van," Margaret said, already bending down to pick up Adelaide's clothes. A bubble of joy worked its way up inside of her and came out in a laugh.

"Why are you laughing, Mom? Did we make a joke?"

Adelaide often missed the subtleties of humor, and she felt self-conscious about it. "No. I'm just happy."

"Oh." Adelaide smiled. Margaret knew she didn't understand, and it didn't matter. She'd been happy earlier, but now she felt simply giddy. Her daughter was going to be home for Christmas!

"We have to eat early," Margaret said. "We are decorating the tree tonight, and Aiden and Hailey and Emma are coming over to help."

"Yay! Come on, Dad. We have to hurry." She grabbed her suitcase and dragged it out to the back. Then she screeched.

Margaret hurried to the back. Bernadette was right behind her.

"What's wrong?"

"That's Lizzy and Butterscotch!"

Margaret grinned. "Yes, and they are at home, waiting for you."

"But where's Oreo?"

"I haven't painted him in yet. I think he'll go on the ledge by the ox."

"Oh. Okay." Adelaide turned to Allan. "Hurry, Dad. We have to go."

Margaret and Bernadette watched them leave. Then Margaret realized Bernadette had been the silent witness to the entire scene. She turned to her young artist friend, trying to think how she would explain.

Bernadette grinned.

"Family." She shook her head. "You just never know what's going to happen."

"That is an understatement," Margaret replied.

Chapter Thirteen

A delaide!" Aiden's face lit up when he saw her, and he rushed into the house, arms wide for a hug, not stopping to remove his coat or boots or hat.

"Adaway!" Three-year-old Emma echoed her brother, rushing in to join in a group hug. Their cousin Hailey stayed by the doorway, removing her coat. Shelley was right beside her.

"Aiden, Emma, come take off your coats," Shelley called after them, but they ignored her, or didn't hear her as they embraced Adelaide, who had dropped to the floor to greet them.

The joy on Adelaide's face erased any doubt in Margaret's mind that her daughter had made the right decision to stay home. Margaret was so happy that she wanted to get down on the floor and join the hug, but she didn't. She was content to watch the scene unfold. She had invited Shelley's children and niece to help her decorate because Adelaide wasn't going to be there, but what joy to have them all in her living room, enjoying each other.

Allan had strung the lights, so the tree was ready. It was an old artificial tree, but it still had all its branches and most of its needles. Margaret opened the first box of ornaments. From that moment on, pandemonium reigned. It took Adelaide, Shelley, and Hailey together to contain the two small children as they grabbed ornaments and hung them on the tree. Margaret delighted in watching and taking pictures. This was too good to pass up. She might even get some ideas for next year's line of Christmas cards.

"Adelaide, help Emma put some ornaments up higher," Margaret said. Hailey was trying to lift the toddler, who was wiggling and squirming in her arms. At ten years old, Hailey was as tall as Adelaide, but she was slim and gangly, and Emma was not cooperating. She wanted her beloved Adelaide, who had helped Shelley take care of the toddler and her brother many times when Shelley was first starting her baking business from home. That experience had been a catalyst for Adelaide taking child care classes at the college.

Adelaide scooped up Emma and tickled her, making the toddler squeal with delight.

"More, Adaway, more!"

Adelaide laughed and helped Emma place an ornament near the top of the six-foot-tall tree.

"Me, Adelaide. My turn!" Aiden said.

"No! My Adaway," Emma said.

"Let me help you," Shelley said.

Aiden pouted. "I want Adelaide to help me."

Allan came in with a small kitchen step-ladder. "Here, Aiden. You can put the angel on the top of the tree."

Margaret looked at Adelaide. Placing the angel at the top of the tree had always been her job.

Adelaide set Emma down and got the angel out of the box. She carefully, reverently unwrapped it. Then she held it out toward Aiden. "Climb up, Aiden," she said. "I will hand it to you."

To Margaret, it was a defining moment—one of many over the past year for her daughter. Adelaide was passing a torch to Aiden, though he didn't know it. She was taking the role of the adult, helping a child step into a special role: topping the Christmas tree. Though it was unlikely that Aiden would decorate future trees in the Hoskins house, it was significant. Adelaide was no longer her dependent daughter, needing her parents to guide her life. She would always need assistance in some things, but she'd become an adult in her own right. It was a bittersweet moment for Margaret. How proud she was of her daughter, and yet she mourned the loss of her little girl. But Margaret realized it was a step every mother took with her child, watching as her daughter or son became independent. It wasn't Adelaide's defining moment; it was Margaret's.

Shelley clapped as Aiden placed the angel on top of the tree. Hailey started clapping too. It was crooked and looked precarious, but Allan could fix it later. Aiden beamed.

"Yay!" Emma said, dancing around in a circle.

All of the ornaments were on the tree. Many were clustered around the bottom. Adelaide could rearrange them later.

"Are you ready to see it all lit up?" Allan asked.

A chorus of yeses answered. Allan flipped on the switch. The lights blinked on.

"It's beautiful," Margaret said. "You all did a wonderful job. Thank you!"

Held in Adelaide's arms, Emma clapped and giggled. Adelaide beamed at the little girl. Aiden grinned, and Hailey rehung a couple of ornaments that were falling off.

"I have a treat for you all in the kitchen," Margaret said. "I can't compete with your mother's baking, and besides, she probably doesn't want you to have sugar this late, but I have a different kind of treat."

They traipsed into the kitchen, where small bowls of buttons, sequins, and glitter waited in the center of the table, along with some colored marking pens. The craft kits she'd made earlier were placed at each chair. "Your mom said you haven't made Popsicle stick ornaments, so you can each make one to take home with you. You can make a star, like this one," she said, holding up Shane's card. "Or you can make a different shape." She showed them pictures she'd found of other shapes. A tree, snowflakes, snowmen, a sled.

"I want to make a sled," Aiden said. He climbed up on a chair and grabbed a handful of craft sticks.

"Dat," Emma said, pointing to a picture that looked like a reindeer head with a big red nose and a Santa hat made with cotton balls.

"*Hmm*, I can't decide," Hailey said, looking over the pictures. "I think I'll make a snowflake."

Adelaide looked at the pictures. "I like the star," she said. She watched the children for a moment, a look of indecision on her face.

"If you want to help the children now, you can make your own later," Margaret said.

Adelaide's frown lifted, and she smiled. "Sit on my lap, Emma. I will help you."

Emma climbed up on Adelaide's lap. The two of them giggled and laughed as they made her reindeer with Margaret's help.

Shelley sat and watched for a few moments. Aiden and Hailey seemed to be doing fine on their own, and Margaret was there to offer assistance, so she picked up six sticks and began cutting them into lengths with a pair of craft snips. Margaret watched her arrange them into an angel ornament. For twenty minutes, the kitchen table was a beehive of activity. When they finished, Margaret carefully set the ornaments on paper plates and wrapped them so they could carry them home.

Adelaide and Hailey helped Emma and Aiden put on their coats and hats and gloves.

"Thank you, Margaret," Shelley said. "This was fun. I'm so glad Adelaide decided to come home. The kids have missed her."

"So am I," Margaret said. "I couldn't have a better Christmas present."

*   *   *

After Shelley and the children left, Margaret cleaned up the craft mess while Adelaide went to her room. When the kitchen was back in order, Margaret went to the living room and sat down to admire the tree. She couldn't help smiling, thinking about the confusion and the fun of three children and three adult women decorating one little tree. She was glad she'd taken pictures to capture the process.

Adelaide came back out in her flannel nightshirt and placed the two presents from Margaret and Allan, and her present for them, under the tree. Then she sat on the couch next to her mother.

"I liked having Aiden and Emma and Hailey decorate our tree. That was fun."

"I'm glad. It's always been you and your dad and me before. It was fun to include the Bauers."

"We decorated a tree at my home," Adelaide said. Margaret winced when she called it her home, but it was her new place of residence.

"I bet that was fun."

"Yes. We made paper chains and hung them on the tree and all over the house. We drank cocoa and made popcorn strings, but mostly we ate the popcorn. We laughed a lot."

"You like living with your friends?"

"Oh yes. We have fun."

"We miss having you live here. It's awfully quiet without you."

Oreo jumped up on the couch next to Adelaide and rubbed his head against her arm. She put him in her lap and rubbed his head. He pushed his head against her hand and purred loudly. Then he curled up in her lap.

"He misses you."

"I miss him too." As Adelaide petted Oreo, the two female cats showed up and jumped up on the couch. They rubbed up against her, demanding her attention. "Hi, Lizzy. Hi, Butterscotch. Did you miss me too?"

The cats pushed and prodded and purred until all three were lying on her lap. She laughed and petted them. "I miss my cats so much. I wish I could take them home with me."

Again Adelaide's assertion that the group home was "home" made Margaret a little sad. "You can come here to see them anytime." She wanted to tell Adelaide that she could move back home, but she knew that would not be the best thing for her daughter. Adelaide had blossomed in so many ways. She was more outgoing, more self-assured, more decisive. Watching her with Aiden and Emma, Margaret could see the difference. Before, she'd played with them as if she was one of their young friends. Tonight she had played with them as an adult with a child.

"Mom, do you want to see my party dress?"

"I'd love to see your dress, honey. Do you want to model it for me?"

"Yes." Adelaide set the cats aside and jumped up. "I'll go put it on now." She ran into her room and shut the door.

Margaret petted the cats, but they lost interest without Adelaide and wandered off. About fifteen minutes later, Adelaide called her from her bedroom.

"Mom, come help me."

Margaret went to the bedroom door and opened it and peered in. Adelaide had her back to her. She was trying to zip up the back of a sparkly blue dress. Margaret went in.

"Here, I'll get that." She zipped up the long zipper in the back. The dress was a soft knit satin with clear beading that picked up the blue and sparkled in the light. The back had a modest scoop neckline. But when Adelaide turned around, Margaret swallowed a gasp. The neckline plunged. Not dangerously so, but it was cut deeper than anything Adelaide, or Margaret, for that matter, had ever worn before. The bodice crisscrossed in the front and attached to a high waistline and fell to a long, straight skirt.

Adelaide looked . . . gorgeous. And sophisticated. And so wrong in the dress. Sweet, innocent, uncomplicated Adelaide was dressed like a movie star.

"What do you think, Mom?" Adelaide spread her arms wide and turned in a circle to show all sides of the dress. "The lady at the store said it is the latest style and what I should wear to the theater. Cassie said so too."

"It is very beautiful, Adelaide. You are beautiful. And you are lovely in the dress." That was true, and she didn't want to discourage Adelaide.

Adelaide's eyes narrowed and her mouth turned down. "I know it's beautiful, Mom, but I don't like it."

"You don't?" Margaret knew her mouth dropped open, and she shut it.

"I feel funny in it. Like I have to stand very straight and not move."

"Oh. It is very fancy."

"Yes." She gave her mother a look of inquiry. "Is it all right that I don't like it?"

"Oh, sweetheart, of course it's all right. You don't have to wear clothes or buy them to please other people. Wear what you like and are comfortable in." Margaret thought of Bernadette. That's what she was doing, and not everyone liked it. She hoped Adelaide wouldn't pick out clothes that were too wild, but she did need to find her own style preferences.

"Do you think the store would let me give it back?"

"I'm sure they will. Do you have a receipt?"

"Yes. Can we go tomorrow?"

Margaret made a quick assessment of her schedule. Bernadette planned to come in again. The Nativity set was almost finished. She could close the gallery a little early. "Yes. We can go tomorrow afternoon. Maybe we will go out to dinner, just the two of us. You can buy a different outfit, if you'd like."

"Yes!" Adelaide clapped and her mouth turned up into a big smile. Then her smile faltered. "I hope Cassie won't be mad at me."

"I don't think she will be. You bought the dress for the one occasion—*The Nutcracker*. Since you aren't going to it, you won't need this dress."

"Good." Her smile returned.

"Are you disappointed that you're not going to the ballet?"

"No. I want to watch Charlie Brown with you and Daddy."

That was tradition. And it fit Margaret's mood perfectly. Charlie Brown's Christmas started out with disinterest and depression and ended with joy. And that's just how Margaret felt.

CHAPTER FOURTEEN

Allan had gotten up early and made belgian waffles with fried apples and whipped cream for breakfast, in honor of Adelaide's homecoming for Christmas. Margaret would have loved to spend the day with her, but it was Friday, and she needed to open the gallery. Besides, she had a meeting of the friends, and she had so much to share.

"So what are your plans today?" she asked.

Allan and Adelaide exchanged conspiratorial looks.

"I'm going to help Daddy."

"After a bit of work in the shop to finish one more order, we are going to do some serious Christmas baking, right, Adelaide?"

"Right!" She lifted her hand for a high five, and he clapped his hand against hers. They were both grinning.

"That sounds wonderful, and I can't wait to sample everything. But not right now. I'm very full, and I need to get to work. Adelaide, I will come get you at four so we can go do your shopping."

"Yes!" She did something with her fist, holding it up, then bringing it down in sort of a pumping motion. Margaret had seen kids do it before, but it wasn't something she had seen Adelaide do before. She supposed Adelaide had picked it up at school or from her friends. She couldn't help wondering what else her daughter had picked up. Nothing bad, she hoped. Adelaide didn't understand the nuances of people's actions and social behavior. She knew Elsa Kling at the group home watched out for the girls. Their house must seem very quiet with all four girls gone for the holidays.

"Okay. I'm off, then." She could hear talking and laughing as she put on her coat and went out the door. It sounded so good to hear her daughter and her husband sharing with each other in the kitchen. The two had such a close bond. Margaret knew it had been as hard on Allan, having Adelaide gone, as it had been on her.

College classes for the spring semester wouldn't start until the middle of January. Would Adelaide stay with them for the entire winter break? Was that even a good idea for Adelaide? She didn't know, but she could hope.

*   *   *

Margaret went through the back of the gallery and turned the workroom light on and the thermostat up. The stable scene was taking shape. It wasn't finished, but it wouldn't take long. She couldn't wait for her friends to see it. She locked up again and walked next door to the Cove.

Beverly and Diane were already sitting at their table by the back wall with their coffee and pastries. Margaret got in line behind one customer. It was still early, and the rush wouldn't start for another twenty minutes.

"Mornin', Margaret," Brenna said from behind the counter. "What are ya having?"

"I'll have a gingerbread latte, Brenna. That's all. And how are you this fine morning?"

"I couldn't be better." She parked her pencil over her ear and smiled. "No pastries?"

"Not today. Allan fixed a big breakfast. Adelaide is home, you know?" Margaret knew she was beaming. She didn't care.

"Shelley told me! You tell Adelaide to get in he-ah. I want to see her."

"I will. She'll be home for a while."

Margaret got her coffee and joined her friends. Shelley came out of the kitchen to join them.

"I heard you have good news," Diane said.

"You mean Adelaide? Yes, she came home yesterday afternoon." She scooted up onto a chair. They were sitting at one of the taller tables.

"So she changed her mind about going to Boston with her friends?" Beverly asked.

"Yes. I'm not sure what triggered it. They were on their way and stopped at the gallery so she could get a coat and her Christmas presents. She was going to get something she had for us out of her suitcase, and she just sat down on the carpet and announced she wasn't going. She surprised everyone."

"Bless her heart," Diane said. "I bet she got to the gallery and realized how much she missed you and Allan and home. She's never been away from you before, has she?"

"Only when Allan and I went to Paris, and then she was at home and had all of you checking on her."

"Yes, and she missed you then," Beverly said. "I remember my first Christmas away from home. I had a lot to do, but I was so lonely. I'm glad she decided to stay."

"Me too," Margaret said. "And the fancy dress she bought—she wants to return it."

"Really?" Diane asked. "So maybe you're not so old-fashioned after all, eh?"

Margaret laughed. "Yes, I am. But maybe Adelaide is too. We're going shopping this afternoon and returning the dress."

"I'm so happy for you," Shelley said. "Aiden and Emma and Hailey had a wonderful time with Adelaide last night. They loved helping decorate your tree, but I think getting to be with Adelaide was the highlight of the evening for them. I enjoyed it too."

"So did I. It was quite an evening." Margaret knew Diane wanted to talk about the living Nativity, so she changed the subject. "Diane has good news. Did she tell you she got animals for the Nativity?"

"You did? What kind?" Shelley asked.

"Leo found us quite a menagerie, and the owner will be with us as a shepherd to keep the animals in line. So guess what? We. Have. A. Camel."

"No! Really? A live camel?" Beverly asked. "How? Where did he find a camel?"

"Have you ever been to the Desert of Maine?" Diane asked.

"The what?" Shelley put in.

Diane explained about the unusual geological phenomenon that had become a theme park. "They once had a camel. When it became difficult for them to keep him, they turned him over to a rescue farm. So the farmer is bringing us the camel and a donkey for the Nativity. And maybe a Shetland pony."

"That's fabulous," Beverly said. "I remember going there as a child. In fact, I remember the camel. Are you sure it will be all right? I think he liked to nip people."

"He assured Leo that the camel has become gentle in his old age. And Leo will be there too. I'm sure it will be fine."

"It will certainly be authentic," Beverly said. "How is the set coming?"

"Yes, Margaret, how is the set coming? You were very mysterious about it yesterday," Diane said.

"That's my other news." Margaret batted her eyelashes and gave them an innocent look. "I can't tell you. I need to show you. When you finish your coffee, can you all come over to the gallery?"

"Absolutely. I want to see this!" Diane said. She took a big gulp of her coffee. "Come on, ladies. Let's get going."

They all filed behind Margaret to the back door of the gallery. She opened the door and flipped on the light, then led them into her workroom. She had covered the stable with a sheet for dramatic effect. She was so excited.

"Ready?"

"Come on, show us," Diane said in an urgent voice, but her smile belied her impatience.

"Yes, let's see it," Shelley said.

"Okay. Ta-da!" Margaret pulled away the sheet. The overhead spotlight shone right on the stable. Margaret had arranged it so the sides were aligned and held in place with the Velcro straps Shane had attached. "It isn't finished yet," Margaret said. "But I wanted you to see it."

"Margaret, it's magnificent!" Diane said.

"Wow, it's great!" Shelley said. "It even has cats in it. Wait! Are those your cats? I love that!"

"This is perfect," Beverly said. "Did Allan make it?"

"Margaret told me Allan didn't make it." Diane turned to Margaret. "You told me it found you, and you were very mysterious about it. So how did you get it? There's a story here, I just know it."

Margaret laughed. "Yes, there's a story. First I have to tell you about my mysterious Popsicle stick star."

"You asked if Aiden made it," Shelley said. "Did you find out where it came from?"

"I did, and you won't believe it."

"We've seen enough incredible occurrences here to believe anything," Beverly said. "Try us."

"Okay. Last Monday afternoon a stranger came into the gallery. He was passing through town and looking for a painting of a lighthouse for his wife. I was out of lighthouse paintings, except for a very small one. It was getting late and he asked about a place to stay, so I recommended the Landmark. The next day, I saw him at the hardware store." Margaret went on to tell them how Shane inquired about having Allan build a table for him, and how he'd seen her working on the crumbling Nativity pieces.

"So I got home Wednesday night, and Shane was in Allan's workshop, and he'd built the stable."

"That's wonderful!" Beverly said. "But what has that got to do with the Popsicle stick star?"

"That's where it gets really interesting. We invited him to stay for dinner. Afterward, we were in the living room, and he saw the star. He was the one who made it!"

"Wait a minute. An adult, a stranger, made the star and sent it to you anonymously?"

"Yes, but not recently. He made the star thirty years ago. He didn't know who we were. The head of the children's home where he was living sent it to us. But somehow it took thirty years to get here." Margaret raised her hands. "I can't explain it. But there it was, and there he was. Thirty years ago, Allan and I went to Portland with a church choir to put on a program for a group of underprivileged children. We didn't know they came from a children's home. We took presents, and Allan got rooked into being Santa Claus."

"That is amazing," Shelley said. "But how did he happen to come to Marble Cove?"

"Remember when Keeley's owned the hardware store? They used to give out these flat pencils with the store name on them. We did his accounting back then, and Mr. Keeley was always bringing Allan those pencils. He bought a bunch of them one year for advertising. He must have donated some to give to the children at that party. Shane said everyone got one. But he kept his and had it with him. When he got his gift, it was an Erector Set, and he loved playing with it so much that he became an architect. We didn't have anything to do with his gift, but all these years he credited Santa Claus and Mrs. Santa Claus. That was Allan and me."

"You were there, and God used you. That would make a great story for a book," Diane said. "Is he still in town?"

"He was leaving this morning. He's going to get his wife and son in Canada. They're visiting her parents up there. He likes Marble Cove, so he said he might rent a place here next summer."

"That would be wonderful. I hope you get to see him again," Beverly said. "I'd love to thank him for the beautiful Nativity set. That will last for years!"

"Well, that completes what we need for the Nativ—" Diane's cell phone rang. "Hold that thought." She answered her phone, held her finger up to her other ear so she could hear better, and stepped away from them.

"This seems like a miracle to me," Shelley said in a low voice. "Getting that star now, after all those years, and then having the boy who made it show up."

"I agree," Margaret said. "I was feeling blue because of Adelaide moving out, and most unhappy because she wasn't going to come home for Christmas. Having Shane show up and all that happened has made me realize that our joy doesn't come from our circumstances. It's a lot more than that. Joy has to do with giving and finding pleasure in the people around us. It has to do with the love that we share and that others share with us. The love that came to us when Jesus came to us as a baby and changed the world forever."

"That's what I love about doing the living Nativity," Beverly said. "It's such a great reminder of what's really important about Christmas."

"Speaking of miracles," Diane said, coming back to them, "we need one now. I thought we were all set for the Nativity. We have the set, the actors, the costumes, the animals, and everyone is excited to come to it."

"What's wrong?" Margaret asked.

"That was Rita Candleford's daughter. Our angel has fallen. They were skiing, and Rita took a bad fall and broke her ankle. They're at the hospital now. There's no way she is going to be able to play the angel. We have to find a replacement. I asked her daughter if she would do it, but she can't. Any ideas?"

The room was silent for a few moments.

"I think we've asked everyone in town to participate," Beverly said. "They're either already involved or they can't. I'm sorry, but I can't think of anyone."

"Neither can I," Shelley said.

"Me either," Margaret said. "Poor Rita. So what do we do now?"

"I don't know," Diane said. "There's only thing we can do, I suppose. We've experienced more than our share of miracles here in Marble Cove. It seems like it's time to pray for another one."

Love's Pure Light

Camy Tang

CHAPTER ONE

The winter wind was brisk against her cheeks as Beverly Mackenzie—formerly Beverly Wheeland until a few months ago—ran along the beach. It was late afternoon, with the sun still hanging above the horizon, and several Marble Cove residents were walking, running, or being walked by their dogs on the boardwalk promenade that ran up to the lighthouse.

One of those was her friend and neighbor Diane Spencer, who was coming from the direction of the lighthouse, with her dog Rocky trotting alongside her. Diane smiled and waved at Beverly, but her smile was weary.

Beverly paused, jogging in place. "You look tired. Are you doing okay?"

"I needed to get out of the house," Diane said. "Ever since I left the gallery this morning, I've been calling people, trying to get someone to fill in for Rita Candleford as our angel. Margaret and Shelley have been calling people too, but we've had no takers."

"I would guess people are hesitant to do something like that," Beverly said. "When you asked me to be one of the three wise men, my first reaction was to refuse, even though as mayor, I should be used to standing up in front of crowds of people. Being the angel is kind of like a 'performance,' so it might give people the willies."

"Some people are definitely uncomfortable doing it," Diane said, "but unfortunately, most people I talked to already have plans and can't commit to being at the living Nativity for the entire time."

"Has anyone heard from Rita? How's her ankle?"

"I gave her a call just before I came out walking. She sounds cheerful, but there's something in her voice that makes me think she's still in a lot of pain."

"What a terrible accident. I'm glad she didn't get a concussion or anything more serious when she fell." A biting wind whistled between the two women, and Beverly shivered, despite her thermal running outfit. "I'd better get back to my run so you can get indoors."

"Is this your second run of the day? Usually you run in the mornings."

"I didn't run this morning—I overslept and only had time to make our coffee time. But it's nicer running at this time of the day because it's warmer than it was when I woke up. See you."

Diane gave a friendly wave as Beverly turned and jogged down the boardwalk toward the lighthouse. Soon her blood was pumping again and she was a little warmer.

She'd been at work all day, both carrying out her mayoral duties and consulting her own business clients with last-minute phone and video conference meetings. Many of her clients had important end-of-the-year events, and she'd been helping with some problems that had come up unexpectedly.

Just like the living Nativity. Poor Rita, and poor Diane. The timing of this was terrible. If Diane had an extra week or two, there might have been more people able to fill in, but today was Friday and the living Nativity was set to take place Sunday and Monday nights.

Now that Beverly's client work for the day was done, maybe she could help find someone to replace Rita Candleford as the angel in the performance. Diane, Margaret, and Shelley were probably all calling people from their churches, but would someone from city council be willing to fill in? She'd have to ask her friends later for a list of who they called, so Beverly wouldn't overlap and contact people who'd already been asked.

Beverly reached the lighthouse and paused to place a hand on the cold stone of the exterior. She glanced up at the white expanse of the wall high above her and suddenly felt reassured by the stalwart solidity of the structure. This lighthouse had been what had brought her and her three friends together. They might only have been friendly acquaintances if not for the fact that they had all seen mysterious lights in the lighthouse. She hadn't been very religious before, but her friends and her own experiences had helped her to grow in her faith, and she now knew that it was God who had drawn them together—not just as neighbors, but as close friends.

She started jogging back to her home on Newport Avenue. Even though it had only been half a year since she'd moved to the new home she shared with her husband, it felt as if she'd been here forever. The renovations she and her husband, Jeff, had done made their house seem newer than it was, and she'd finished unpacking the last box last month, so they were finally fully moved in. It had amazed her how many things she and Jeff had both accumulated over the years. At the same time, she'd been able to revisit treasured mementos that she'd forgotten she owned as she put them in new places in her home.

This would be her first Christmas married to Jeff, and in their new home. It filled her with more excitement than she'd felt about Christmas in a long time.

An especially brisk wind sliced through her, and she picked up her pace as she jogged down the wooden boardwalk. She scanned the beach, which was empty now that the afternoon had grown late.

Suddenly something on the shore caught her attention. Rather than gray or black or sand-colored, it was a dull green, and it looked like it had been washed up by the tide.

She realized that if it was trash, she should stop to pick it up and throw it away. So she veered off her normal course and picked her way to the shoreline, careful with her footing on the slick rocks. The wind seemed colder nearer to the water, and she shivered in her running clothes.

As she drew near, she realized that the object was an artificial wreath, but a very old and badly damaged one. About half of the plastic green needles were gone, stripped from the rusted metal frame, and those that were left were faded from exposure to the salt water.

What was curious was that several ornaments still clung to the limp fake branches like barnacles. The ornaments were all shell ornaments, fairly common here on the coast of Maine. Some were badly damaged, but there were five that hadn't been too badly broken by the wreath's journey in the ocean and being tossed up onto the shore.

The five ornaments were all musical instruments—a saxophone, a violin, a guitar, a trumpet, and a drum. The tiny shells making up each ornament had been painstakingly glued into place, and while there were a few holes where a shell or two had fallen off, they were mostly intact.

As she peered at the ornaments, she froze in shock. She . . . she felt that she knew this wreath.

The ornaments stirred a memory for her. Music. She heard a strain of piano music but couldn't place what it was. It was a warm memory of Christmas from some distant place in her childhood, but she couldn't completely remember what had happened.

Beverly bent to pick up the wet wreath, the cold of the water seeping through her running gloves. She realized her hand was shaking. How did she know this wreath?

Then reason asserted itself. It couldn't be the same wreath from her childhood, surely. Shell ornaments like these were not unusual. Since she lived in this area of the East Coast, around Christmastime every year she'd seen dozens of them, including shell ornaments shaped like musical instruments. Her family and neighbors all had at least one type of shell ornament on their trees.

But she couldn't shake the strange feeling that this particular wreath was special to her. She remembered the unexplained lights she'd seen in the lighthouse, and other strange things she and her friends had witnessed over the past few years. She was no longer so quick to dismiss things she couldn't completely understand.

She headed home with the bedraggled wreath in her hands. She passed one or two people out for a walk and saw the perplexed looks they cast her way, but she simply gave a polite smile and continued toward home.

She left the wreath outside the back door, since it was rather dirty and she didn't want to track sand into the house, but she took a long look at it before heading inside. The house was almost uncomfortably warm when she opened the door and pulled her sandy shoes off in the small mudroom-cum-laundry room. The open doorway led to the kitchen, where her husband, Jeff, was whistling as he finished cooking dinner. The smell of coconut teased her nose, an unusual contrast to the normal smells of the Christmas season.

"What's for dinner?" she asked as she slid her sock-clad feet into some house slippers and shuffled into the brightly lit kitchen.

"I hope you like it," Jeff said. He turned to give her a peck on the cheek in greeting. "I got the recipe from my mother."

Beverly gave him a look of mock alarm, and he laughed. His eccentric mother had spent a life of adventure traveling the world, working first in the Peace Corps and later on various humanitarian efforts, following wherever her whims took her. It had been Jeff's grandparents who had raised him in the absence of his mother. Jeff had her adventurous streak, but with a firm grounding in practicality and responsibility from his grandfather.

"Don't worry," he said. "The recipe seemed both easy and tasty, if a little exotic—roasted pork tenderloin, with a spinach–coconut milk sauce. It's from some famous chef in Hawaii who's apparently good friends with my mom."

"That doesn't surprise me," Beverly said. "I'm game to try it, but I'm not sure Father will like it."

"He already tried some of the sauce when he came over earlier," Jeff said. "I made him taste it, and he liked it, so I think he's willing to give it a go." He stirred the creamy sauce in the small pot on the stove. "You have a few minutes to shower while I slice the pork, then we have to go to your dad's place."

Beverly raced into the bathroom, peeling off her clothes to hop into the shower. The hot water soothed her muscles from her run, but there was still that uneasiness in her heart. Why was that wreath familiar to her? Why had it triggered that memory, and that line of music in her head? She could hear the strain of piano music as if it were being played from far away, but she couldn't hear enough of it to try to figure out what piece it was.

The more she pondered it, the more she became convinced that at some point in her past she'd seen these particular five musical instrument shell ornaments, all on a fake wreath. She could almost picture it in her mind's eye, hanging on a dark-paneled wall high above her. But whose wall? Which house? It wasn't any of her childhood homes.

After getting dressed, she helped Jeff carry their dinner over to her father's house across the street. The primary reason they'd bought their house was because it was so close to her father's. She could check in on him almost as regularly as when she was living with him, and they had family dinners at least twice a week, usually more often.

The back door was open, and they headed inside. The dining room table had been neatly set, either by Beverly's father or, more likely, Mrs. Peabody or her granddaughter Belinda, who traded off on checking in on her father during the day when Beverly was at work. Mrs. Peabody's fierce New England pride kept her from being entirely comfortable that Beverly compensated her for "being neighborly," but Beverly was more than grateful for the light cleaning she did and the hot lunches and dinners she made for her father.

Her father was dozing in his chair in the library, and Beverly touched his shoulder gently. "Father, we're here. Time for dinner."

He came awake slowly, and there was a faint smile on his face. "Eh?"

"Sorry, you look like you were having a good dream," Beverly said.

"Oh." He cleared his throat. "Just remembering Christmas with your mother." He cleared his throat again. "You're late," he said gruffly as he got to his feet.

"Sorry about that." Beverly followed him as he slowly made his way to the dining room. He didn't like it much when she helped him like an invalid, but the cold weather made his joints ache, and she felt a little uneasy sometimes watching him totter on the smooth wooden floors.

"I just hope that husband of yours isn't trying to poison me with that foreign food he's cooking."

He had been entering the dining room as he said it, and Jeff, unfazed, gave him a grin.

"Father, it's Hawaiian," Beverly said. "Hawaii is one of the fifty states, so it's not really foreign."

"I'll decide that when I've tried it." He sat in his seat at the head of the table.

His cantankerous mood didn't affect Beverly. She knew that beneath his gruff words lay a merry heart, and he dearly loved these family dinners, regardless of what she or Jeff cooked.

They joined hands and bowed their heads, and Jeff said grace for the meal. "Heavenly Father, thank You for all You've blessed us with. We are especially grateful during this season as we're reminded of the gracious gift of Your Son, Jesus Christ. Please bless this, um . . . unusual food . . ."

Beverly's eyes were closed, but she knew her husband was biting back a smile as he said it.

"And thank You for providing it. And we also pray for healing for the lady in the living Nativity who got injured, and ask that You help the living Nativity committee find someone to replace her. In Jesus's name, amen."

"Amen," Beverly and her father said.

"What's that about the living Nativity?" her father asked.

"Rita Candleford was supposed to play the angel," Beverly said, "but we just found out she fell and broke her ankle."

"Have you heard from her?" Jeff asked as he served slices of pork with a spoonful of creamy spinach sauce over it.

"She sounds all right, considering the circumstance."

"So who's going to replace her?" her father demanded. "Isn't it the day after tomorrow?"

Beverly felt a bubble of panic at the base of her throat. "Yes, so Diane's scrambling to find someone, but no luck so far." She reached for her water glass.

"Well, there's no help for it," her father said. He had a serious expression, except that his eyes were twinkling. "I'll have to be the angel."

Jeff guffawed, and Beverly almost choked on her sip of water. "Father!" she said.

"What?" he asked innocently. "I think I'd be a great angel. Terrible and frightening, like how I used to frighten any disobedient kids in my classes when I was still teaching social studies."

"You're incorrigible," Beverly told him.

He flashed a smile at her, then tasted his pork. His eyebrows lifted, and then he was chewing happily.

Beverly tasted the meal also, and was pleasantly surprised at the savory spinach sauce, only slightly sweet from the coconut milk. The pork loin was so tender that she could cut it with her fork.

"See?" Jeff said with a grin. "'Foreign' food can be fun."

"You have to admit, a Hawaiian recipe this close to Christmas is a little odd," Beverly said.

"I once spent Christmas in Hawaii on a photo shoot," Jeff said. "The best part was being on the beach at sunset and watching the waves. It was hard to believe it was Christmas."

Mention of the beach reminded her of her run this evening. "I found something strange on the beach today. A fake wreath."

"Lots of trash is getting washed up on the beach these days," her father said. "It's a shame people can't throw their rubbish away properly."

"This was more than just a piece of trash," Beverly said. "I think I remember this exact wreath from somewhere in my childhood."

"Oh?" Jeff looked up at her.

"A wreath?" Her father's wrinkled forehead wrinkled even more. "What kind of wreath?"

"It has only shell ornaments on it, and five of them are of musical instruments. Do you remember anything like that, Father?"

He shook his head slowly. "Your mother and I never had anything like that. She had that one angel shell ornament, but none on a wreath."

"I remember the angel," Beverly said. "I was so upset when I accidentally broke it a few years ago because Mother had made it herself."

"You couldn't repair it?" Jeff asked.

"No," she said sadly. "It had fallen on the floor, and I pretty much pulverized it when I dropped a heavy gift box on top of it." She thought a moment. "Mother didn't make any shell ornaments in the shape of musical instruments?"

"Your mother liked fresh wreaths and not fake ones," her father said. "So putting shell ornaments on a fake wreath seems out of character for her."

"You're right." Beverly sighed. "I wish I could remember where I've seen the wreath before."

"You brought it home with you?" Jeff asked.

She nodded. "I left it outside the back door. It's pretty filthy."

"Why don't you take a closer look at it tomorrow?" he suggested. "You never know. It might reveal its secrets to you if you look hard enough."

Dinner continued with comfortable chitchat, but Beverly's mind was never far from the wreath. If it really was the same wreath from her childhood, how had she happened to be the one to pick it up on the beach all the way here in Marble Cove?

Like the lighthouse, the bell tower at Old First Church, and the abandoned train station, here was another mysterious occurrence she had encountered. She had a feeling this wreath was significant . . . and that it would bring some sort of change into her life.

Chapter Two

The next morning dawned bright and clear, but Beverly cut short her morning run in order to head over to Diane's house. She carried the wreath in a large black garbage bag, but she also brought a notebook and pen in her purse.

When Diane answered her front door, she smiled and looked curiously at the bulky trash bag. "Early Christmas present?"

Beverly chuckled. "You won't be hoping that when you see what's inside it."

"Come on in. Did you want a cup of coffee?"

"Oh, no need to bother . . ."

"How about one of Shelley's cranberry-orange muffins?"

"Well, twist my arm." Beverly grinned and sat on Diane's sofa, setting the bag on the floor beside her. She saw a notepad on the coffee table with a list of women's names, most crossed out. "Are these people you've asked to take Rita's place in the living Nativity?" Beverly asked as Diane carried two coffee mugs to the table.

"Yes." Diane sighed. "I'm trying not to panic and trying to remember that it's all in God's hands at this point, but I can't stop sending up 'reminders' to Him that it's *tomorrow*."

Beverly winced. "You already have so much to do. Why don't you let me find someone to replace Rita?"

"Would you?" The relief was evident in Diane's voice. She plopped down hard on the sofa, making the cushions jump. "I can't begin to tell you how that helps me out. But do you think you could find someone?"

"There has to be someone, perhaps from the city council, who's available. And if we need to, we could have two or three people do it, trading off as they become available, so no one has to do it for the entire time on both days."

Diane looked thoughtful. "That might work. There were a few people who could only make it on one day, not on both days. I think I marked that down next to their names." She picked up the notepad, then tilted it toward Beverly and pointed to two names. "The only problem is that one of them is really much too tall to fit into Rita's angel costume. If we have more than one person do it, they both have to be about Rita's size." Frances, Shelley's mother-in-law, had stepped in to organize a team of seamstresses to create new costumes when the old ones could not be found.

"Oh, I hadn't thought about the costume," Beverly said. "You're right, since we don't have time to alter it before tomorrow night. And if two people are trading off, we really can't alter it much at all." Her job suddenly got a little harder, but she was determined to take this off Diane's plate. "Don't worry, I'll take care of this for you. Can I have your list? That way we won't call anyone twice by mistake."

"Of course." Diane tore the page off the notepad and handed it to her. "And thank you so much for doing this for me."

"No problem." Beverly tucked the paper into the notebook she'd brought with her.

"Here, have a muffin—you'll have earned it."

"I haven't yet." But Beverly took a muffin eagerly, and although she tried to only nibble at it, she couldn't help taking a larger bite. It was wonderfully moist and sweet with a hint of tart. Shelley's baked goodies were always delicious.

"So I'm dying of curiosity—what's in the bag?" Diane asked.

"After I saw you yesterday, I found this on the beach." Beverly opened the bag and pulled the sides down so Diane could see the bedraggled wreath, but she didn't completely take it out so she wouldn't get sand and dirt and falling plastic fir needles on the carpet. "I thought at first it was just some random trash washed up with the tide, but I had a really strange feeling about it. I think I know this particular wreath. I remember seeing it on a wall in my childhood at some point."

"Really?" Diane peered at it. "Are you sure it was this particular wreath?"

"Well, I remember those ornaments clearly. But I can't for the life of me recall where I've seen the wreath. It wasn't among my parents' Christmas decorations."

"Each of us has been receiving some sort of mystery object the past couple weeks. Why not you too?"

Beverly blinked. "I hadn't really thought of this wreath like your and Shelley's ornaments and Margaret's card. I mean . . . it's a whole *wreath*."

Diane laughed. "It still showed up in an unexplained way. How are you going to discover the mystery behind it?"

"I was going to focus first on the living Nativity."

"Beverly, you are the most organized person I've ever known. You can multitask."

"I don't know where to start. It's old and in sorry shape."

"But these ornaments aren't too badly damaged." Diane reached out to finger the shell guitar. "And these are definitely handmade. You don't see intricate shell ornaments like these at one of those big box stores."

"You might be right."

"I know!" Diane snapped her fingers. "Margaret might be able to help. If these were made by a local artisan, Margaret might know someone who knows someone who makes shell ornaments."

"That's a good idea. At least I have a place to start, which was more than I had before I came here. I knew you'd have some sort of suggestion for me."

"I'm glad I could help."

As Beverly was about to leave with the list of names and her wreath, Diane said, "I'll be praying we can find someone today to replace Rita. Thanks again for doing this for me."

Beverly waved to her and walked across the street to her house.

She spent about an hour calling people. She called everyone not yet called on Diane's list, and she pulled a few names from her own personal address book to ask if they could help. She left messages for about half the people she called, but of the ones she spoke to, no one was available, not at this late date. She talked to only one person, whom Diane had also called earlier, who was Rita's size and could do part of Monday's living Nativity, but not the entire evening, and not on Sunday. Beverly began to feel some of the panic Diane had mentioned, but she took a deep breath to calm herself. God would surely provide.

After calling the last person, she decided to go see Margaret. She grabbed her purse and the wreath—still in its plastic garbage bag—and walked across the street to Margaret's house.

Allan answered the door. "Oh, hi, Beverly. You just missed Margaret— she headed to the gallery today with Adelaide to work on some last-minute orders she has to ship this afternoon."

Everyone had been excited for Margaret and Allan's daughter, Adelaide, who had Down syndrome, when she'd left her parents to live independently in a group home. She hadn't moved far away, but Beverly admitted she missed seeing Adelaide's warm smiles as often as she used to. And now she had returned home for Christmas.

"I know they'd both be happy to see you, if you want to stop by the gallery," Allan told her.

The day had warmed with the winter sun, and as Beverly walked to downtown Marble Cove, she hoped the clear weather would last through the two living Nativity nights. It would be perfect if there was no wind, rain, or snow.

Main Street seemed to have more people than usual, but perhaps she shouldn't have been surprised since it was one of the last shopping days before Christmas. There were three people in the Shearwater Gallery when Beverly pushed open the door—two looking at the last of Allan's woodworking projects on display and one studying some of Margaret's paintings. Margaret and Adelaide were behind the counter, working together to wrap a large framed painting in butcher paper. Margaret smiled in greeting, but Adelaide's grin was pure sunshine.

Margaret was quietly glowing. She'd been feeling a bit down earlier because Adelaide had originally not planned to be with them over the holidays. Beverly had invited Margaret and Allan to her home for Christmas, which had cheered Margaret up quite a bit, but the events of the last week, including Adelaide's unexpected return, had restored her Christmas joy.

"So I'm guessing you won't be coming to our house for Christmas dinner?" Beverly asked Margaret.

"Oh, Beverly, I almost forgot about that," Margaret said. "I can't tell you how much it meant to me. But now that Adelaide's home, I'm looking forward to a cozy family Christmas dinner."

"You're welcome to come by for dessert," Beverly said. "I'm making a German chocolate cake—it's Shelley's recipe, actually."

"*Ooh*, we'd love that. What do you think, Adelaide?"

Adelaide grinned. "I love cake."

Margaret eyed the trash bag, which Beverly had set on the floor. "I'm guessing that's not garbage?"

"I found this on the beach, and it's certainly beat up by the ocean, but there's something about this wreath that's nagging at me."

"Let's have a look at it." Margaret moved the painting aside and cleared a small section of the counter.

Beverly hoisted the bag onto the counter and gingerly unwrapped it so that none of the fraying fake fir needles and sand would fall out. "I thought at first it was just trash, but the more I look at it, the more I'm convinced that I saw this exact wreath when I was a child. I can picture it on a wall, and the five shell ornaments in the shape of musical instruments."

"They're definitely handmade." Margaret turned each one over, careful not to detach it from the old wreath. "I don't see any signature from an artisan either. There's usually at least something small."

"They're pretty." Adelaide tugged gently at one of them. "They're glued on to the wreath."

"And somehow they survived the waves. We should remove them," Margaret said. "That will make it easier to study them closely."

Margaret used a pair of wire cutters to snip the fake fir boughs from the larger wreath, and then she and Adelaide used a cotton swab to dab an array of different solvents—from oil to vinegar—on to the glue that connected the ornament to the branch. Then Margaret managed to remove the ornaments by gently easing them free with a tiny pair of pliers, with the tip scraping the ornament away from the glued branch.

Margaret did the first ornament, then had Adelaide do the others while she studied the first one, which was the saxophone ornament. "This is beautifully done, but it looks very old."

"How can you tell?"

"I'm not positive, but it seems the glue is discolored and faded from age—I don't think that's from the trip in the ocean. This looks like it might be the type of glue people commonly use for arts and crafts projects, nothing industrial."

"It's not made by any of the local artists you know now?"

"No, I don't think so. I still don't see an artist's signature, and they're usually pretty careful about that since this is a work of art for them. This especially took a long time to make, I can tell."

"So it could have been made by anyone?" Beverly sighed. "I really don't know how to figure out where I've seen this wreath. No, more specifically, it's these ornaments. They make me remember something, and it's been bugging me that I don't know more."

"What do you remember?" Adelaide glanced up from where she was removing the drum ornament.

"I see it on a dark-paneled wall high above me, and I have a warm, happy feeling. I'm really young, I think."

"I'm assuming it didn't belong to your parents?" Margaret asked.

"No, Father didn't know anything about it. I'm not entirely sure if that's accurate or he simply forgot—if I'm as young in the memory as I think I am, it would have been around forty years ago. I'm amazed that the sight of these ornaments made me remember it at all."

"I'm not," Margaret said. "Art often evokes memories—pictures in your mind, smells, sounds . . ."

"Oh, I forgot, I also remembered a strain of piano music."

"You did? What piece was it?"

"That's just it. I don't know. It was only a few measures, and I can't place it."

"I wonder how the sight of these ornaments would trigger a piece of music for you," Margaret mused. "If you can't place the visual memory, maybe you should try to figure out the piano piece."

"I hadn't thought of that," Beverly said. "I've been so focused on the wreath that I forgot about the music."

"That might be the key," Margaret said. "Memory is a funny thing—get one piece, and the rest falls into place."

"Here you go. It's the last one." Adelaide looked at the violin ornament. "This one's missing two shells. Do you want me to fix it?"

"You could do that?" Beverly asked.

"I think so," Adelaide said. "It would be a challenge. The shells are really tiny."

"Thank you. I'd love that," Beverly said. "I could put them on a new wreath, or on our Christmas tree."

"Sure," Adelaide said. "I'm home all week with Mom and Daddy."

The answer to the living Nativity's problem suddenly hit her like a smack in the head. "Adelaide!" Beverly said suddenly.

Adelaide jumped. "Huh?"

"Do you think you could be the angel in the living Nativity?"

"The living Nativity?"

"Rita Candleford was supposed to be the angel, but she broke her ankle," Beverly said. "You're about Rita's size. Are you free to do it tomorrow night and Monday night?"

"I guess so, but . . ." Adelaide bit her lip. "It'll be in front of a lot of people."

"I would be the last person to try to force you or nag you into doing something you don't want to do," Beverly assured her, "but you would really save the event if you do it. Diane and I have been calling everyone we know, and we can't find someone at this late date."

"Why don't you think about it?" Margaret asked Adelaide. She turned to Beverly. "When do you need an answer?"

"Probably tonight, so we can get the costume to her to try on tomorrow," Beverly said. "It might need some adjusting."

"I'll think about it," Adelaide said slowly, but it was obvious she was reluctant to do something like that. Beverly didn't blame her. She was now the mayor, and she'd agreed to be one of the wise men, but she still had a feeling of trepidation doing anything in front of people.

One of the customers came up to Margaret then, so Beverly bade her friends good-bye and headed back home, leaving the ornaments for Adelaide to repair and taking the ragged wreath back in the trash bag to dump in her rubbish bin. Beverly felt energized—not just because Adelaide might be the angel for the living Nativity, but also because she now had something she could actively do to get one step closer to finding out what memory those ornaments on the wreath had triggered for her. She was determined to sit at her piano until she could figure out that piano piece, if it took her all day!

CHAPTER THREE

Beverly stopped at her father's house to check in on him first. Harold Wheeland was reading—or perhaps dozing—in his leather chair in the library, but he smiled up at her when she walked into the room.

"Jeff just stopped by," he said.

"He did?" Beverly glanced at the clock. Jeff had left earlier this morning.

Her father looked at the clock also. "Oh, maybe it was a while ago when he stopped by. He said he was going on a photo shoot. Some engagement photos on a beach."

"Yes, it's for one of his photographer friends. The couple used a different photographer originally, but the photos on the beach turned out badly because the photographer wasn't very good with outdoor shots like that, so the groom asked Jeff to do some new photos for him."

"He said it was a ways away—two hours, I think?"

"Yes, he'll be gone most of the day today. Do you need anything?"

"Nope. Er . . ." He looked at his coffee cup, which had now gone cold, sitting on the table. "Maybe some coffee."

"I'll have some too." Beverly made a fresh pot and brought her father a mug, then sat and chatted with him about general things while she drank from her own mug. She left him reading his biography of Dietrich Bonhoeffer and headed to her own home.

After leaving Margaret's gallery, she had wanted to immediately sit in front of her piano to try to figure out the piece, but she had needed to check in on Father. After all, the Christmas season was the time for family and celebrating the love between family members. She was glad she'd spent some quality time with her father.

She sat at the piano now, running her fingers over the keys. This piano had been in her father's house and they'd brought it over to their new home, but it had no sentimental meaning for her. She missed her mother's piano, a beautiful rosewood upright piano that her father had bought for her mother for a wedding anniversary gift before Beverly was born. However, five years ago, a leak in the roof had caused extensive water damage to the piano and her father had been forced to get rid of it. Her mother had been dead for over a year, and Beverly had been in Augusta, so he had bought a cheap secondhand piano to take its place.

Beverly closed her eyes and thought of the line of music. She had a hard time at first, but then she pictured the shell ornaments and immediately the strain came back to her. She began fiddling with the keys.

How strange. Her right hand vaguely remembered the fingering for the melody of the piano piece—in fact, the more she played it, the more sure she became of the music. But when she tried to play the left hand, her fingering was clumsy, and it took her considerably longer to figure out the notes. It was as if she'd learned to play only the right hand of this piece when she was younger.

The thought of playing only the right-hand portion suddenly made a memory flood into her mind. She was a child, sitting at her grandmother's piano at her mother's parents' home at Christmas. She was playing the right-hand side to a piece her mother was teaching her, and when she looked up, she could see the wreath hanging on the wall above the piano.

That was it! That's where she'd seen the wreath! But what was it doing in the ocean? Was it the same wreath? With the handmade ornaments, surely it must be. But how did it manage to be found by her, of all people?

But now that she knew she'd seen the wreath in the house of her grandparents, she knew where to ask for help. She immediately dialed her mother's younger sister, her aunt Helen.

"Hello, Beverly," her aunt said as she answered the phone. "It's so nice to hear from you."

As had happened before her wedding a few months ago, the sound of her aunt's voice caused a wave of nostalgia in her. Aunt Helen's voice was so very much like Beverly's mother's voice. "Hi, Aunt Helen. How are you doing?"

"Busy." She sighed. "This time of year, it always turns out that way, doesn't it? Just when we should be slowing down to enjoy our time with family."

"You and Uncle George are still coming to our family gathering on New Year's Day, aren't you?"

"Oh, of course. There won't be many people, will there?"

"It'll be a relaxing, informal dinner," Beverly said. "Just family, from both my mother's side of the family and my father's side too."

"That'll be something to look forward to," Aunt Helen said. "I haven't seen anyone from the Wheeland side of your family in ages."

"Speaking of family, I'm calling about Grandmother Harkness."

"My mother?"

Beverly explained briefly about finding the wreath on the beach, then asked, "Was there a wreath with those types of shell ornaments above the piano at Grandmother Harkness's house?"

"Oh my goodness, yes." Aunt Helen sounded amazed.

Beverly blinked. "Really?"

"It was a fake wreath with shell ornaments. In fact, your mother made it."

Beverly was speechless. Her mother!

Aunt Helen continued, "Back when Eunice was in high school, she went through a phase when she was making lots of shell ornaments. I declare, she was glued to her glue gun, she made so many."

Beverly chuckled.

"The last ornaments Eunice made were for our mother, your Grandmother Harkness. There were a few delicate ornaments in the shapes of snowflakes, but the five main ones were in the shapes of musical instruments. She glued them to a fake wreath and gave it to our mother one Christmas."

"Aunt Helen, the wreath I found must be the same wreath somehow. It had those five ornaments, and while it looked like there had been some other ornaments attached, if they were more delicate, they'd have been easily washed away." She'd missed her mother so much during her wedding, and finding the wreath now was like a gentle reminder that her mother was still watching over her.

"Your Grandmother Harkness always hung the wreath above the piano during Christmas," Aunt Helen said. "How in the world did it turn up in Marble Cove, of all places? I can't believe it. I haven't seen that wreath since . . ." There was a sudden strange silence.

"Aunt Helen?"

Her aunt paused before answering, and when she did, an uncomfortable hesitation had crept into her voice. "This was all when you were still in elementary school. My parents were in a car accident—a truck slid on the ice and crashed into them. My mother died instantly, and my father died a few weeks later from complications with his injuries."

"I do remember when Grandfather and Grandmother Harkness died," Beverly said slowly. "I remember the funeral, because it had been only a few months after my Grandfather Wheeland died."

"I remember that now—it was so tragic, both sets of your grandparents dying within a few years of each other."

Beverly cleared her tight throat. "So what happened to the wreath after the funeral?"

"Well." Aunt Helen hesitated again, as if deciding how much to say about the subject. "Do you remember my older brother, your uncle Dudley?"

"Oh." Beverly hadn't thought of him in years. He had died only a year after Grandmother and Grandfather Harkness. "Yes, I vaguely remember him. Wait . . . I remember an argument between Uncle Dudley and my mother. It made her very upset. What happened?"

Aunt Helen sighed. "We tried to keep our disagreements from you kids, but it was very difficult. What happened was that only a few days after my father died—in fact, even before the funeral—Dudley went to our parents' house and simply took whatever he wanted without consulting me or Eunice."

Beverly choked. Uncle Dudley's actions seemed incredibly indelicate and rude. "Why would he do that?"

"When Eunice and I went to speak to Dudley, he insisted there was nothing wrong with what he'd done. He said he'd only taken the things that were promised him. Since our father was dead, Dudley said that there was no need to wait to take what he wanted."

Beverly couldn't believe how callous he sounded. She remembered Uncle Dudley as being loud and boisterous, but she hadn't known him well before he died, and had no idea of this side of him.

"You must understand: Eunice and I didn't want a great deal from the house," Aunt Helen said. "We only wanted a few mementos of our parents, and certain things they had personally promised to give to each of us. For instance, there was a pearl necklace our mother had promised to give to Eunice one day, and a pearl bracelet that I was to have. There were a few other trinkets we would have liked to have had for sentimental reasons, but Dudley was welcome to the rest."

"I'm so sorry, Aunt Helen." Now that she thought about it, Beverly vaguely remembered overhearing a conversation between her mother and Aunt Helen at her wedding to her late husband, Will. Her mother had said something along the lines of, "If only he hadn't taken it, she could have worn it." She hadn't understood that sentence at all at the time, but now she wondered if she had been referring to that necklace.

"But Dudley stopped speaking to us no matter how we tried to reconcile with him. He accused us of only wanting to talk to him in order to nag him about giving us items from the house. I suppose he might have been right," Aunt Helen added, "but we also didn't like the rift between us. And then Dudley died of a heart attack only a year later."

"I remember Mother had been terribly sad at the funeral."

"We both were," Aunt Helen said. "We had both become bitter about what Dudley had done, but we were also very regretful that we hadn't been able to reconcile with him before he'd died. After all, we were family. We should have been able to repair our differences."

"So . . . the wreath was one of the things Uncle Dudley took from the house?"

"He took all the Christmas decorations," Aunt Helen said bitterly.

"*All* of them?"

"There were some very valuable antique ornaments that belonged to our mother, but he took everything—probably so he wouldn't have to take the time to find the valuable pieces. There was also an angel tree topper that I had given to my mother—I had sewed and embroidered the angel's robes myself, you see, and my mother had promised to give it back to me one day. But now it's lost."

"You couldn't go to Uncle Dudley's wife to ask for it back?" Beverly asked. "What was her name again?" Uncle Dudley had been her second husband, Beverly remembered, and she had brought her two children by her previous husband to her marriage with Uncle Dudley.

"Yes, Malvina," Aunt Helen said. "I'm surprised you remembered—she'd only been married to him for two years before he died. She moved away with her children to live with her parents and never kept in touch with me or Eunice. But I would have thought that all those things Dudley took from our parents' house must have gone with her."

"Do you know where her parents lived? Or what their last name was?"

"I only know that they lived somewhere in Maine," Aunt Helen said. "I don't know her maiden name, but her children's last name, by her first marriage, was Lemmon, with two m's."

"I think I remember them too," Beverly said. "Albert and Mabel, right?" They had been teenagers when she'd known them, and unwilling to play with an elementary school child, so Beverly had played more with her cousin Charlotte.

"Yes, you have a good memory."

"Maybe I can try to find them," Beverly said. "They'd be able to get me in touch with their mother."

Aunt Helen paused, then said, "You can definitely try, but I feel I should warn you that I'm not sure how Malvina will react if someone from the Harkness family reaches out to her, asking for her help."

"Were things uncomfortable between you and my mother and Malvina too?"

"Eunice always thought that Malvina was the one who instigated Dudley's unfeeling behavior after our father's death," Aunt Helen said. "We never found any proof of that, of course, but your mother—and me too, I admit—we couldn't quite let go of our resentment against Malvina and Dudley."

"Would you rather I didn't try to contact her?"

"Of course not," Aunt Helen said quickly. "So much time has passed, and we should try to reconcile with Malvina since she's family."

Even though Malvina wasn't a sister by blood, Aunt Helen spoke so positively that Malvina was part of their family. It reminded Beverly of what her mother had always said, that it wasn't that you *had* to love your family, but that you *could* love your family, no matter what. And Beverly's mother would also consider Malvina to be family.

"I had better go," Aunt Helen said. "I hope this hasn't been too upsetting for you."

"No, I apologize for bringing up a rather painful subject," Beverly said.

"Oh, it happened so long ago, and it's probably good that you've brought it up. I'd like to try to resolve it somehow," her aunt said.

"Will you be coming to our living Nativity?"

"Oh yes, I'll be coming, not on the first night, but we'll be there on Monday."

"I'll see you then."

But as she said good-bye to her aunt, Beverly wondered if she might be opening a can of worms. It was hard not to feel some resentment against Uncle Dudley and Aunt Malvina on behalf of her mother and aunt.

Her mother and her aunt would and could consider Malvina to be family—but could Beverly?

CHAPTER FOUR

Beverly blinked, realizing she had hung up the phone and was simply staring blankly at it for some minutes. What should she do next? Should she try to contact Malvina or her stepcousins, Albert and Mabel, or should she just let this go? Was her desire to understand how the wreath ended up in Marble Cove strong enough to justify stirring up those long-ago memories and feelings? Wasn't it enough that Beverly was 90 percent sure that this wreath was the one her mother had made for her grandmother?

Her waffling back and forth was interrupted by the doorbell, and she was surprised to see Shelley standing outside the door. "Hi, Shelley."

"Hi, Beverly. I came by with your costume." Shelley held up a bundle of jewel-toned fabric. "It was just finished. Let's try it on."

Beverly had tried to put playing one of the wise men out of her mind, but she now felt that familiar nervousness in her stomach at the thought of performing in front of people. It had always been this way for her, and even though she had to speak in front of crowds sometimes as part of her mayoral duties, she never seemed to get used to it enough that the jitters got any better.

"Good grief, you just turned white as a sheet," Shelley said. "Do you need to sit down?"

"I'm fine. I just remembered about the performance tomorrow night."

Shelley laughed. "I understand how you feel. I'm sorry you got roped into doing something that obviously makes you uncomfortable, especially when you've already done so much for the living Nativity, including all the publicity."

"Well, we needed someone, and I was happy to help. I'm just not very good at calming my nerves beforehand."

"Well, if it makes you feel any better, the headdress for this costume covers part of your face."

Beverly laughed, but it actually did make her feel better. She had to admit, as she stood in her living room and Shelley adjusted the fit, pinning here and there, that the costume was gorgeous. As befitting a rich ruler, the fabric was a mix of blues and purples, with some flashes of crimson edging. The headdress had long fabric edges that framed the sides of Beverly's face.

"Your mother-in-law and her friends did a great job on this. So do I get a beard too?" Beverly asked, partly joking.

"Actually, you do." Shelley grinned. "And you'll get some heavy eye makeup. That'll hide your face even more."

"Maybe being a wise man isn't so bad then."

Shelley helped her out of the costume. "I'll get someone to do the hemming and tucking so it'll fit you better. I'm sure one of Frances's friends can do it. By the way, Diane said you were helping her out by finding someone to replace Rita Candleford as the angel. Any luck?"

"Well, I asked Adelaide if she'd be the angel, but she's still not sure if she wants to do it."

Shelley's eyes lit up. "Adelaide would be perfect! Frances is finishing up the angel costume right now. As soon as she's done with it, maybe I'll take it to Margaret's house for Adelaide to see and try on. That might convince her to agree."

"Well, I don't want to pressure her into it, but she really would help us out a lot."

"Plus she'd be a perfect angel. I don't know why none of us thought of it before."

"Probably because we thought she wouldn't be here. How are things going with your parents?" Beverly asked. Shelley had been surprised with her divorced parents both showing up for a Christmas visit with their spouses, and things had been a bit tense and crazy for a while, but in a near-miraculous turn of events, peace had been restored.

"Things aren't perfect, but they're not as bad as they were before," Shelley said. "I remind myself that it's Christmas and I really do love them all, and they love me and my family. Isn't that what the Bible says? 'Love covers over a multitude of sins.'"

The Bible verse that Shelley quoted suddenly struck Beverly to the core. Wasn't that perfectly applicable to the struggle Beverly had been having only moments before?

"Beverly, what's wrong?" Shelley looked concerned.

"Nothing bad," Beverly assured her friend. She explained briefly about her aunt Malvina, which led her to backtrack and explain about finding the wreath on the beach because Shelley hadn't heard about it yet.

"That's amazing," Shelley said. "It seems like all of us are getting mysterious Christmas presents this month. Diane and I got those ornaments and Margaret got that card."

"I don't know if I'd really considered this a Christmas present. After all, I found it on the beach. It probably classifies more as trash."

"But if it really is your mother's wreath, that's something out of the ordinary."

"I'm not sure it's my mother's wreath. I could be just a coincidence."

"But even if it is a coincidence, maybe you're meant to explore it a bit. After all, it brought up a lot of family secrets that you hadn't known about before. Maybe there's a reason for all this."

Beverly frowned, thinking hard. "Do you really think it would be wise to continue to dig into what happened to my mother's wreath? It might only dredge up bad feelings."

Shelley took Beverly's hands in her own. "At the very least, maybe you need to deal with this for yourself and your own peace of mind. I can tell you from experience with my parents that you need to deal with estrangement. It's not good to just ignore it."

"Maybe I should wait until after Christmas to reach out to Malvina. It's a busy time of the year."

"Well, it's up to you, but I think now is the perfect time," Shelley said. "What I've been learning over the past week or two is that Christmas is when we're reminded of the love between family members, because of the love God showed in sending His Son."

Beverly sighed. "I know you're right, but I don't like conflict, and knowing I'm going to deliberately try to bring up old hurts is frightening."

Shelley squeezed Beverly's hands. "I know it's hard—I had to deal with a lot of emotions when I started interacting with my dad again. But ultimately it was a good thing. I don't regret it."

"Thanks, Shelley." Beverly gave her friend a hug, and Shelley left to take the costume back to her home for adjusting.

Shelley was absolutely right—Beverly shouldn't be holding a grudge against Aunt Malvina over something that happened so long ago. Aunt Malvina was family, and even if Beverly didn't find out anything about the wreath, she should try to bridge the years-long gap between their families. Beverly was grateful that she had gained such good friends here in Marble Cove over the past three years who could give her such wise advice.

Beverly went online and began searching. There were no Malvina Harknesses or Malvina Lemmons in Maine, but there were several other people whose last names were Lemmon. One of them might be related to Malvina and her children.

She made a few cold calls to the people with the last name of Lemmon whose numbers were listed in the phone book, but none of them had heard of Malvina, Albert, or Mabel Lemmon.

When she set the phone down, she realized her heart was racing. She'd been both hoping to find Malvina and also dreading it. She stopped to take a deep breath, then said a quick prayer for help from the Lord to calm her. This was harder than she could have imagined, but the more she persevered in doing this, the more she knew it was the right thing to do.

Beverly then went on social media sites and left messages for people with the last name of Lemmon, explaining that she was looking for her aunt and cousins by marriage, Malvina Harkness, formerly Malvina Lemmon, and her children Albert and Mabel Lemmon, although Malvina and Mabel may have both married and changed their last names.

After she was done, Beverly sat and contemplated her computer screen. She felt physically drained, as if she'd run a marathon on the sand in blazing-hot weather. She hadn't really realized how frightening it would be to try to find her relatives while knowing there might be very ugly feelings between them and her mother's family.

No, she shouldn't focus on the negative aspects of this situation. She could focus on the positives—she might have found her mother's wreath, the exact same one that hung above Grandmother Harkness's piano. It was like an invisible cord connecting her to her mother's love after all these years.

Speaking of piano, now that she realized the wreath had been at her grandmother's house, Beverly could again try to figure out the music piece she kept hearing in her head. She left her office and headed down to the living room, where the piano sat.

She flipped through her old piano books, but none of them had the strain of music she was remembering. The piece was very simple, so perhaps it had been a song from one of her elementary music books, which she no longer had. She even tried using an app on her cell phone to try to identify the music, but the app didn't work, perhaps because she was manually playing the piece and the app's database used only recorded songs, or maybe because she wasn't playing it exactly as it had been written.

She played the piece through again, this time figuring out more of the left-hand notes from the stronger memory of the song in her mind. Yes, she must have been very familiar with this song. She and her mother must have played it many times together.

As the notes died away, she felt a squeezing in her heart. How she wished her mother were still here to play the left-hand part with her, to spend Christmas together with her family. She had a feeling that her mother would have liked Jeff and his grandfather, who had raised him. As had happened just before her wedding, she felt the void of her mother's presence in her life. She realized her eyes were wet with tears, and she wiped them away.

And yet finding the wreath and the ornaments was almost like receiving a gift from her mother from beyond the grave—almost, because Beverly still wasn't entirely sure how Aunt Malvina would respond to her tentative olive branch.

Beverly shook her head. Maybe she was being too biased against Aunt Malvina. She closed her eyes and tried to remember those long-ago family gatherings at Grandmother Harkness's home. She remembered that they were a little more subdued than those with her Wheeland relatives, but there was always lots of good food, even if it was just an informal visit. Grandfather Harkness loved to barbecue, and Grandmother Harkness would make lots of side dishes. Even in the wintertime, Grandfather Harkness would use his Weber smoker to smoke ribs or chicken in the covered open-air patio out back. Beverly could remember watching him bundled up on the patio, tending to his smoker.

Beverly also could remember music. Grandmother Harkness had been very good at the piano, and the family would stand around and sing choruses or popular songs while Grandmother Harkness accompanied them. When not playing piano, her grandmother loved to listen to classical music. There had been an old turntable and a vast record collection in the corner of the living room, which had been almost all her grandmother's music. She had never bothered to get her music on cassette tape since the turntable worked fine, and CDs hadn't been invented yet.

Beverly couldn't remember any of her other relatives playing piano except for Grandmother Harkness, Beverly's mother, and herself. No, she did remember her stepcousins Albert and Mabel playing around at the piano sometimes, although they hadn't been as proficient as the adults.

Since Albert and Mabel had been teenagers, they had watched television or played card games with each other rather than playing children's games with Beverly and her cousin Charlotte, who were close in age. They hadn't been unfriendly, but the age gap had prevented them from interacting more. For example, once Mabel had yelled at her because she and Charlotte had been playing tag in the living room while Mabel was trying to paint her nails, and Beverly had knocked into Mabel's hand.

Aunt Malvina had been a presence next to her uncle Dudley, but Beverly couldn't remember interacting much with her except for expressing thanks for Christmas and birthday gifts. Aunt Malvina and Mabel had looked very much alike, with long black hair and heavy-lidded blue eyes.

Aunt Malvina hadn't despised the children by any means, but she hardly ever played with them or even talked to her own children at those family gatherings, instead talking almost exclusively with the adults. In contrast, once in a while Beverly's parents or Charlotte's parents would leave the adults and play with her and Charlotte, or talk with Albert and Mabel.

Beverly couldn't remember Uncle Dudley when he was single, before he married Aunt Malvina. He had been a large man, taller and wider than Grandfather Harkness, with a loud laugh. He'd had beautiful wavy brown hair with gold glints in it and a thick mustache. As Beverly searched her memory, she remembered Aunt Malvina's happy expression as she looked at Uncle Dudley. They had been very much in love.

Yes, people were complex. Beverly had been simplifying her viewpoint of her aunt and cousins. Everyone made mistakes, everyone was selfish, and yet people could also love very deeply.

Reaching out to Aunt Malvina might turn out to be a great blessing. Beverly hoped so.

A sudden knock at the door made her jump. How long had she been lost in her own thoughts? She hurried to open it.

"Hi, Beverly!" Adelaide said. Margaret stood behind her.

"Hi, Adelaide, Margaret. Do you want to come in?"

"We don't have time—we're just on our way home to lunch," Margaret said. "But we wanted to stop by to tell you something." She touched her daughter's shoulder.

"I'll be the angel for the living Nativity," Adelaide said. She still looked a little nervous, but she was smiling.

"That's wonderful!" Beverly gave her a hug. "I'll let Shelley know you'll be the angel. She'll be so happy. They're working on the angel costume right now."

"I hope I do a good job," Adelaide said.

"I think you'll be absolutely wonderful," Beverly told her. "I'll be there too as a wise man, so you won't be alone."

"Oh, good." Adelaide sighed in relief.

"Thank you so much for doing this, Adelaide, and on such short notice," Beverly said.

"You're welcome." Adelaide waved good-bye, and she and Margaret turned toward their home.

Beverly grabbed her coat and stuffed her feet into her boots to race to Diane's house to tell her the good news, then to Shelley to tell her about the costume. How wonderful that Adelaide would take the angel part in the living Nativity. God had certainly come through for them!

CHAPTER FIVE

The next morning, Beverly woke up well before her alarm. She decided to go for her run earlier than usual and headed out. It was still dark and very cold, but she dressed in thermal running clothes and she enjoyed the air stinging her cheeks and the quiet of the early morning. The boardwalk along the shore was lighted with streetlamps, although she ran beside it on the sand in case the boards were slippery with ice. The sound of the ocean waves seemed louder at this time of the day, and she felt all alone with God as she ran.

She returned home and showered, but Jeff was still asleep, so she made a pot of coffee and sat in front of her computer to check her e-mail. She hadn't had time to check it last night because after telling Diane about Adelaide being the angel, they'd both gone to Margaret's house. Allan had been making a huge pot of clam chowder, and he'd invited them—and Jeff—over for dinner. They'd spent the evening talking to Adelaide about how she'd been doing as a college student and a young woman living away from home, and they'd gotten home a little late.

She sipped her coffee and answered a few e-mail questions about the living Nativity, which was opening that night, and then she was surprised by a sudden e-mail that arrived at that moment.

Beverly gasped as she read the e-mail. It was her stepcousin Mabel, who had married and changed her last name to Murdock. She now lived in a town several hours south of Marble Cove. One of the Lemmons Beverly had messaged on social media yesterday was Mabel's cousin, and he had contacted Mabel about Beverly. Mabel gave her phone number and said Beverly could call her anytime.

Beverly checked the time. Jeff would be waking up soon and they'd be getting ready to go to church, but there was still more than an hour before they had to leave the house. Since the e-mail came only a few minutes ago, Mabel was probably awake. Beverly was too impatient and decided to chance calling Mabel so early on a Sunday morning.

As she dialed the number on her cell phone, her heart was pounding so hard that she felt like she'd just come back from her run all over again. She hadn't spoken to Mabel in years. What was she like now?

"Hello?" Mabel's voice had a pinched tone, but she spoke politely.

"Hello, Mabel. This is Beverly Wheeland. You might remember me as Anna." A few years ago, to signify a new start after her first husband died, Beverly had begun using her middle name rather than her first name, Anna. For the same reason, Beverly also felt it would be better to give her maiden name rather than her current married name. "I just got your e-mail. Thank you so much for getting in contact with me."

"Well, I must say I was surprised to hear you were looking for me," Mabel said. "It's almost too little, too late."

"Um . . . excuse me?" Beverly wasn't sure what she was talking about.

There was a slight pause, then Mabel said, "Excuse you? Is that all?"

Beverly took a breath because the conversation was already getting too jumbled in her head. "I'm sorry, Mabel, I'm afraid I'm a bit confused. What did you mean, 'too little, too late'?"

"I'm talking about what your family did to my mother and stepfather, of course."

"My family? Do you mean my mother and aunt?"

Mabel gave a huff of irritation. "Are you saying you don't know anything about what happened after your grandfather died?"

Beverly began to realize that what Aunt Helen had told her might be different from what Mabel knew of the incident. "Do you remember what happened? I was only in elementary school at the time."

"Do you mean you don't know?" Mabel sniffed. "Really, Anna, I thought you were calling to apologize for your family." She sounded huffy that it wasn't the case.

All the time Beverly had spent at her job as an analyst and also as mayor came to the forefront and enabled her to take a deep breath and answer in a calm, polite voice, "I hope it won't be too difficult, but would you please tell me what you remember?"

"My stepfather, as the eldest son, had always known he was entitled to your grandparents' personal effects, but he was terribly hurt when your mother and aunt tried to challenge him out of his own inheritance."

"Er . . . what did they challenge him about? Were they after my grandparents' home?"

"They wanted everything for themselves. Well, I suppose not the house itself, but they wanted all the contents of the house."

Beverly wanted to hear both sides of this issue, but she knew both her mother and her aunt, and couldn't imagine them trying to take Uncle Dudley's entire inheritance from him. "Do you mean they didn't want Uncle Dudley to be able to have anything from the house? Shouldn't they have divided the estate among the three of them?"

"Why would they do that?" Mabel demanded. "The entire estate belonged to my stepfather. He didn't have to split anything."

"Perhaps he misunderstood, and they only wanted a few items from the house," Beverly said. "Surely they wouldn't have wanted to steal his inheritance from him completely."

"That's exactly what they did," Mabel said.

Beverly was conflicted. What had really happened? She was tempted to simply dismiss Mabel's version of events because she couldn't imagine her mother or aunt acting in that way. It would have been completely out of character for either of them. "Do you know when all this happened?"

"Oh . . . before the funeral, I believe. All this sibling squabbling when your grandfather had just died. Of course, I'm sure they were all very sad about that—your grandparents' deaths were very sudden," Mabel added, as if as an afterthought.

"I see." Beverly didn't see, not at all. What had really happened?

"You didn't just ask your mother about this?" Mabel asked.

"My mother passed away several years ago."

"Oh. Well, I'm very sorry about that." She sounded contrite.

"I was hoping to get in contact with you and your mother and brother again," Beverly said. "After all, we are family." She almost didn't say it, but she knew this was important, regardless of what had really happened between her uncle, her mother, and her aunt.

"My mother died over ten years ago," Mabel said. "If you didn't know anything about this, why were you trying to get in contact with me?"

"I had two reasons," Beverly said. "First, I wanted to invite you and your brother and your families to a gathering at my house on New Year's

Day. I'm inviting family from both my father's and mother's sides of the family, and you are all part of my mother's family."

There was a pause, then Mabel said in a more subdued voice, "Well, that's very kind of you, Anna, but I'm afraid we have plans. What's the second reason?"

Beverly's throat tightened, because she had a feeling Mabel would be offended by what she was about to say. "The second reason is because I was trying to track down a Christmas wreath that my mother made, which had been in the Christmas decoration boxes at my grandparents' house."

"You are just like your mother," Mabel snapped, "trying to take what's not yours."

Beverly gritted her teeth, and again had to don her polite and conciliatory "mayoral hat" as she replied, "I'm sorry you feel that way. Until you told me just now, I had no idea that it seemed that my mother had been trying to take your stepfather's inheritance from him."

"Uh . . ." Mabel seemed at a loss for words as she processed that logical conclusion. She herself had just explained to Beverly what had happened from her point of view, so she couldn't accuse Beverly of trying to do the same thing as her mother when she hadn't known about it. Mabel gave a sniff, then said, "What wreath are you talking about?"

"It was an artificial fir wreath that hung above Grandmother Harkness's piano," Beverly said. "It had shell ornaments on it."

"Yes, I remember that wreath. Why would you want that ugly old thing?"

Beverly cleared her throat, then said evenly, "My mother made those ornaments."

"Oh." Mabel's voice was terse, perhaps with embarrassment. "Well, I'm afraid I don't know where it is. When Mother died, everything was divided between Albert and me, and I certainly don't have it. I don't remember seeing it among the Christmas things that Albert got."

Beverly had to bite her tongue so she wouldn't say something about how Mabel and Albert had split their mother's estate, and yet she'd been offended when Beverly's mother and aunt had expected the same from their own brother.

"You don't think you might have thrown it away?" Beverly wouldn't really be surprised—or blame her—if she had. After all, it hadn't been a nice, professionally made wreath.

"No, I know I didn't," Mabel said with a touch of irritation.

"Would you perhaps be willing to give me Albert's phone number? I'd like to invite him to the New Year's party and also ask him if he knows what happened to the wreath."

"I most certainly will not give you his number," Mabel said huffily. "I am not in the habit of giving my brother's contact information to just anyone who asks."

Beverly counted to ten and then realized that Mabel probably considered Beverly the same as a stranger since she hadn't seen Mabel or Albert in years and they weren't related by blood. "Then would you please give my contact information to Albert and ask him to call me?"

"I suppose so," Mabel said grudgingly. "But I can't guarantee he'll call you."

"That's fine." Beverly wasn't sure she would want a second dose of hostility from Albert too, if he were of the same mind as Mabel. But if he had the wreath, then she would know that the ornaments she'd found weren't her mother's.

She heard sounds from the kitchen and knew Jeff must be getting breakfast ready. "Thank you for your time, Mabel. And thank you for taking my call this morning."

"Well, I can't say it's been a pleasure, Anna," Mabel said. "I don't know why you have to go bringing up hurt feelings after all these years."

"I assure you, that wasn't my intention. Thank you for telling me what happened."

Mabel sniffed again, then said good-bye and hung up.

Beverly's hands were shaking as she set her phone down. She had expected the call to be emotional, but Mabel's reaction had been a shock, and the turmoil going through her now was difficult to deal with. Maybe she should have tried to prepare herself better for how unfriendly Mabel had been. Beverly hadn't had to deal with many people so ill-disposed and antagonistic.

Was Mabel really correct in what had happened? Or was her perspective skewed? Or was Beverly just *hoping* Mabel's perspective was skewed because she didn't want to believe her mother and aunt would be so unreasonable?

No. Beverly knew her mother, and she'd gotten to know her aunt better over the past year. She knew with 100 percent certainty that her mother wouldn't have tried to do something like take all of Uncle Dudley's inheritance from him, and she couldn't imagine Aunt Helen being the same way.

She had wanted to let go of her resentment against Mabel's family but this phone call only seemed to deepen her feelings of injustice and frustration. If it wasn't so soon before church, she would have gone right out for a second jog to try to relieve her vexation.

What would Diane do in a situation like this? Diane would tell Beverly to calm down and pray. Beverly sat in her office chair, taking deep breaths to try to calm her mind, but it was easier said than done.

God, help me! she prayed, but the prayer didn't seem to help her feel better.

She headed into the kitchen, where Jeff was making pancakes. The buttery smell didn't lift her spirits like it usually did.

He smiled when he saw her, but then his eyes grew concerned when he noticed the expression on her face. "What's wrong?"

Beverly sighed, then explained about Mabel.

Jeff turned off the stove and set down the spatula, then went to embrace her. "It'll be all right," he said in her ear. "Your finding that wreath is pretty unusual—it could be that you really need to connect with your family right now, for some reason."

Beverly leaned into his shoulder, finding comfort from the fresh smell of his soap mixed with the scent of the frying pancakes. She needed that comfort more than she realized.

Was this really the right thing to do? What good could come from her opening this emotional can of worms right before Christmas?

CHAPTER SIX

Beverly had a hard time focusing on Reverend Locke's message in church. It was about how God showed His love for everyone by sending His Son to be born. It was only with difficulty that Beverly could imagine what it would have been like to be a king and then to become not only a commoner but a helpless baby. She knew that God loved her, but sometimes understanding that love was hard.

The reverend also mentioned the living Nativity just before he dismissed the congregation. Beverly was surprised when, as she and Jeff mingled with some of the other members of the congregation after the service ended, one older woman came up to her and said, "I just heard about a living Nativity tonight."

Beverly was a little frustrated that after all her publicity efforts, there were still people who hadn't known about the event. "Yes, it'll be at the old train station. It's a community event that's been put together mostly by members from the different churches in Marble Cove."

"That sounds interesting," the woman said. "There hasn't been a living Nativity in Marble Cove in so many years. Will there be live animals there too? Maybe I could take my grandchildren."

"Yes, our local vet, Dr. Leo Spangler, is getting the animals for us," Beverly said. "We're even going to have a live camel."

"A camel! Really?"

"I can't wait to see if he can pull it off," Beverly said. She suddenly noticed Shelley hovering at the woman's elbow, politely waiting for Beverly to finish her conversation. Earlier that year, Shelley and her family had started going to Old First, where Dan's parents were long-standing members of the congregation, though Shelley sometimes still went to Light the Way Chapel.

"Well, that sounds wonderful," the woman said. "I'll most certainly come tonight."

"I'll see you there," Beverly said as the woman turned to speak to someone else. "Hi, Shelley. What's up?"

"Your wise man costume is ready," Shelley said. "I'll come by later today to drop it off."

"No need," Beverly said. "I can come by to pick it up. When will you be home?"

"We're heading home right now," Shelley said. "There are still a lot of little things to be finished for the costumes before tonight, so we're having a quick lunch at my house and then working to get everything done."

"I'll come by after I have lunch with my father," Beverly promised.

They went home, and Beverly baked macaroni and cheese. She loved the contrast of the crispy breadcrumb topping and the creamy sharp cheese, and it seemed especially perfect for such a cold winter day as today. She and Jeff brought it over to her father's house, and he seemed to enjoy it, humming pleasantly to himself as he ate.

"What will you do this afternoon?" she asked her father.

"I wanted to rest up, to be sure to make it to the living Nativity tonight," he said, "but the light went out in the bathroom."

"I'll change it for you," Jeff said. "Do you have spare lightbulbs?"

"I don't remember," her father said. "I'll have to look."

"I'll look for them," Beverly said, but Jeff interrupted her.

"No, I'll help look for them," Jeff said. "If there aren't any, I can go to the store to get some."

"Are you sure? I don't have a lot to do this afternoon."

"You never know what might come up since the living Nativity is tonight," Jeff said, "and you have to get your costume, don't you?"

Beverly nodded.

Jeff turned to her father. "Harold, I'll drive you to the living Nativity when it opens at seven tonight."

"Sounds good," he replied.

Beverly headed over to Shelley's house while Jeff and her father went looking for spare lightbulbs.

She knocked on the door, and even before it opened, she could hear the voices chattering on the other side. When Shelley opened the door, the sounds of women laughing spilled out of the house.

"You're just in time," Shelley said. "Margaret and Adelaide are here trying on the angel outfit."

"How does it fit?" Beverly headed eagerly into Shelley's living room, where Adelaide stood in the center of the room, surrounded by women. Some were working on other costumes, but two or three were fussing with the angel costume that Adelaide wore. It was composed of swaths of lovely white fabric that draped around her in graceful folds.

"It fits perfectly," Shelley said with a grin. "It's like a miracle."

"How do the wings stay up?" Beverly asked. Peeking out from the fall of fabric at the back were two elegant wings. They were made from a wire frame with white fabric stretched over it and white feathers glued to it, so they were both lightweight and strong.

"They're attached to a shoulder harness," Shelley said. "It's hidden under the costume."

"It's not heavy," Adelaide said, shrugging her shoulders.

"They're beautiful," Beverly said. "I can't believe they were made in such a short time."

"Actually, one of the seamstresses had them in her attic," said Frances Bauer. "She had made them for a high school production of *The Swan Princess* that she had helped with. We only needed to clean them and add more feathers."

"Are you going to be warm enough?" Beverly eyed the floating fabric of the angel's robes, which looked ethereal and beautiful but not very good protection against the cold.

"She put on winter long johns under the costume," Margaret said. "And it's long enough that she'll be able to wear her fleece-lined boots underneath and no one will be able to tell."

"And the innermost layer of the costume is wool," Frances said.

"Wow, all that's really well hidden," Beverly said.

"Wait. I'll go get your costume." Shelley stepped out of the room for a moment, then returned with the jewel-toned costume Beverly had seen earlier. She helped Beverly put it on.

"It fits great," Beverly said. She moved her arms and took a few steps. The hem was just the right length, and it was just roomy enough in the shoulders.

"Here's the headdress." Shelley set it on Beverly's head, and the rich fabric framed her face.

Shelley brought out a cardboard box. "And lastly, pick your wise man gift box." Inside the cardboard box were two cheap music boxes, heavily gilded and very flashy, which looked like jewel-encrusted treasure chests, as well as the redecorated pirate chest Shelly's son Aiden had found at the antique store.

"*Ooh*, those are so pretty," Beverly said.

"We wanted them to be extra flashy so they'd be easier for the audience to see," Shelley said. "And see? Your box will fit into this neat pocket in your costume."

"That's so clever!" Beverly said. The box nestled comfortably against her thigh inside the rich robes.

"Make sure you arrive a little early," Frances told her. "We'll do your makeup and put on your beard."

"You won't look like yourself at all," Shelley joked.

The doorbell rang again, and some other people arrived for their costume fittings, so Beverly moved closer to the hallway to make room for them in the living room. Shelley came with her to help her remove the costume.

Just as Beverly had finished putting her clothes back on, she suddenly heard some yelling from the direction of Aiden's room.

"Oh dear." Shelley headed to the bedroom, and Beverly followed behind her.

"Mine!" Emma, Shelley's daughter, yelled at her older brother Aiden while wrapping her arms around their dog Prize.

"You have to listen to me," Aiden yelled back, obviously continuing some argument they had been having. "I'm older." He tried to take Prize away from her.

"Hey," Shelley said, stopping the fight. "What's going on?"

"I want to play with Prize now," Aiden said.

"Mine," Emma insisted.

Beverly remembered that Shelley had mentioned that Emma's vocabulary had been growing, but she unfortunately had a fondness for words like "mine" and "no."

"You played with Prize earlier," Shelley said. "It's Emma's turn."

"But I'm older," Aiden insisted. "She has to listen to what I say."

Shelley knelt in front of her son and gently pulled him a little ways away from his sister. Beverly knelt in front of Emma and cooed to her while petting Prize, who looked bewildered at being fought over. She could hear Shelley speaking to Aiden, however.

"Aiden, we know you're older than Emma, but you should treat her fairly because she's your sister."

"But I'm older," he said. "How come I have to give way to her when I'm older?"

"Aiden, do you remember what Reverend Locke talked about today in church?"

Aiden wouldn't meet her eyes and stuck his bottom lip out in a classic expression of belligerence.

"He was talking about how Jesus was a king up in heaven, but He humbled Himself to become a helpless baby at Christmas. Remember?"

Aiden nodded slowly.

"Do you remember why Jesus did that?"

Aiden didn't answer.

"It's because Jesus loves us so much," Shelley said. "He wanted to teach us to love each other the same way He loves us, so He became an example, even though He was a king."

Aiden's lower lip no longer jutted out, but he still couldn't quite meet Shelley's eyes.

"Do you love Emma?" Shelley asked.

Aiden nodded.

"So can you love Emma like Jesus loves us and be a humble older brother to your sister?" Shelley asked him.

"I guess," he mumbled.

Shelley hugged him. "I know Jesus is proud of you. And I am too."

Emma saw the hug and reached her arms out to her mother for her own share of hugging. Shelley gathered Emma with her other arm so that it was a sweet three-way embrace before she released both of them.

"Hey, where's Prize?" Aiden asked.

Beverly looked down and realized the dog was no longer by her knee. "Uh . . ."

A woman's surprised shriek from the living room had Aiden running out the door to retrieve his dog. Beverly followed, but he already had a firm grasp of Prize's collar.

"Sorry, Meemaw," he said to Frances.

"No harm done," Frances told her grandson. "Just don't let it happen again. It'll be better after the costumes are done and you don't need to keep your dog in your room." Despite her gently chiding words, Frances's love for Aiden was obvious in the way she ruffled his sandy hair before he turned to lead the dog back into the bedroom.

"Sorry, Mom," Aiden said to Shelley, who had come up behind Beverly in the hallway.

"It's all right. As your grandma said, no harm done. Just keep Prize in your room for the afternoon, okay?"

"Okay." He closed the bedroom door after him.

"You did a nice job back there," Beverly told her.

Shelley laughed. "I was sweating bullets for a while. I wasn't sure exactly what to say or where I was going with that. Most of the time parenting is just flying by the seat of your pants."

"Well, if it makes you feel better, what you said to Aiden helped me too," Beverly said.

Shelley's eyebrows rose. "Really?"

Beverly explained about her early morning phone call with Mabel.

Shelley's cheeks grew rosy with indignation for her friend. "What a conversation to have first thing in the morning!"

"I don't know what really happened back then between my mother, my aunt, and my uncle," Beverly said. "But you reminded me that Jesus suffered a lot, all because He loves us. The least I can do is try to love Mabel."

Shelley sighed. "I can relate to what you're feeling, both the frustration and also how you want to try to heal the relationship. But just remember, Mabel may not respond no matter what you say."

"I know, but I'm realizing that I have to at least try. I need to not let my or my mother's resentment color my relationship with my stepcousins. They're family."

Shelley gave a rueful smile. "That's true. It's what I've had to learn with my own family."

Beverly gave the wise man costume back to Shelley and said goodbye before she headed back to her own home. Diane had the majority of the work already done for the living Nativity, but she was in charge of publicity and she wanted to make sure the programs would be ready.

She placed a call to the printer, who was making up the program for tonight. It was only a single piece of paper folded in half with the names of the living Nativity participants, but Beverly had called yesterday to replace Rita Candleford's name with Adelaide's. The printer assured her that the correction had been made and the programs would be printed and delivered that afternoon to the train station.

She had just disconnected the call with the printer when the phone suddenly rang in her hand. It was a phone number with an area code outside of Marble Cove or Augusta, and she wasn't familiar with it, but she answered the phone anyway. "Hello. This is Beverly Mackenzie."

There was a slight pause, then a man's voice said, "I'm sorry, I must have the wrong number. I'm looking for Anna Wheeland."

"I apologize—this is Anna. These days, I go by my middle name, Beverly. Beverly Mackenzie now."

"Oh." The man cleared his throat, then said, "Beverly, this is Albert Lemmon."

Albert! Beverly hadn't expected to hear from him—after all, she'd spoken to his sister only this morning, and Mabel hadn't exactly been eager to pass along Beverly's message to her brother to call her. "Oh, hello, Albert. Thank you for calling me." She kept her voice carefully neutral. After her experience with Mabel, she wasn't sure what to expect from Albert.

"Yes, Mabel called me early this morning to tell me about your conversation."

For a moment, Beverly wasn't sure how to respond. Did he share his sister's opinion about the long-ago events over his stepfather's inheritance? Was he also upset with Beverly? At the same time, Beverly was hesitant to mention to Albert about her tense conversation with Mabel.

From Albert's voice, it seemed he also was trying to be careful in his tone and how he phrased his words, so Beverly hoped that they were both striving for a polite conversation rather than the heated exchange she'd had with Mabel. "I haven't seen you in a long time. I hope you're doing well?" She realized guiltily that she had never gotten a chance to ask Mabel about her own family.

"Yes, I have two grown children now. How about you?"

"No children. I was widowed a few years ago, but I recently remarried this year. I'm living near my father in Marble Cove."

"Ah, good, good." He sounded distracted, and Beverly could hear a woman's voice in the background of his phone. "Mabel mentioned you were looking for a Christmas wreath?"

"Yes. It was an artificial wreath with only shell ornaments decorating it, and it used to hang over Grandmother Harkness's piano."

"I'm afraid I don't recall it, but we still have several boxes of Christmas decorations in the attic that I haven't gone through in years. At least one or two of the boxes were decorations I received from my stepfather. Why don't you come to my house tomorrow and look through the boxes yourself?"

The invitation surprised her. For one thing, she hadn't expected Albert to be so accommodating. He certainly wasn't effusively friendly, but then again, when she knew him as a child, she remembered him as always being reserved and logical, and he was scrupulously polite to her now, in contrast to Mabel.

The suddenness of the invitation also made her wary. She hardly ever made spur-of-the-moment plans like that—it went against her careful personality, which she'd gotten from her father. "Tomorrow? Are you sure?"

"Well, tomorrow is more convenient for me, time-wise. We're pretty busy with engagements from Christmas Eve until after New Year's, and I assumed you'd want the wreath in time for Christmas, right?"

He had a point, although in reality, Beverly only wanted to know if the wreath she had found was her mother's wreath or if the real wreath was still with the Christmas decorations that had been taken from her grandmother's house. Ought she to tell him the truth about that? "Actually, Albert . . ."

Suddenly, however, she again heard that strain of piano music. Before, it had been playing in her head, but this time, it sounded like it was being played from the next room, even though she knew she was alone in the house. It was so mysterious and so sudden that she stopped speaking.

"Yes?" he prompted her.

The music strain played again, and she heard it clearly. Taking her phone with her, she walked to the hallway, peering in the rooms and peeking at the living room, where the piano stood silently. Was there a reason she'd suddenly heard the piano music? Did it mean something? She couldn't shake the feeling that it was some sort of message to her.

She decided not to explain to Albert about finding the wreath. "I would be happy to come see you tomorrow," she said. "Thank you for offering to let me search through your Christmas decorations."

"Here's my address." He gave her an address that was a little outside of Thorndike, Maine, which was about an hour away from Marble Cove. "If you could arrive around nine o'clock, that would be best," he added.

"Certainly," Beverly said. "I also wanted to invite you and your family to a New Year's gathering at my house in Marble Cove, if you're available."

"I'm afraid I'll have to ask my wife first," he said. "I'll talk to her this afternoon and let you know tomorrow."

"Of course. Thank you, Albert."

They said good-bye and hung up, but Beverly stared at her phone for a moment in confusion. She ought to be relieved, she supposed, that Albert had been polite and not hostile to her. Yet this cool conversation told her nothing about how Albert felt about her or the old family feud. Perhaps he didn't feel anything about it since it didn't have to do with himself or even his blood relatives. Yet that attitude was markedly different from Mabel's, who was still upset over the incident.

She decided to take this as an indication that Albert might be open to healing the breach between their families. After all, this was Christmas, and they were still family.

Her thoughts were suddenly interrupted by the ringing of her cell phone once again. From the caller ID, she could see that it was Diane. "Hi, Diane. What's up?"

"Oh, Beverly, I'm sorry to bother you, but could you please come down to the train station?" There was a thread of strain in Diane's voice. "I'm afraid we have a problem and I need your help."

Chapter Seven

Anxiety churned in Beverly's stomach as she drove to the old train station. Several vehicles were there, with a few bearing the company logo of Wayne Stover, Dan's boss. They must belong to the electricians who were setting up the wiring for the outdoor lights that illuminated the different sets of the Nativity.

As she got out of the car, she happened to spot Dr. Leo Spangler, the Marble Cove veterinarian. He waved to her and walked to her car.

"Hello, Beverly. What brings you here so early?"

"Diane called and asked me to come down. She said she needed my help for something."

"Uh-oh. I hope it's not serious."

"I hope so too. What are you doing here?"

"Well, the animals are scheduled to arrive soon, and I'm setting up the pens for each of them." The vet turned to point out two college-age young people who were pounding stakes into the gravel of the dirt area outside the train station building. "I commandeered my neighbor's kids, Levi and Audrey, to help me."

"I can't believe you managed to get a camel for the living Nativity tonight," Beverly asked. "I know Diane was hoping you could, but it seemed like it was touch and go for a while there."

"I can hardly believe it myself." Leo grinned. "But we did. He's a long-lived old fellow and a bit ornery, but as long as people don't get too close to him, he'll be as dignified a camel as ever bore a wise man from the East."

Beverly laughed, then caught sight of Diane exiting the train building. She waved, and Diane headed toward them.

Diane's smile seemed a bit relieved as well as welcoming. "Thanks for coming."

"No problem," Beverly said. "What's up?"

"I'll have Wayne explain it to you when we get inside the building."

Diane turned to Leo with a warm smile. "When are the animals coming? I can't wait to see them."

"They should be here within the hour," he said. "Hey, if we're in the way of the electricians, just let us know. We're almost done making the animal pens."

"Oh, you're fine," Diane said.

At that moment, Margaret's minivan and Shelley's car drove up to the train station and parked. Allan, Margaret's husband, drove the minivan with Margaret in the passenger seat, and Ralph, Shelley's father-in-law, was sitting in the passenger seat of Shelley's car. Allan and Ralph were the two other wise men who would be acting alongside Beverly tonight.

Shelley climbed out and waved at them. "We're helping Margaret put up the last pieces of the Nativity set."

"I can't wait to see it," Diane said.

"Me neither," Beverly said.

"What are you all up to?" Margaret asked as she walked up to them.

"Diane called me," Beverly said.

"We'd better go inside," Diane said. "Wayne's waiting for us."

"I'm glad you're here," Leo said to Margaret, Shelley, Ralph, and Allan. "We're making the pens for the animals so we can figure out where best to put the stable set and the straw for the shepherd set. What do you think of . . ." He continued walking and talking to them as they headed toward where Levi and Audrey were still working on the pens.

"Oh, there's Wayne," Diane said.

Wayne Stover, who had volunteered to be in charge of the on-site electrical teams, had exited the train station and headed toward them.

"Hi, Wayne." Beverly shook his hand.

The tall electrician gave her a not-unfriendly nod, but his steely blue eyes were worried. "Thanks for coming out here, Mrs. Mayor."

Beverly smiled. "Just Beverly, please."

"Hi, Beverly," called a voice behind her, and she turned to see Shelley's husband Dan. He had apprenticed under Wayne when he was just starting out as an electrician, and now he worked full time in Wayne's company. "Did Diane call you? Thanks for coming out here," Dan said.

"We appreciate you guys doing this for us," Beverly said. Dan had been quick to volunteer his time because of Shelley's involvement in the living Nativity. Wayne was volunteering his services because of his friendship with Dan and Shelley, and also because he was well acquainted with Diane through them.

Wayne nodded to her again. "Not a problem. Well, maybe I shouldn't say that, because obviously there's some sort of problem. We just can't figure it out."

"How can I help?" Beverly asked Diane.

Diane nodded to Wayne. "I'll let Wayne explain."

"We've been working on the wiring all day—we did an evaluation last week so we knew it wasn't bad, and we weren't expecting any major problems. We set everything up, but for some reason we aren't getting power to the outdoor lights." He gestured to the large outdoor spotlights that illuminated the various scenes for the living Nativity. "We've double-checked all the wiring and we're flummoxed as to why it doesn't work. Then we discovered an area of the building that isn't in the plans we got."

"Not in the plans? Could I see it?"

"Sure."

Wayne led them all inside the train station building. After being declared a historical landmark, the town of Marble Cove had plans to renovate it and turn it into a museum and gift shop, but they hadn't completed the work yet so it was still empty of any furniture or display cases. Someone had been assigned to keep the inside tidy in the meantime so that it was much cleaner than it had been when Beverly and her friends had first found the train station, abandoned and forgotten, about a year ago. The ticket counters were like empty eyes along one wall, but the broken windows had been repaired, and the paint, which had been peeling from the walls, had been stripped so that the interior looked clean and neat, if a bit bare.

A few volunteers were arranging tables and chairs for refreshments for the people who attended the Nativity. In the corners they'd also set up some industrial space heaters and would later bring hot water pots and coffeemakers as well as snacks and goodies.

Beverly, Diane, and Wayne went behind the ticket counter and down a hallway into a room in the back. Wayne pointed to a section of the wooden wall that had been cut out to expose the wiring. "This isn't in the building blueprints that we got from you last week."

"Do you think this area is what's causing the power not to work?"

Wayne shrugged. "There's really no way to know without the blueprints."

Diane turned to Beverly. "Since you were kind enough to get us these blueprints, we were hoping you could see if there's an older set of blueprints or building plans for the train station that might show this wiring."

Beverly nodded. "I'll go check."

"Thank you." Diane gripped her hand tightly. "We have to get those blueprints fast because the living Nativity is set to open in only a few hours, and we need electricity for those outdoor lights and the hot drinks inside the building."

"I think I know where the plans might be," Beverly said. "When I got the blueprints for the building to you last week, I also saw where the old archived building plans are stored in the municipal building."

Beverly hurriedly drove to her office at the municipal building annex, which was actually a converted Victorian house. The only people around this Sunday before Christmas were a few officers who could be seen through the windows of the police station in the main municipal building next door. Beverly let herself into the annex with her key.

She headed down the hall to the rooms that housed the city planning office and the storage rooms where the building blueprints were stored. Last week, she'd spent at least twenty minutes searching for the right drawing, but today she remembered exactly where she'd gotten the plans for the train station. She checked the shelf around where it had been. If there were older blueprints for the station building, they'd be here. For other buildings in the town, the new and the older blueprints for the same building were stored together on the same shelf.

However, she couldn't find anything. Beverly checked each shelf around the area but still came up with nothing. What could she do? The electricians needed to know about that older area of the building in order to set up the lights for the living Nativity.

Beverly had left the door to the room open, and she was huffing in frustration at the blueprint shelves when movement at the door caught her eye. She turned to see Angela, the municipal office receptionist, standing in the doorway and staring at her. Angela held aloft a heavy ceramic vase as if getting ready to throw it. Beverly recognized it as the vase that usually stood on a table in the reception area, holding a lavish flower arrangement that was replaced twice a week.

"Beverly!" Angela lowered the vase. "You scared the socks off me. I thought we had a burglar or something."

"Sorry," she said with a smile. "What are you doing with that vase? You could have just run over to the police department next door to report the intruder."

Angela looked sheepishly at the vase in her hand. "I wasn't really thinking, I guess. All I knew was that I heard noises from the storage room."

"What are you doing here on a Sunday afternoon?"

"Oh, I forgot my wallet at my desk," Angela said. "I took it out of my purse on Friday to get change for someone, and I just put it in my desk drawer because we were so busy that day—last day before the holidays and all. I didn't even remember I'd left it until today when I tried to buy lunch at the Cove."

Beverly winced. "Oh, you were driving without your license all weekend?"

"I know, scary, right?" Angela blew out a breath. "Good thing nothing happened. Why are you here today?"

"I'm hoping to find an older blueprint for the train station," Beverly said.

"Didn't you get the blueprint last week?" In fact, Angela had been the one to help Beverly find it.

"The one I gave to the electricians doesn't have an area of old wiring, so I was hoping to find an older one that might have it."

"It couldn't wait until Monday?"

"The electricians are having problems getting the power to work, but the living Nativity is tonight."

"Oh, that's right." Angela tapped her chin as she thought. "It might be in one of the archive rooms. I know that the blueprints are normally all stored together, but we had to clean this room out a few years ago because it was getting too full, so some of the older blueprints were shuffled to an archive room."

"Do you know where it might be?"

"I think so." Angela led the way down the hallway to an older section of the building. She set the heavy vase down on the floor before a door and used her key to open it.

The room was full of freestanding metal shelving that had everything from file boxes to rolled-up papers. Angela and Beverly searched the shelves for blueprints but didn't find any.

"It's probably in one of the other rooms." Angela unlocked a second door in the hallway, which was again filled with freestanding metal shelving. However, this time, as Beverly was searching one corner, Angela gave a triumphant cry.

"Here they are. The old train station, you said?"

Beverly joined her, and they searched through the blueprints piled on the shelf. They were all older, with more brittle paper than the blueprints in the other room. It was Beverly who found the one that said, "Maine Central Railroad, Marble Cove Branch" on the corner, and the date, 1935.

"The one I gave Wayne was for 1947," Beverly said. She wasn't very proficient in reading blueprints, but she saw that the difference in this older building and the one standing now were some rooms in the back, including the one where the strange wiring was. It looked like there used to be more rooms, but each was smaller. The building now had fewer but larger rooms. That must have been the reason for the 1947 renovation when the newer blueprints were placed in the municipal building.

"Do you think this will help?" Angela asked.

"I hope so." Beverly rolled up the blueprint. "Is there some sort of tube I can put this in?"

"Oh, I know. There's a roll of Christmas wrapping paper in my office."

"Perfect." Beverly followed Angela to the reception area and tucked the blueprint inside the wrapping-paper tube. It was a little short, but at least it afforded some protection.

They walked out of the building, and Beverly locked it again. "Thanks so much, Angela."

"No problem. Merry Christmas!"

Beverly got in her car and made a beeline to the train station. She handed the blueprint to Wayne, who laid it out on the wide ticket counter inside the train station.

"*Hmm.*" He studied the drawing, tracing lines with his finger. Then his gray eyebrows rose. "That wasn't on the other blueprint. They might have just forgotten to label it."

He continued to mumble to himself for a few minutes, then he and one of the other electricians went to the back room. Beverly and Diane stood by the door. The two men did various things that made no sense to her, but then after a while they stood up.

"Okay, let's try it," Wayne said.

They went outside to where the outdoor lights were set up. "Ready? Punch it," Wayne called to one of the men.

There was a metallic clang, the sound of a few clicking levers, and then suddenly the lights flared up.

"All right!" Beverly and Diane hugged each other. A couple of the electricians cheered, and Wayne gave a satisfied smile.

"Let's leave them to their work and see how the sets are doing," Diane said.

In only the short time Beverly had been gone, Margaret and Shelley had erected the stable set. It was beautifully done, really looking like the inside of a stable. The walls were painted to look like old, handmade clay blocks with mortar and stucco coming off. She had also painted some freestanding animals—a lamb and ewe tucked up together, a goat, and an ox. The animals all had large gentle eyes that looked almost real—and shining as if in anticipating of being the first to see the Christ child.

But what was most precious were three cats painted on the walls of the stable—a striped tabby, an orange cat, and a black-and-white cat. Beverly knew these cats by name: Lizzy, Butterscotch, and Oreo—Adelaide's pets.

"The entire set is so beautiful, Margaret," Diane said, and Beverly voiced her agreement.

"It's not done yet." There was a mischievous gleam in Margaret's eyes as she turned and called out, "Okay, Shelley, now!"

From behind the stable suddenly rose a star, hoisted by ropes and pulleys. The star was made of several slats of wood painted with golden glow-in-the-dark paint. Strings of crystal-white Christmas lights were draped from the bottom like beams of light streaming upon the scene. Dan's head appeared above the stable roof as he climbed a short ladder, guiding the star into place. Beverly saw that Allan and Ralph were pulling the ropes to suspend the star directly above the stable.

"That's going to look so magnificent shining in the darkness," Diane said with a delighted smile.

"Let's anchor the Christmas lights so that they look like streams of light shining down from the star on to the roof of the stable," Margaret said.

"That's a good idea." Dan climbed down from the ladder and soon appeared around the corner of the stable. He placed the ladder so Allan could climb up and grab the end of one of the "streams" of lights. In no time, the streamers had been fastened to the front edge of the stable roof.

"I can't wait to see how that'll look tonight," Beverly said.

At that moment, some trucks pulling animal trailers drove up the main access road to the train station.

"Oh, good," Leo Spangler said as he appeared from around the back of the stable. "The animals for the Nativity are here."

"Need help?" Allan asked.

"We could use a hand with the sheep," Leo said. "We just need people to body-block them to get them to head into the pen over there." He pointed to a pen that had been built where the shepherds would be "watching over their flocks by night."

Beverly and her friends also helped with the sheep while Leo unloaded the donkey. The sheep were a bit skittish but docile and seemed to easily be deterred from wandering by just seeing someone step into their path. The "shepherds" managed to get the six animals into the pen with no problems.

Then the owner of the animal rescue farm came out of the largest trailer leading the camel.

"Wow, he's bigger than I expected," Beverly said to Diane.

"But he looks rather regal, don't you think?" They watched as the owner led the camel to the pen that had been erected behind the stable set.

Leo headed toward them. "Beverly, I know you're one of the wise men. Who are the other two?"

"Actually, it'll be Ralph and Allan." The men had agreed, albeit reluctantly, to step in when two cast members dropped out due to illness. Beverly beckoned to the two men, who were helping to guide the donkey into a small pen to the side of the stable.

"Who'll be leading the camel?" Leo asked the three of them.

Ralph and Allan both immediately looked at Beverly.

"Me?" she choked.

"You're the highest-ranking member of the wise men, Mrs. Mayor," Ralph said with a twinkle in this eye.

Beverly rolled her eyes, but then said, "All right. Leo, I'm it."

"Come and meet your costar." Leo led the way behind the stable set to where the camel's pen had been erected. Calmly standing in the center was the camel, who looked curiously at Beverly as she approached. Ralph and Allan followed a few steps behind her. Already there, standing outside the pen and looking at the camel, were Margaret, Diane, Shelley, and Dan.

"This is Leo," Leo said.

Everyone burst into laughter.

"Yes, I know," Leo said in a long-suffering voice. "I didn't name him. He's an old fellow who was a fixture at the Desert of Maine for many years."

"He lives at a rescue farm now, right?" Diane asked.

Leo nodded. "The owner is letting us borrow Leo for both nights of the Nativity."

Up close, the camel was even larger than Beverly expected. "Will he bite?" she asked tentatively.

"Oh no," Leo assured her. "He's more obedient than most dogs I see at the clinic. But, um . . . there's one thing you'll have to watch for."

Beverly's shoulders tensed. "What?" She had a vision of the camel bolting into the woods with herself hanging on for dear life.

"Leo, uh . . ." The vet cleared his throat. "Leo drools. The camel, I mean."

Beverly blinked at him. "Huh?"

"As I understand it, he's actually drooled for years," Leo said. "But he's a sweetheart, I promise."

Allan, Dan, and Ralph were hooting in laughter, and Beverly's friends were trying to hide their amusement. Beverly's vision now morphed into the camel drooling liberally onto her head as she said her wise man lines.

"Come meet him." Leo opened the gate to the pen and beckoned Beverly to follow him.

She followed him warily. Up close, Leo the camel was even larger than he appeared from the safety outside the pen walls. He had a rather unusual, musty odor that rose above the normal smell of the thick layer of straw lining the bottom of the pen, but he didn't smell terribly dirty.

And yes, he drooled. She didn't notice it at first, but then suddenly his tongue appeared, hanging out of the side of his mouth, and drool dripped from the tip onto the ground.

"Oops, there he goes," Dr. Spangler said cheerfully.

Beverly whimpered. "Leo . . ."

"Me or the camel?" he asked with a grin.

"Leo, do I really have to do this?"

"It's not too bad if you stick to his right side. He only drools when his tongue hangs out of his mouth, and typically that's his left side. Also if you stay a little behind his head, that will keep you out of the target zone too."

Beverly groaned. Dan, Ralph, and Allan went into a fresh round of laughter.

"Dan! Ralph!" Shelley scolded her husband and father-in-law.

"Allan," Margaret tried to admonish him, but there was humor in her voice as she said his name.

"Leo's really not as bad as other camels," the vet assured her. "I've seen others where the drool is just dripping constantly from their mouths."

Beverly blanched. "I could have really done without the visual."

"Go ahead and pet him," Leo said. He held on to the camel's harness.

Beverly approached warily, but there was no sign of drooling at the moment. She reached out to stroke the rough brown hide. It was thicker than she expected it to be, and warm. Leo the camel was covered in several woolen blankets in various jewel tones that would match the wise man costumes and keep him warm in the cold Maine winter temperature when the sun set tonight.

Leo the camel turned to look at her with eyes that seemed to say, "Hello. Your head looks yummy. May I nibble on it?"

Beverly gulped.

"Good boy," Dr. Spangler said enthusiastically, petting Leo's other shoulder, and the camel turned his gaze away from Beverly and on to the vet.

As Beverly exited the pen, Ralph said, "See? You'll do fine."

"Easy as pie," Allan added.

"Have you ever made pie?" Beverly demanded nervously.

"Of course," Allan replied with a smile.

Beverly sighed. Of course, since Allan was a rather good cook, he probably made better pies than she did. Hers always turned out with rather ugly-looking top crusts.

"Allan, be considerate of poor Beverly," Margaret said.

"Yeah," Shelley said. "After foisting the camel on her, at least try not to laugh at her."

Diane's eyes were still twinkling, but she put an arm around Beverly. "You'll do fine, and Leo the camel will be a perfect gentleman. Don't worry about it."

"Hey, that's right, you three are in the living Nativity," Shelley suddenly said. Just then her phone rang, and she glanced at the display. "It's Frances. When were you supposed to meet her at my place to get your costumes?"

Beverly gasped and checked her watch. "We're late! We were supposed to be there half an hour ago!"

CHAPTER EIGHT

Beverly's beard itched. She scratched at her jaw again for the hundredth time and turned to the other two wise men. "How do men stand having a beard all the time? I've only had one for ten minutes and I'm ready to shave it off."

Ralph and Allan both laughed. The three of them stood to the side of the living Nativity set about an hour before it was scheduled to start. They had already gone through a dry run with the entire cast, including the choir led by Maddie Bancroft.

Allan said, stroking his own natural snow-white beard, "It's too bad you're the only wise man who had to wear a false beard."

Beverly wasn't very short, but she was still shorter than the two men. With the beard, she could pass for a slender young man under the rich robes of the wise man costume.

Leo was talking to the shepherds near the shepherd set, where the pen of sheep was. Dan and Detective Fred Little were shepherds, but one of the shepherds was also the owner of the animal rescue farm who had lent them to Leo and had come to keep an eye on the venerable beast. He seemed to be answering questions from Leo, Dan, and Fred.

Leo then turned and headed toward Beverly and the two other wise men. "Good evening, gentleman," Leo joked. He had a knitted cap covering his head and ears and a scarf around his neck.

"You're bundled up pretty well," Ralph said. "Will you be outside during the Nativity?"

"Yep, I'll be taking care of the camel while he's not on set," Leo said. "Levi and Audrey will be in charge of the animals in the stable, but the camel needs a little more TLC, so I'll hold him in the pen behind the stable until you need him, Beverly."

She nodded. She was glad Leo would have charge of the camel most of the time.

The vet continued, "Just before your wise man scene, come out to his pen to get Leo. You'll lead him a few feet to the edge of the stable set, and when the last scene is done, just lead him back."

"He'll follow me?"

"Oh, he's very docile, very well trained. Just tug firmly on his harness, and he'll follow you and stop when you do."

"Hey, cast and crew!" It was Diane calling to everyone from the area in front of the sets. "Let's pray before we open for guests." All those on the set, including the people doing the lights and the sound and the people handing out refreshments, gathered in a large circle in the parking lot.

Diane raised her voice and prayed, "Dear heavenly Father, thank You for this opportunity to celebrate the birth of Your Son with this living Nativity. I pray You'll bless everyone who comes, and also everyone who has volunteered their time to help and participate. We lift tonight and tomorrow night into Your hands. In Jesus's name, amen."

"Amen!" everyone repeated, and there was a spontaneous round of applause and cheering.

The cast members remained hidden behind the sets while people started to arrive. The entire Nativity was only fifteen minutes from start to finish, so they waited about five or ten minutes before starting the first round.

Noah Henry, the young descendant of the town's founder who had recently come to Marble Cove, was the narrator. He held a microphone hooked up to the speakers placed at strategic places among the sets. He quietly began, reading Luke's beloved narrative from the King James Version of the Bible. "And it came to pass in those days, that there went out a decree from Caesar Augustus that all the world should be taxed. (And this taxing was first made when Cyrenius was governor of Syria.) And all went to be taxed, every one into his own city. And Joseph also went up from Galilee, out of the city of Nazareth, into Judaea, unto the city of David, which is called Bethlehem; (because he was of the house and lineage of David:) to be taxed with Mary his espoused wife, being great with child."

Levi and Audrey, who were playing Mary and Joseph, were dressed in simple woolen garments, and Audrey sat on a real donkey, which the young man led by a harness. They walked to the stable set and were met by the innkeeper, played by Brenna McTavish, who worked at the Cove. Like Beverly, Brenna also had a fake beard to go with her woolen robes.

"Innkeeper, we need a room," Joseph said.

"Sorry, but we're full," Brenna said.

"But my wife is about to give birth."

"I'd like to help ya, but we're stuffed to the gills. I got people sleeping in the hallways." Brenna's strong Maine accent came through, which made the scene a bit comical, in Beverly's opinion.

"Isn't there anywhere she can rest?"

"Well, I feel bad, but the stable's free. I'll get some clean straw for ya."

The light grew brighter and illuminated Margaret's wonderfully painted stable. Joseph led the donkey to a small area to one side that had been carpeted with straw, and he helped Mary down.

They froze, and the lights dimmed, and the narrator continued, "And so it was, that, while they were there, the days were accomplished that she should be delivered. And she brought forth her firstborn son, and wrapped him in swaddling clothes, and laid him in a manger; because there was no room for them in the inn."

The lights suddenly went up on the adjacent set, which was the shepherds. They stood next to the pen of real sheep. Shelley's Emma was by far the tiniest shepherd and looked adorable in her little costume. She seemed a bit nervous and clung to the hand of her ten-year-old cousin, Hailey, who was another shepherd.

The narrator then said, "And there were in the same country shepherds abiding in the field, keeping watch over their flock by night."

Dan spoke as one of the other shepherds: "I'm tired. I think I'll get some sleep."

Fred Little said, "But you can't. We have to watch over our flock of sheep." He gestured to the penned sheep.

Suddenly, one of the spotlights was turned on full power and the bright light was almost blinding. The shepherds shielded their eyes and crouched on the ground.

"What's that?" Hailey asked. "I'm scared!"

Then the light dimmed back to normal, but Adelaide had appeared, standing atop a short ladder. She looked breathtaking in her angel costume, and one of the spotlights shone softly from behind her so that she seemed to be in a halo of light.

Adelaide hesitated slightly, then spoke slowly and clearly, "Fear not: for, behold, I bring you good tidings of great joy, which shall be to all people. For unto you is born this day in the city of David a Saviour, which is Christ the Lord. And this shall be a sign unto you; Ye shall find the babe wrapped in swaddling clothes, lying in a manger."

The narrator then said, "And suddenly there was with the angel a multitude of the heavenly host praising God, and saying, 'Glory to God in the highest, and on earth peace, good will toward men.'"

Then through the speakers came musical accompaniment, and the choir started singing a short snippet of the "Hallelujah Chorus" from Handel's *Messiah*. It only lasted a minute or so, but Beverly could see the crowd gathered around smiling at the joyful music.

Somehow, the sight of the shepherds humbly kneeling and the beautiful angel, combined with the richness of the music, made Beverly almost feel as if she were there two thousand years ago, and the heavens were celebrating the birth of the King. The scene made the emotions rise in her chest, the awareness of Jesus's immense love for all people, so great that He would come to earth as a baby to save everyone. Beverly found herself forgetting that it was her friends playing the parts. Instead, it was as if she were watching the actual events, and the play became very real to her.

The light shone brightly again, and when it dimmed, the angel had disappeared. The shepherds rose to their feet.

"Do you think that really happened?" the first shepherd asked.

"The angel said it did," the second shepherd said.

"And the Lord has made it known to us," the third shepherd said.

"Bethlehem is close by. Let's go see the baby," the first shepherd said.

The shepherds left their sheep in the pen and walked to the stable, where they found Mary and Joseph and the babe lying in a manger.

"We're on soon," Ralph whispered to Beverly.

She started in surprise. She'd been so caught up in watching that she'd forgotten she had a part to play. The wise men would enter in a few minutes, after the shepherds spoke to Mary and Joseph.

Beverly went to retrieve Leo the camel. Dr. Spangler was standing in the pen behind the stable set, holding on to Leo's harness. Beverly unlatched the gate, and the vet led the camel out of the pen. He pressed the leather harness lead into Beverly's hand. "Here you go," he whispered.

Beverly felt like a trembling leaf in a cold winter wind. She couldn't possibly do this with Leo the camel. She worried she would do something wrong and he'd go rambling off the set and into the crowd, or maybe he'd drool all over her and it would be gross and terribly embarrassing.

"Leo," she began, turning toward her friend. But the veterinarian just smiled and laid a hand on her shoulder.

"You can do this," he whispered. He turned her around and gave her a gentle push.

The shepherds, having gone to tell everyone about Jesus, returned to the stable with the six people from the choir, including Maddie Bancroft, and Aiden Bauer as a little drummer boy. His small drum hung at his hip, strung around his shoulder Civil War–style, and he had a huge grin on his face.

Beverly heard Noah Henry, the narrator, say, "Behold, there came wise men from the east to Jerusalem."

For a moment, Beverly froze. But then Leo the camel grunted, and she remembered that she was acting as a wise man in the living Nativity, and she had a drooling camel to keep in check. She would make sure to do her part.

Beverly, Ralph, and Allan all walked out from behind the stable set, and suddenly the beautiful star blazed above them. She wasn't sure how it happened, but she really felt like they were the wise men coming to see the Christ child.

The first wise man said, "Where is he that is born King of the Jews? for we have seen his star in the east, and are come to worship him." He gestured to the star above them.

The narrator said, "And, lo, the star, which they saw in the east, went before them, till it came and stood over where the young child was. When they saw the star, they rejoiced with exceeding great joy."

Beverly walked on to the stable set, pulling the camel. He came obediently, just as Leo said he would, and he stopped when Beverly stopped walking. When he grunted again and smacked his lips, she automatically took a small step away from him just in case he was planning on using her headdress as drool target practice. But no, he only drooled on his left side, just as promised. She kept Leo the camel standing over a pile of straw to catch stray dribble.

"We have come to worship the king of the Jews," Allan said. Then he and Ralph sank to their knees in a posture of worship toward the baby in the wooden manger.

Beverly hesitated. She was supposed to kneel too, but would Leo stay still if she did? She kept a firm grip of the leather lead and gently got to her knees, while sneaking looks at Leo in case he decided to do something unexpected, but he just stood there. He even gave a sigh as if bored.

Beverly sighed too, but with relief, as she bowed toward the manger with Allan and Ralph.

The three of them rose to their feet, and then each of them withdrew an ornate box from the pockets of their robes.

"I have brought gold for the king," the first wise man said. He laid his box at the feet of Mary.

"I bring frankincense for the Son of God," the second wise man said, and also put his box on the ground.

"I bring myrrh for the Savior of the world," Beverly called out in as deep a voice as she could muster, and put her box next to the others.

Then the little drummer boy stepped forward and said in a loud voice, "Little baby, I'm a poor boy too, and I don't have a gift to give to You. Can I play my drum for You?"

Mary nodded, and then the musical accompaniment for "The Little Drummer Boy" sounded in the speakers. The choir launched into the gentle carol.

Beverly had heard the song dozens of times and even played it herself on the piano, but now, with the scene before her of the people who had come to worship the baby Jesus, the lyrics held extra poignancy for her.

I played my drum for Him
Pa rum pum pum pum
I played my best for Him
Pa rum pum pum pum

Beverly felt tears gather in her eyes, and she blinked to keep them from falling and ruining her heavy black eye makeup. She didn't mean to, but she glanced at the audience to see if anyone noticed.

She was astonished. The faces of the people in the audience were enraptured. Some were smiling; some were obviously touched by the song and the scene. One or two wiped away a tear. Apparently Beverly wasn't the only one affected by this live performance.

This living Nativity seemed to have brought the true meaning of Christmas to many of the people in Marble Cove.

The narrator concluded by quoting John 3:16, "For God so loved the world, that he gave his only begotten Son. . . ."

The choir and cast members sang "Joy to the World" to end the living Nativity. After the carol, everyone took a bow and the audience applauded.

Leo gave a series of grunts and snorts as if to remind Beverly that he was there, and she hurried to return him to his pen. "You were so much more well behaved than I expected," she told him. "I ought to give you a treat."

"Better not," Dr. Spangler said as he came to meet her and take Leo's harness. "Food makes him drool more."

They had a break, during which children were permitted to pet the sheep and the donkey under supervision. Leo also allowed the kids to pet Leo the camel, but from behind the rails of his pen.

Then they did the living Nativity again for another crowd of people. It was easier for Beverly to say her lines this time. The camel actually did drool quite a bit more over the course of the evening, but Beverly's costume remained unstained, and the animal remained calm and obedient. In between performances, the actors and helpers filed into the train station to warm up with coffee, tea, and hot cocoa. Beverly made sure to get some hot drinks to the people supervising the impromptu animal petting zoo—the rescue farm owner, Levi and Audrey, and Leo.

After the last performance of the night, everyone sang "Joy to the World" with a little more exuberance than normal. The crowd, at its largest for this performance, gave the production hearty applause.

Beverly and the other actors hurried to change out of their costumes. Like most of the cast members, she wore long thermal clothing under her costume and kept hand warmers in her pockets, but even with that, she wasn't as warm as she was in her thick winter jacket and gloves.

She had just finished changing in the women's changing room—one of the rooms in the back of the train station—when the door opened and her friends peeked in. Most of the other women had already changed and left the room, so it was relatively empty.

"Mom!" Adelaide ran to Margaret for a hug. "How did I do?"

"You were so wonderful," Margaret said.

"You were a perfect angel," Shelley said.

Adelaide beamed at them. "I'm going to find Dad." She left them alone in the room.

"You were great too," Diane said to Beverly.

"I was scared to death something would go wrong," Beverly said.

"I'm sorry for laughing at you earlier," Margaret said. "That camel was *really* drooling."

"But you were still incredibly dignified," Diane said.

"Drooling camel aside, I thought it went really well," Shelley said. "I only caught the last performance since I was helping with refreshments, but the set and costumes were beautiful."

"I was really surprised to find that there's something about a live performance of the Nativity that makes it really hit home," Margaret said. "Actually seeing how the angels and the people responded to the birth of Jesus reminds me of how special this season really is."

"I think so too," Beverly said. "I even teared up a couple times."

"I'm really glad you pushed for Marble Cove to do this living Nativity, Diane," Margaret said to her. "I was feeling a bit down last week, but the Nativity has reminded me how Christmas is all about Jesus and how He came to save the world—and each one of us."

Beverly was surprised to see tears in Diane's eyes. "I'm so glad you feel that way. Originally I wanted to organize this to honor my mother's memory, but when I saw the performances tonight, I also realized how this Nativity has helped remind me of the true meaning of Christmas. I think I know now why my mother was so excited about organizing a living Nativity for her community."

"I think she'd be so happy to see you organizing ours this year," Shelley said.

"It's like she left you a legacy that has ended up blessing so many more people than you could have expected," Beverly said.

"I couldn't have done it without all of you encouraging me," Diane said.

"Even if we weren't that encouraging at first," Beverly said.

"Now, now," Diane said, with a smile. "You all came through with flying colors, as far as I'm concerned."

"Group hug!" Shelley said, and the four friends embraced warmly.

"I'm going to find Allan and Adelaide," Margaret said.

"I need to find my family too," Shelley said.

"I want to thank Leo for getting those wonderful animals," Diane said. "I can't believe he found that camel!"

As they filed out of the room, Beverly remembered to hang up her costume for tomorrow night. She had been touched by how the shepherds, the wise men, and the audience had responded to the Nativity, but she also remembered what the Bible had said about how Jesus's mother had reacted:

"Mary kept all these things, and pondered them in her heart."

Beverly would do that too, and it would help her remember the real meaning of Christmas even after the Nativity had finished.

CHAPTER NINE

The next morning, Beverly awoke to the smell of coffee brewing. Jeff handed her a steaming mug, fixed just the way she liked it, when she walked into the kitchen.

"I'll drive up with you," he offered.

"To see my cousin? I don't think it'll be very interesting for you," Beverly said.

Jeff put an arm around her waist. "It doesn't matter if it's interesting or not. I'm coming to give you some moral support. You might need it."

Beverly hugged him. "Thank you so much. I don't know what I'd do without you."

The truth was, she'd been feeling apprehensive about going to see Albert, and having Jeff with her gave her more courage.

"I even have a surprise for you," he said. "I made cranberry-orange bread yesterday for us to take to your cousin's house."

"You really are worth more than rubies," Beverly said, grinning up at him.

Beverly wanted to enjoy the time she could spend alone with Jeff during the drive to Albert's house, but her stomach was in double and triple knots, and she didn't feel much like talking. Jeff seemed to understand, and every so often he'd hold her hand and give a comforting squeeze.

Albert lived in a quiet suburb that had the same feel as Marble Cove, with its mix of different types of older houses in his area, and Beverly could see the roofs of several newer housing developments a few miles away. There was even the same cobblestone main street lined with small shops, although this street was named Stone Boulevard.

Albert's blue-and-cream-colored house was a simple craftsman that seemed to be lovingly cared for. Its paint looked fresh, and the yard, although snow-covered and empty of foliage in the middle of winter, had defined lines where there would be flowers come spring.

Beverly paused before ringing the brass doorbell. She could only hope that talking with Albert wouldn't be a repeat of her conversation with Mabel. She took a deep breath, then pressed the button.

When Albert opened the door, Beverly was immediately brought back to when she was a child in elementary school, looking at her stepcousin's round face. He had the same soft brown eyes, although his brown hair was now more ash-gray. She had forgotten about his slow, wide smile until it appeared on his face now.

"Beverly, how nice to see you again." He had a low, calm voice, but it was the expression on his face that showed his joy in seeing her again. "You look exactly the same as the little Anna I remember."

"You look just like you used to as well," Beverly said. "This is my husband Jeff."

"Nice to meet you." Albert held out his hand and shook Jeff's. "Please come in."

"We brought some cranberry-orange bread for you and your wife." Beverly handed him the cake, which was in a Christmas-decorated plastic container.

"Thanks," he said. "We can have it with coffee."

Albert's living room was dominated by a lovely Christmas tree in the corner to one side of his brick fireplace, but it looked like Christmas decorations had exploded all over the cream-carpeted floors and the chintz-upholstered furniture.

Albert disappeared through an open doorway into his spacious kitchen, where he poured mugs of coffee. "Sorry for the mess," he said. He brought the coffee and the cranberry-orange bread container into the living room and set them on the coffee table, then cleared space for them on the sofa. When they sat, he took a seat in an overstuffed chair adjacent to them. "After we talked on the phone, I got all the other Christmas decorations from the attic and started looking through them for the wreath you mentioned."

"You didn't have to go through all that trouble," Beverly said. "We'd have been happy to look through them instead. I feel terrible that you took the time searching for something that only has meaning to me."

Albert didn't answer at first, but simply gazed sightlessly at a box of ornaments. "I remember, you know . . . the argument my stepfather had with your mother and your aunt."

Beverly floundered for something to say in response.

"I was in high school at the time," he continued, "so I was treated like a child who didn't have to concern myself with what was happening, but I was old enough to understand."

"I was only in elementary school," Beverly said. "I wasn't aware of what happened, and my mother never spoke of it to me."

"She didn't?" Albert looked up at her. "Well, I'm not surprised. I remember Aunt Eunice was like that. Whenever Dudley and Aunt Helen had a disagreement, she would always try to help them to get along."

Beverly remembered, too, a few instances when her mother would talk soothingly to her siblings to get them to compromise when they had an argument.

She then felt Jeff touch her shoulder. She looked at him and saw in his eyes an urging for her to ask what she wanted to ask. "I've heard different versions of what happened back then," she said hesitantly.

"Don't listen to my sister," Albert said quickly. "She got the story from our mother and didn't witness firsthand what happened, but I was there. I saw what Dudley did and heard him arguing with his sisters."

"Please tell me what you saw," Beverly said.

"It was only three days after your grandfather died in the hospital," Albert said. "The funeral hadn't even taken place yet. Dudley took me with him to your grandparents' house—I had no idea what he was going to do. I thought maybe he needed something for the funeral arrangements. But he walked into the house and seemed to be looking around. And then he just started taking things and telling me to put them in the car."

Beverly bit her lip. It sounded so terribly callous when Albert spoke of it like that, seeing what Uncle Dudley had done with his own eyes.

"I asked him what he was doing, and he said he was only taking his things. I suspected he was lying, but I was only a teenager—I was too frightened to say anything more to him."

"That wasn't your fault," Beverly said. "It wasn't your place to question him."

"I thought my mother might say something to him, but when we returned home, she just asked whether he had gotten the china set."

Beverly's chest tightened. That valuable china set had belonged to her grandmother's grandmother.

"It took him three days, and your mother and aunt had no idea what he was doing," Albert said. "So finally, I called your mother. I said I was the son of a neighbor and I asked her why her brother was taking so many things from his parents' house."

"You did that?" Beverly was astonished. "You could have gotten in trouble with your stepfather."

"At that point, I didn't care. But it was too late. Dudley had already called a moving company and taken what he wanted of the furniture— that was the last of it that he took. All I did was cause your mother and aunt to argue with Dudley over what he'd done."

"What you did was very courageous," Beverly said.

Albert sighed and ran his hand over his thinning hair. "It felt cowardly. And if I had been really courageous, I would have contacted your mother and aunt after my mother died to try to heal the rift between our families. However, it was so many years after the incident that I convinced myself not to reach out. It would only bring up bad feelings, and nothing could be done about what had happened."

"I can understand completely," Beverly said. "I almost didn't try to reach out to you and Mabel for the exact same reason. I didn't even recall the incident, and I didn't know how you would feel to hear from my family again."

"I'm sorry if Mabel was antagonistic toward you," Albert said. "She and I don't see eye to eye on many things, and one of them is our mother's account of what happened between Dudley and his family. My mother and Mabel didn't like Dudley's family very much, but I always enjoyed Christmas and holidays at Grandmother Harkness's house."

From what he'd been saying, Beverly had already suspected that Albert didn't hold grudges about what happened between his stepfather and her mother, but now it was confirmed. She had been prepared for—and afraid of—more of the same type of haughty attitude she'd received from Mabel, but Albert's attitude was so markedly different from his sister's that Beverly thought it was almost too good to be true.

"Well, let's look for your mother's wreath," Albert said. "I feel that might help erase some of the past, even though we two had very little to do with it."

Beverly thought that some of the past had already been erased, and she was glad of it.

"I feel I should confess about the wreath," Beverly said. "I actually found a shell wreath on the beach at Marble Cove that looks a lot like my mother's wreath. I've been trying to track down my mother's wreath to try to figure out if the one I have might miraculously be hers."

Albert looked confused. "You found it on the beach?"

Beverly explained about everything that had happened, and Albert was amazed. "I almost hope we don't find the wreath here," he said. "It would be fantastic if that wreath found its way to you that way."

They each took a corner of the room and started sorting through the boxes. There were a surprising number of ornaments, far more than could fit on the tree, and Beverly thought she recognized one or two from her grandmother's house, but she chose not to say anything about them.

"By the way, Beverly, how's your mother?" Albert asked.

"Oh, she passed away a few years ago," she said.

Albert sat back on his heels. "I'm sorry to hear that. I liked Aunt Eunice. I would have liked to go to her funeral."

"At the time, we did send an announcement to the last address we had for your family, but it got returned."

"Yes, we moved out of Dudley's house very soon after he died, but Mom didn't want to give any of the Harknesses our forwarding address."

"I still see Aunt Helen every so often," Beverly said. "I think she'd love to hear from you."

That reminded her of how Aunt Helen had regretted that Uncle Dudley had taken that angel tree topper. Should she mention that to Albert? Would that make it seem like Beverly only wanted Albert to return the things his stepfather had taken? She reasoned that if Albert reached out to Aunt Helen at a later date, her aunt could mention the tree topper to him then.

"Albert, what do you do?" Beverly asked.

"I'm a radio engineer," he said. "I help plan and maintain cellular towers, depending on the signal strength needed in various areas, to ensure even coverage."

"So if my cell phone drops a call, I can blame you?" Jeff joked.

Albert laughed. "My job isn't really that important. But I've been working for the same cellular service company for most of my adult life—it used to be a plain telephone company, but they moved toward mobile phones back in the nineties. I'll be up for retirement in a few years, but I still really enjoy what I do."

"That's a gift," Beverly said.

"How about you?" Albert asked her.

"I used to be a budget analyst for the Maine State House of Representatives, but a couple of years ago I quit to start my own business consultation service. I have several clients, although most of them are outside Marble Cove."

"I should have my wife speak to you," Albert said. "She embroiders Christmas stockings and sells them online, but she wants to ramp up her business."

"Sure." Beverly dug in her purse. "Here's my card. I also was just elected mayor of Marble Cove a few months ago."

"You must be really busy," Albert said.

"Being mayor is more of a part-time job," Beverly said, "but it helps that I can control the hours I spend on my clients."

"How old are your children?" Jeff asked. He held up an old ornament frame holding pictures of a boy and a girl, both younger than five years old.

Albert laughed. "That's an old ornament, and it's falling apart, but my wife and I can't bear to part with it. My kids are both graduated from college and starting their careers now."

"What do they do?" Beverly asked.

"My son, Albert Jr., started a moving company of his own. He worked for one when he was in high school and college, and the owner always hired students, or veterans, or recovering alcoholics—anyone in need of a job. The owner died while Al was in college, and he wanted to have a company that would do the same thing. He works closely with some local rehabilitation homes to offer jobs to people who would otherwise have a hard time finding work."

"That's great," Jeff said.

"I'm impressed by your son's initiative when he's still so young," Beverly said. "I still didn't really know what I wanted to do when I was just out of college."

"My daughter is like that," Albert said. "She's always wanted to be an artist, and she went to an art school, but she still isn't sure she wants to paint for a living or if she should try to get a more stable job such as a teacher or work for a museum. She's doing temp work for my wife's brother's company while she decides if she's going to go for more schooling or not."

"My friend Margaret is an artist," Beverly said. "She used to be an accountant, but when she retired she decided to pursue her art and now she runs an art gallery in Marble Cove."

"Do you think your friend would be willing to chat with my daughter? That might be the kind of wisdom and insight she needs to make her decision."

"I don't think she'd mind at all. Why don't you give me a call, and I'll get you in touch with Margaret."

"Thanks. Jeff, what do you do?"

"I'm a professional photographer."

"Really?" Albert's entire face lit up. "I'm an amateur photographer. What do you photograph?"

"Mostly nature, travel, and documentary shots, but I've done a couple of weddings for friends. I like candid poses contrasted with colorful foreground shots of the wedding decorations."

"Another reason I enjoy my job is being able to erect cell towers in remote areas," Albert said. "So much of the area around here is beautiful. I like to take photos of the landscape from the towers."

"Those shots must be so gorgeous," Beverly said.

Albert and Jeff talked more photography while they slowly went through all the boxes, but Beverly grew concerned when they didn't find the wreath. It should be here—after all, in terms of probabilities, there should be no way for the shell ornaments she found on the beach to be the same ones made by her mother. Yet where was the original wreath?

They finally went through the last box. They found two old wreaths that had belonged to Albert's wife's mother, decorated with painted wooden ornaments.

But there was no wreath from Grandmother Harkness's house. The shell ornament wreath that her mother made wasn't here.

CHAPTER TEN

Beverly wasn't sure how to feel. Where had the wreath gone if it wasn't here with her Grandmother Harkness's Christmas decorations? Did Mabel have it after all? But Albert said that was improbable, and Beverly didn't think Mabel had any reason not to give Beverly an old and handmade shell wreath if she did have it, or to tell her what she'd done with it. Maybe Malvina had gotten rid of it for some reason?

She supposed she shouldn't be surprised if the wreath had found its way to Marble Cove against all odds. After all, hadn't she and her friends experienced several unexplained things in the past few years? Maybe this was yet another instance of something mysterious and strange happening to her.

But the analyst side of her, the logical side, wanted a definitive answer to where her mother's wreath had ended up, and she had thought she'd find that answer here.

Except the wreath wasn't here, nor were the answers she'd hoped to find. Too bad you can't prove a negative.

Albert looked at the clock. "My wife is returning from her breakfast with her sisters soon. She wanted me to keep you here until she had a chance to meet you, but I wonder if she may know something about the wreath."

"It could be that you never got it at all from your mother," Beverly said. "Maybe Mabel has it, or maybe your mother threw it out."

"No, my mother never threw anything away. She was a bit of a hoarder. I doubt Mabel would have it—after our mother died, Mabel didn't take many of the Christmas things from our mother's house because she tends to like very modern, matching Christmas decorations."

They sat back on the sofa and chair again, and Albert got them fresh coffee to enjoy with the cranberry-orange bread. "So tell me how you two met," Albert said.

Beverly laughed. "It's a long story. I guess you could say the Marble Cove lighthouse brought us together." She talked about the mysterious lights she and her friends had seen there, and Jeff described tracing his grandfather's history with the old lighthouse.

They were in the middle of their story when a door opened and a short, energetic woman bustled inside. "I'm home! Oh, thank goodness you're both still here. I'm Sabrina, Albert's wife." She shook hands with both Beverly and Jeff, while still talking. "I'm so sorry I couldn't be here when you arrived, but I and my sisters—I have five of them— have breakfast a few days before Christmas every year, and of course I couldn't miss it. So I told Albert to keep you here until I returned even if he had to handcuff you to the Christmas tree!" She laughed. "Not that he'd actually handcuff you. Don't worry. He's such a sweetheart. Did you find what you were looking for?"

After that whirlwind of words, Beverly was a little dazed, but she managed to answer, "No, I'm afraid not."

"Sabrina, maybe you can remember if we had a wreath with shell ornaments," Albert said. "We couldn't find it in the Christmas things, and I know this is all the boxes we had in the attic."

"Shell ornaments?" Sabrina leaned on one hip and screwed up her face as she thought. "I tend to like flashy, metallic ornaments, so I don't know that I'd have kept it."

"Did you throw it away?" Albert asked. "I didn't know you'd thrown any Christmas decorations away."

"No, but I remember giving a box of decorations to a thrift store many years ago," Sabrina said. "I don't specifically remember a wreath, though . . ."

"Oh." Beverly happened to look at Albert at that moment, and his face showed the same disappointment and perplexity that she felt. Had the wreath even been in the box of Christmas decorations that Sabrina gave away? None of this answered her question of how the wreath might have ended up in Marble Cove. She had been hoping for a definitive answer to her question—if the wreath had been here, she would have known it wasn't her mother's wreath. If Sabrina had definitely remembered that she'd given the wreath away, that might have explained why it ended up as trash on the beach at Marble Cove. But this vagueness was difficult for Beverly because it wasn't an answer at all.

"I'm sorry, Beverly," Albert said. "I guess we might have given it away."

"You don't need to apologize for it," Beverly said.

"You might never have had it either," Jeff said.

"I should explain about the wreath," Beverly said to Sabrina, and told her story again about finding the wreath on the beach and trying to track down the real one.

"Well, I'm with Albert," Sabrina said when she was done. "I'm almost glad it's not here. It would be so amazing if your wreath was actually your mother's."

"Is there anything else you'd like to take with you?" Sabrina asked. "As you can see, we have so many decorations, and I know many of these are from Albert's mother—and, from what I understand, many of those are from your grandmother, right? I'm sure there must be some ornaments that hold sentimental value for you."

Beverly hesitated, remembering the angel topper Aunt Helen had mentioned. Would it be all right to ask Albert and Sabrina for it? She felt a nudge at her elbow and saw that Jeff was again looking at her with an expression of encouragement, urging her to speak up.

"I hope it's not too rude of me," Beverly said, "but my Aunt Helen mentioned an angel tree topper that she had made for my grandmother years ago."

"An angel topper?" Sabrina asked. "I think we have more than one of them, but I don't know that either of them is handmade. They were both from Albert's mother, I believe."

"I saw one in this box." Albert went to a box in the far corner.

"I saw one too," Jeff said, and searched through another one.

Both were beautiful tree toppers, but Beverly had no idea which one her aunt had meant. "Why don't I call my Aunt Helen to ask her to describe the one she made?" She pulled out her cell phone and called her mother's sister.

"Hello, Beverly," her aunt said.

"Aunt Helen, you won't believe where I am now," Beverly said. "I'm visiting Albert Lemmon, Aunt Malvina's son."

"Are you really?" Aunt Helen sounded absolutely astonished.

"He invited me to his home today to look for my mother's wreath. We've had a lovely morning just catching up with each other."

"How is he doing?"

"Would you like to speak to him?"

Aunt Helen hesitated, then said firmly, "Yes, I would love to."

Beverly handed the phone to Albert, and he smiled as he said, "Hello, Aunt Helen."

Beverly, Jeff, and Sabrina only heard Albert's side of the conversation, but he told Aunt Helen about his wife, his children, and his job, and it seemed Aunt Helen said she hoped to have them over for dinner or something like that, because he said, "We'd love to come. Let me give you my phone number, and we can set up a date when we're all free to see each other." He gave her his number, and it seemed there was a glow of joy to his face as he said, "I can't tell you how wonderful it is to speak to you again. I missed Christmases at Grandmother Harkness's house."

Sabrina poked at his shoulder and whispered, "The angel topper. Mention the angel topper."

"Aunt Helen, Beverly said that there was an angel topper that you made and gave to Grandmother Harkness, but my stepfather took it. I got a bunch of Christmas decorations when my mother passed away and I'd love to give it back to you, if I have it."

Even Beverly could hear her aunt's cry of joy from the cell phone.

"We have a couple of angel toppers, so could you describe it?" Albert asked. He then repeated Aunt Helen's words to his eager listeners. "It has a porcelain head, but she made the dress . . . burgundy velvet, with gold ribbon trim."

"This is it." Sabrina picked up the angel that Albert had found. "I declare, I thought it was professionally made. It's exquisite. Albert, give me the phone."

Sabrina put out her open hand, and Albert grinned as he said, "Aunt Helen, my wife wants to speak to you . . ."

He'd barely finished speaking before Sabrina snatched the phone away and said, "Hello, Helen. This is Sabrina, Albert's wife. Your angel is amazing! Did you make the two petticoats too? The inside one, made of cotton—did you make the ruffle at the hem yourself? I've never seen such a tiny ruffle. And the second petticoat, where did you get that figured muslin? And the lace at the hem, is it brussels lace? It's divine. Yes, I love to sew too! My children hated when I sewed for them because they wanted name-brand clothes instead, although I offered to embroider a Nike swoop for them if they wanted . . ." Sabrina laughed into the phone. "Yes, we really should get together to talk sewing. I'm so glad Beverly reached out to us. I'll let you go before I talk your ear off. We'll make arrangements to get the angel back to you. Good-bye!" She handed the phone back to Albert, who also said his good-byes and hung up before handing the phone back to Beverly.

"Are you sure about the angel?" Beverly asked. She was still bemused by Sabrina's enthusiastic one-sided conversation with Aunt Helen and guessed that her aunt probably felt the same way.

"Of course," Sabrina said. "The tree topper we have now was our children's gift to us for our wedding anniversary a few years ago, so we only use that one now." She gestured to the gold star on the Christmas tree in the corner of the living room, which was beautifully decorated with different metallic colors so that it almost looked like stained glass.

"It would be great if we could get the angel to your aunt before Christmas," Albert said. "Maybe we should drive to her home to give it to her."

"I have a better idea," Beverly said. "Aunt Helen is coming to the living Nativity in Marble Cove tonight. Why don't you two also come? You can give her the angel topper and spend some time with her."

Albert and Sabrina looked at each other, and it was as if they were silently communicating with just that one glance.

"That sounds like a wonderful idea," Albert said.

"Yes, let's have an early dinner and drive to Marble Cove tonight," Sabrina said.

Beverly gave them the information for the living Nativity, including the address and the time it would be open. "Aunt Helen said she'll be coming later in the evening, so why don't you also come near the tail end of the living Nativity? Then I can make sure you get a chance to talk to her."

"That sounds good," Sabrina said. "Thank you for inviting us, Beverly."

"Did you see any other Christmas decorations from your grandmother's house that you'd like?" Albert asked. "I feel terrible that the one thing you wanted isn't here."

"No, that isn't your fault," Beverly said. "I have other mementos from my mother that make me feel like she's close to me."

"Do you know what I miss?" Albert said. "I remember Grandmother Harkness would play the piano whenever we had a gathering at her house. I always enjoyed when she played songs for us to sing, like carols at Christmas."

"I remember that," Beverly said. "It was always fun."

"Didn't you and your mother play?" Albert asked. "I think I remember a few times when you and Aunt Eunice would sit together and play."

"Yes, Mother taught me to play when I was in elementary school," Beverly said. "You played too, didn't you?"

Albert made a face. "It was Dudley who forced us to take lessons. Mabel and I didn't care for them, although I liked them better than she did."

"We did the same and forced our kids to take lessons," Sabrina added, nodding to the upright piano tucked away in a dark corner of the living room, "but they did it very grudgingly and they stopped once they left for college."

"There was that one piece you and your mother played over and over. How did it go?" Albert hummed a few notes.

It was the same piece of music that had been running through Beverly's head. "Yes, I remember playing that! I can't believe you remember it too after all these years."

"Actually, the only reason I remember it is because when our kids were taking lessons, the teacher assigned that same piece to them to learn."

Beverly's heart skipped a beat. "Really? Do you happen to know what it was?"

"Uh . . ." Albert gave a helpless shrug. "I'm afraid I don't know the name or composer. But I do remember which book it was in." He went to the upright piano and moved away the boxes of Christmas decorations that sat on top of the bench. He opened the hinged bench and rummaged among the music books inside, finally pulling out a beige-colored book that was so well used the binding was cracked and some pages were loose, peeking out from the edge. "This is it." He handed it to Beverly.

She carefully opened it. It was a book of sonatinas, easy enough for a moderate beginner to play. Some of the songs had their page numbers circled, so she assumed those were ones the teacher had assigned to Albert's children. She looked at each song, and very quickly found what she thought might be the piece she'd been hearing—Sonatina op. 36, no. 1 by Clementi.

"May I?" she asked, nodding to the piano.

"Of course. We have it tuned once a year, although it hasn't been played since our kids left for college," Albert said.

Beverly sat at the piano, which was a sturdy upright Knight piano with a warm brown wood finish. It was well taken care of, with the hinged cover over the keys smoothly folding back. She caught a whiff of something, perhaps the oil used on the wood, that seemed familiar to her, but it was only a wisp of a memory.

She set the book on the shelf and began playing. Yes, it was the exact piece she'd been trying to place for the past few days. It was a sprightly song, and even though Beverly hadn't played it in years and sight-reading was normally difficult for a classical piece, this was an easy sonatina and her fingers seemed to remember the notes and even the fingering.

The notes brought her back to her grandmother's house, and to the feeling of her mother's presence beside her on the piano bench. She could almost pretend her mother was playing the left-hand notes. As she finished, she was embarrassed to realize she had tears on her lashes.

Everyone clapped when she finished playing.

"That's it," Albert said. "That's the piece I remember."

"I can't believe I could still play it after all this time," Beverly marveled. "Thank you so much, Albert, for helping me to remember this piece."

Sabrina suddenly gave a little gasp. "Albert, how about the piano?"

He froze for a moment. Then he looked toward his wife, and they had that strange silent communication like they'd done before. His face lit up like one of the spotlights at the living Nativity. "Sabrina, that's a great idea."

He turned back toward Beverly. "Do you recognize this piano?"

Beverly stared hard at it. She again smelled that strange woodsy odor that had stirred her memory. "You don't mean . . ."

"It's your grandmother's piano," Albert said excitedly. "It was one of the last things Dudley took from her house—well, he had movers take it away."

That's why Beverly recognized the smell—the piano was made of solid teakwood. She remembered her mother going to her grandmother's house and oiling it for her a few times, explaining that the piano needed a special teakwood oil.

Albert said, "We would love to give it to you, as something to remember your grandmother."

"Oh no, I couldn't . . ."

"It's only a glorified bookshelf these days," Sabrina said. "Albert and I wish we were more musically inclined, but we realized we should just settle for enjoying a few concerts in Augusta a few times a year."

"But you shouldn't give it to me," Beverly said. "I'm sure it's quite valuable."

"We'd be happy to give it to you if you'd only pay for the movers to take it away," Albert said. "In fact, my son's moving company might be able to do it."

"I think he could," Sabrina said. "When he called yesterday, he was complaining that things were slow because not many people moved just before Christmas."

"But . . . ," Beverly began, but then Jeff interrupted her.

"We would be honored if you'd give it to us." Jeff touched her shoulder. "The cost of the movers would be more than worth it for you to have your grandmother's piano."

She couldn't believe this was happening. It felt as if both her mother and grandmother were embracing her. "Thank you from the bottom of my heart," she said to Albert and Sabrina.

"Don't be too quick to thank us," Albert joked. "This piano's been through two kids running around this house. It's got a few battle scars that weren't there when it was in your grandmother's house."

"If I remember correctly, my other cousin and I also ran around our grandmother's house," Beverly said. "I'm sure there are a few scars we caused too."

"I'll call our son to ask if he can move it for you," Albert said. "What's your address?" After Beverly gave it to him, he went into the kitchen to use the phone.

"Would you like more coffee?" Sabrina asked. "Oh, and is that cranberry-orange bread? That's my favorite. I simply must have a slice before I expire."

Beverly and Jeff had a good time chatting with Sabrina, although she did most of the talking. She was so lively and energetic, with an expressive face that was so different from Albert's habitually calm expression.

Albert returned to the living room. "It's all arranged. You should have the piano at your home by noon tomorrow."

"That's amazing," Beverly said. Everything seemed to be moving so quickly, which wasn't what she was used to.

However, Jeff seemed to take it in stride, and he was her anchor in the midst of all this change. "I appreciate your doing that for us," he said to Albert.

"Oh, you're doing us the favor by giving our son work just before Christmas."

They chatted over another cup of coffee, but then Beverly and Jeff rose to leave when they heard that Albert and Sabrina had to get ready for Albert's office holiday gathering.

"We're having a New Year's dinner," Beverly said. "Please say you'll come."

"We'd be delighted," Sabrina said. "Call me later with the details."

At the door, Jeff shook Albert's hand, but then Beverly gave him a hug, and gave one to Sabrina too.

"I'm so glad we reconnected," Albert told her. "Although we weren't related by blood, I have fond memories of your grandparents' home and the Harkness family. You accepted me and my sister and made us feel welcome. I never got along well with my mother or my sister, but I loved Dudley's family."

"I'm glad we reconnected too," Beverly said. "And we'll definitely keep in touch more from now on."

As Jeff drove them away from Albert's house, Beverly waved to Sabrina and Albert. Her heart felt like it was overflowing with sunlight.

"I really regret the bad feelings within my family that kept us from a closer relationship with Albert and his family, and which almost prevented me from reaching out to him," she said.

"I'm glad I could come with you today," Jeff said. "It was nice to see someone from your past."

Yes, in this Christmas season, when people came together with family, she had gotten her long-lost cousin back.

CHAPTER ELEVEN

That evening at the living Nativity, Beverly was on pins and needles as she waited for Albert and Sabrina and Aunt Helen and her family to arrive. She wanted to make sure to ask Aunt Helen to stay until after the last performance so she could introduce her to Albert and Sabrina, but neither group seemed to have arrived yet. Beverly hoped they would make it in time to see the living Nativity.

Beverly tried to scan the faces of the crowd as she did her wise man part, but it was difficult to concentrate on her lines and on Leo the camel when she was also looking at the audience, so she stopped doing that.

It was even colder tonight than it had been last night, so the actors and the people in charge of the lights and sound would hurry into the train station for hot beverages in between performances. Shelley was again helping with refreshments, and Beverly headed straight toward her.

"Hi, Shelley," Beverly said.

"It's pretty cold tonight, isn't it?" Shelley said. "Want some coffee?"

"Actually, could I get four cups?"

"You're going to be going to the bathroom every thirty minutes," Shelley teased her.

"It's not for me—Leo, Levi and Audrey, and the owner of the animal rescue farm are all still out in the cold supervising the animals."

"Oh, that's right. I think it's great they're allowing kids to pet the animals in between performances."

"The kids absolutely love the camel," Beverly said.

"I'd never seen a camel in real life before seeing him last night," Shelley said. "He's pretty sweet, in spite of being so big."

"Are your kids enjoying themselves tonight too?"

"Hailey's a little bored with doing the performance over and over, but Emma is thrilled because she gets to stand next to the sheep all the time, and Aiden said he's stood next to the donkey so often, he's pretty sure it will let him sit on top of it. However, Dan and I did a firm veto on that, at least until after the last performance—Leo said that having an excited kid on top of it might make the animal a little nervous, and I don't want to ruin the living Nativity."

"Yes, that donkey does seem a little high strung," Beverly said. "Levi is pretty good at keeping it firmly under control, but he always has its rein in hand and he's paying close attention to it all the time."

Shelley handed Beverly four cups of coffee, and she headed out to pass them to the animal supervisors, who were all grateful for the hot drink. It wasn't windy, but steam rose from the animals in the icy air.

Beverly was about to head to Leo the camel to give the last cup of coffee to Leo the vet when she suddenly caught sight of Aunt Helen in the crowd. "Aunt Helen!" Her aunt looked around but didn't seem to see Beverly, so she walked up to her. "Hello, Aunt Helen."

Her aunt gave a little yelp, then laughed. "Beverly! I didn't recognize you in your costume."

Beverly laughed too. She'd forgotten about the beard, the heavy black eye makeup, and the brightly colored headdress she was wearing. "Sorry about that. I forgot I was in costume."

"You look magnificent, like a real ruler from the East."

"Thank you." Beverly smiled. "Did you just arrive?"

"Yes. We missed the earlier performance. Charlotte was sorry to have to miss it, but her boys came. Looks like they're over checking out the petting zoo." She gestured to where they stood with Uncle George.

"I'm afraid I'm on the clock," Beverly said. "I have to deliver this coffee before our next performance. Will you be able to stick around after the last one?"

"I think so. I'll ask George, but it should be fine. Why?"

"I have something to give to you," Beverly said, giving her a mysterious smile and then heading toward the camel pen. She hadn't told Aunt Helen about Albert and Sabrina arriving tonight, and hoped to surprise her. That is, if Albert and Sabrina were able to make it. From the looks of it, there would be only two more performances before the end of the night, and she hadn't seen either cousin yet.

She almost cried out in relief when, in that next performance, she saw Albert and Sabrina smiling as they stood in the audience. She realized she never told them she'd be performing, nor that she'd be a wise man, and they didn't seem to recognize her as she said her lines.

Afterward, remembering Aunt Helen's startled reaction, she approached them cautiously. "Albert, Sabrina, it's Beverly."

Sabrina gave a little start, then a laugh. "Oh, goodness, Beverly, you're certainly in disguise. Nice job."

"I'm so glad you two could make it," Beverly said.

"We almost didn't," Albert said. "There was an accident on the highway, and we had to take a detour."

"I'm afraid I don't see my aunt Helen at the moment, although she and her husband could be inside the train station, getting something to drink. Do you think you could stay until after the last performance? I'll find each of you then."

"Sure thing."

They started the last performance a little later than planned, so the living Nativity would end a little after the time on the schedule. As with last night, the crowd for this last performance was large. Beverly was impatient for the performance to end so she could see the look on Aunt Helen's face when she received her angel tree topper.

But just as the performance started, Levi seemed to be having problems with the donkey. It hadn't been the most docile actor during the living Nativity, and it seemed to have reached its limit. Rather than walking the few feet into the stable set with Mary on its back, the donkey began to bray. With gusto.

The narrator, Noah Henry, hesitated before speaking his lines because the donkey was so loud. Joseph tried speaking softly to the donkey, but it only seemed to make the animal complain harder. It finally quieted when poor "pregnant" Mary got off its back and walked to the stable on her own while Joseph bullied the donkey into following her.

The scene went smoothly up through the shepherd scene and into the wise man scene. But then, just as Beverly was about to speak her lines and offer her gift to the Christ child, the donkey began to bray again, in short, honking bursts.

Beverly froze. What should she do? Should she pretend the donkey wasn't braying and speak louder to be heard over the animal? Should she wait until it stopped making that racket? She met Ralph and Allan's wide eyes—they apparently weren't sure what she should do either.

Everyone was surprised when Brenna, as the innkeeper, suddenly stalked on to the stable set. "You!" She pointed a finger at the donkey. "Shut your trap. You'll wake the baby."

And wonders of wonders, the donkey stopped.

There was a moment of stunned silence, then Brenna nodded to Beverly, and Beverly went on with her lines. "I bring myrrh for the Savior of the world." She laid her gilded box near the other wise men's gifts on the ground and stepped back. She was dimly aware of muffled laughter from the audience, and she wanted to giggle nervously herself, but it wouldn't look very dignified for a rich young ruler from the East to be laughing hysterically.

Beverly was never more relieved when the cast sang "Joy to the World" at the end of the performance. The audience sent up an especially loud cheer.

Shelley was the first to come up to the assembled actors, and she went straight for Brenna. "Brenna, you saved the day!"

Brenna's cheeks colored. "I didn't even think. I just did it."

"That's better than I could do," Beverly said. "I just froze."

"It wasn't as awful as you might think it was," Diane said as she walked up to them. "It was rather funny, but most people understand that's the price to pay when you work with live animals. Didn't W. C. Fields say, 'Never work with animals or children'?"

"We saw the truth of that!" Brenna said.

Everyone laughed.

"Despite the mishap, I think it was really great that we had live animals," Shelley said.

People seemed reluctant to start taking down all the sets and getting out of the costumes, as if they wanted to prolong the evening a little. Beverly chatted briefly with the narrator, Noah Henry, and with Shelley's kids, who were hanging around the sheep pen. Then she saw Aunt Helen and Uncle George and ran up to them.

"Hi, Aunt Helen, Uncle George."

Her uncle hadn't seen her in costume before the performance, so he gave a little start before laughing. "Hi, Beverly. Nice outfit."

"Thanks! How did you like the performance?"

"It was so touching!" Aunt Helen said. "Even with the donkey braying every so often, the scene with the shepherds was incredibly moving, and I liked the little drummer boy near the end too."

"Aunt Helen, there's someone here I want you to meet," Beverly said. "Let's find them. Uncle George, is it okay if I steal her away for a little while?"

"Fine with me. I'm going inside to get a cup of hot coffee."

Beverly worried that, with the number of people there at the living Nativity, she wouldn't be able to find Albert and Sabrina again, but she easily found them gawking at Leo the camel, who looked dignified, if a little bored, in his pen. Then he ruined the dignified image by sticking his tongue out and drooling. The children nearest the stream of drool shrieked and laughed as they jumped back. The live animals had proved to be a huge hit with the younger members of the audience.

"Albert, Sabrina," Beverly called to them, and they left the circle around Leo's pen. "Do you remember Aunt Helen?"

Albert's face split into a grin as bright as Adelaide's angel. He spread his arms wide and embraced her in a hug. "It's so nice to see you again, Aunt Helen. I really missed you."

There were tears in her aunt's eyes as she returned the embrace. "It's been too long, Albert. It's good to see you again too."

"This is my wife Sabrina," Albert introduced her. "Aunt Helen would always help me with my history homework. She had lots of little tricks to help me remember dates and events."

"Oh, you were such a good student. It was a joy to study history with you," Aunt Helen said.

Albert's eyes grew sad. "I'm sorry about what happened with my stepfather. I have so many regrets about that."

"Oh, Albert." Aunt Helen cupped his cheek with her palm, the way Beverly had seen her do often with her daughter Charlotte. "It wasn't your fault. Dudley and I were adults—we should have been able to resolve our differences. I just made the mistake of thinking we had plenty of time."

Beverly's throat grew tight. She had almost not reached out to Albert, wanting to let the past remain as it was. She had thought all the ugly feelings that had occurred would be dug up, which wouldn't accomplish anything except cause more emotional stress. That had happened, to some extent, with Mabel, but with Albert, she and her family had been given a chance to heal from the past and move forward in renewed relationships with her estranged cousin.

Beverly realized that she should never shy away from difficulties in reconciling with family, even if it might cause her or someone else pain temporarily. Family was too important to risk living with regret, as Aunt Helen and Albert had done.

"I know this won't erase the unhappy memories of the past, but we wanted to give this to you." Albert took the brightly decorated Christmas gift bag that Sabrina handed to him, and he gave it to Aunt Helen.

Aunt Helen unwrapped the tissue paper inside and gasped as she saw the beautiful angel tree topper. "Oh, Albert. I can't tell you how much this means to me."

"We wanted you to have it in time for Christmas," Sabrina said. "And, I admit, I wanted a chance to talk sewing with you. The handiwork on that angel is exquisite."

"What do you like to sew?" Aunt Helen asked.

"I've done everything, although I love making costumes the best," Sabrina said. "I belong to a local theater group and I always love when we choose a period piece to perform because then I can let my creativity run wild when making the costumes. Victorian is my favorite time period."

Albert rolled his eyes good-naturedly at Beverly. "When Sabrina gets talking about sewing, there's no stopping her."

"I knew Aunt Helen did quilting, but I had no idea she'd done something so intricate as that angel dress," Beverly said. And Aunt Helen looked absolutely intrigued as she talked about costumes with Sabrina.

"Beverly!"

She turned to see Margaret heading toward her. "Hi, Margaret. This is my cousin, Albert Lemmon. Albert, this is my friend who owns the art gallery."

"Nice to meet you," he said, shaking her hand.

"So you're Beverly's cousin," Margaret said. "It's nice to meet you too. I'm so glad she was able to find you and reconnect after all these years."

"We're really glad too," he said.

"Aunt Helen came tonight, so I was able to get them together," Beverly said. "Aunt Helen's talking with Albert's wife about sewing right now."

"But I'm used to that," Albert said with a laugh. "It's what happens when you have artistic family members. And I have two of them."

"That's right, your daughter was an art major," Beverly said.

"Was she?" Margaret perked up. "What kind of art?"

"Painting mostly," Albert said. "But she's still wondering what she wants to do with her degree. I hope it's not an imposition, but do you think you'd be willing to talk to her?"

"Of course, I'd love to. Here's my card."

They exchanged cards and chatted for a little while as Beverly stood by and listened. She never really expected it to mean so much to her, but she was glad her friends got along with her relatives.

Then Albert turned to her with a sheepish grin. "Beverly, I'm sorry for monopolizing your friend."

"Oh, not at all," she said.

"I'll let you two talk," he said. "I'm going to get some coffee, since I don't think Sabrina's conversation will be over anytime soon."

"I'll see you both before you leave," Beverly said. "I have the information about the New Year's party at my house."

"Sure thing." He waved to them and headed to the train station building.

"I think the living Nativity went really well," Margaret said to Beverly. "Although maybe I should have tried to repair the freestanding donkey so we wouldn't have to use a real one."

Beverly chuckled. "I felt bad for Levi. That donkey gave him such a hard time!"

"I wonder if the real Mary and Joseph had to scold their donkey for waking up the baby."

Margaret and Beverly laughed at that, but then Margaret suddenly froze, her eyes caught by something she saw in the crowd. "Oh my goodness," she breathed.

"What is it?"

"I can't believe he came." Margaret waved her hand. "Shane!"

A tall, nice-looking young man in the crowd saw Margaret and waved back. He hurried toward her, followed by a young woman and a little boy about six years old.

He came up and took both of Margaret's hands in his, and his wide smile showed slightly crooked teeth. "Did I surprise you?"

"Did you ever! Why didn't you tell me you were coming to the living Nativity?"

"I wasn't sure if you'd be here, but I wanted to show my family the stable set." He put his arm around the young woman, who had long dark hair and a shy smile. "This is Marissa, and that's Anthony."

"It's so nice to meet you," Marissa said to Margaret, shaking her hand. "When Shane showed up at my parents' house in Canada, I was completely shocked. But then he told me about meeting you and what you'd done to encourage him when he was a young boy at the orphanage."

"I heard so much about you too," Margaret said warmly. "Shane told me he would be going to Canada to see you, but I had no idea he'd be back in Marble Cove so soon, or that I'd get a chance to meet you. This is my friend Beverly."

"Nice to meet you." Beverly shook hands with them, and with little Anthony too.

"Beverly, this is Shane, who made the stable set background," Margaret said. The original background they had found from the old living Nativity was falling apart, and Shane had volunteered his own time and made a new one in Allan's shop.

"I was glad to do it," Shane said. "And it was fortuitous, since I found out your husband had been the Santa Claus who gave me that Erector set all those years ago. I wouldn't have become an architect if not for him."

"The set is beautiful," Beverly said. "I'm so grateful for all the people who helped us put the living Nativity together. I've been blessed to be a part of it this year."

"You were a wonderful wise man, even with the donkey braying," Marissa said to Beverly.

"That donkey was funny," Anthony piped up, giggling.

"Would you like to see him?" Beverly asked. "Let's see if he's up for being petted. Although I don't know if he deserves it since he was so loud." Anthony giggled again, and Beverly looked to Marissa and Shane. "Is it all right if I take him to the donkey pen?"

"Of course. We'll be there in a minute," Shane said.

While they walked to the donkey pen, Anthony talked about how his dad got him a sailboat kit when he was in Marble Cove, and he let him open his present early and was helping him put the boat together. "But I don't want to be a sailor," Anthony said. "I want to build buildings like my dad."

Ironically, the donkey seemed to be enjoying all the attention it was getting in its pen. Maybe it had been so vociferously complaining during the Nativity because it had wanted to be the center of attention. It stood patiently while children petted him, and seemed almost to be grinning.

Levi was holding on to the donkey's reins and supervising the animal while the children petted him. "You did a good job today," Beverly told him.

He groaned. "Dr. Spangler will have words with me later. I was supposed to keep the donkey in line."

"Well, there are some things that can't be helped. I doubt Leo will blame you."

"Well . . ." The young man's eyes were focused on a point in the crowd around the donkey. "You might be right, but I think it's only because he's distracted."

Beverly followed his gaze and spotted Diane standing there. But before she could call out to her, she noticed that Leo was standing next to her. The two of them were chatting, then Leo slipped his arm around Diane's waist and pressed a kiss to her forehead.

Beverly felt a little bubble of joy in her chest. Diane and Leo's relationship had started out when Diane had found her dog Rocky and taken him to the vet for treatment. They'd been only friends for the past three years, but now their relationship was starting to progress to a bit more than that.

This living Nativity had seemed to be the central location for so many connections and reconnections this Christmas—her aunt Helen and cousin Albert, Margaret and Allan with Shane, Shelley, and her parents and stepparents. And it had all been because of Diane spearheading this event. In some ways, the living Nativity had been a way for Diane to reconnect with her mother's memory too.

Beverly couldn't wait for what the new year would hold for her and her friends.

CHAPTER TWELVE

The next day, Albert's son, Albert Jr., showed up at Beverly's doorstep at exactly 12:05 p.m. with a moving truck that had the logo New Beginnings Movers on the side.

Albert Jr. looked exactly like Sabrina, with her friendly smile and dark hair, but he had his father's height. "Hi, Beverly." He shook her hand. "I'm Al."

"This is my husband Jeff."

The two men shook hands, and Al introduced the man who'd come with him, Ollie. "Thanks a bunch for hiring us," Al said. "We didn't have any work this close to Christmas anyway."

"I was a little worried," Beverly said. "Lots of people would rather not have to work the day before Christmas."

"Well, a lot of the guys I hire have family far away, or they don't have family at all," Al said. "I tend to spend Christmas Eve and Christmas Day with them anyway, so it's nice to have a job to do."

"We wondered if you'd be able to do a small side job for us too," Jeff said. "We have a piano in the house now that we'd like to move to Beverly's father's house across the street."

"No problem," Al said cheerfully.

Al and Ollie were quite experienced, because they sized up Beverly's piano in a glance and were able to figure out the best way to move it.

They transferred the piano onto a couple dollies from their van to make it easier to move it over the icy street.

Beverly went to her father's house to warn him about the anticipated commotion. She found him in his library, reading a cozy mystery. "Father, the movers are here. They'll be moving the piano into the living room in a few minutes."

"What?" His eyes were confused. "Movers? Piano?"

"Remember? I told you yesterday that I was getting Grandmother Harkness's piano from my cousin Albert, so we're moving your old piano back into the house."

"Oh, that's right. I forgot," her father said. "Will they be very loud?"

"I don't think so. Oh, they're here," she said as she heard the doorbell ring. She went to open it.

Al and Ollie carefully transported the piano into her father's living room to the spot where it had sat before Beverly married and moved to their new home. The space had been looking forlorn and empty, and now it seemed complete again.

Her father had come to stand in the doorway to the living room to watch the proceedings. "I miss your mother's piano," he said, "the one I bought for her all those years ago."

"I do too," Beverly said to him. "But now I'll have the next best thing—Grandmother Harkness's piano."

"True." Her father's face brightened. "That's the one your mother learned to play on."

Her father ended up following her across the street with the movers and watching as they took a large box from the back of the moving truck. They unwrapped the thick cardboard and layers of bubble wrap and plastic to reveal the teakwood upright piano.

As they were unwrapping the piano, Beverly's friends wandered from their homes to watch the proceedings. "Is that your grandmother's piano?" Diane asked her.

Beverly nodded. "I can't believe I'll have it to sing Christmas carols on."

"I'll be looking forward to that," Shelley said.

"It's beautiful," Margaret said, admiring the teakwood. "I'll have to bring Allan over to see it."

With utmost care, Al and Ollie rolled the piano to Beverly's front door, then lifted it from the dollies. The two men carried it into Beverly's living room and set it gently where the old piano had sat. They did some small adjustments to make sure it sat at the right distance from the wall. Then they returned to the truck to get the piano bench, which was also well wrapped in plastic. They had removed the legs for transport, and now rescrewed the legs back on before setting the bench in front of the piano.

Beverly just stared at that lovely piano, softly lit from the winter light filtering through the wide bay window. She could smell the teakwood oil from the wood, and it brought back a wisp of memory of her grandmother's house.

"Thank you so much," she told Al and Ollie. "This piano is something I never thought I'd see here in my house."

"That's what I love about this job," Al said. "That look when people have a new space, or when they finally have their beloved treasures in their homes."

"And just in time for Christmas," Ollie said.

"I remember all the Christmas carols your mother and your grandmother played," her father said as he looked at the piano. "Too bad there's that painting on the wall, or you could have hung a wreath above the piano, like your grandmother did in her house."

"My dad said there's a surprise for you in the piano bench," Al added with a grin.

Beverly opened the hinge on the piano bench and saw the music book that had the piano piece she'd been hearing in her head since she found the wreath. She picked it up with a glad cry.

"I remember that book," Al said. "Oh man, I hated piano lessons. That book became the bane of my existence."

Beverly laughed. "It might have been a bane for you, but it has a beautiful piano piece from when your dad and I were younger. He helped me to figure out it was in this book. It's a piece with a lot of good memories attached to it."

Jeff paid them for moving both pianos, with a generous tip, and they waved to the two men as they drove off in the moving truck.

Diane tucked her arm in Beverly's. "Let's hear the piano."

"Oh," Beverly said suddenly, "I completely forgot. It probably needs to be tuned first. It had been tuned at Albert's place, but moving a piano always puts it out of tune. I'll have to call our piano tuner after Christmas."

"Aw, no Christmas carols?" Shelley asked.

"If you wait about five minutes," Jeff said, looking at his watch, "you might get another Christmas surprise."

"Huh?" Beverly asked.

"When I talked to Albert yesterday about moving the piano, he mentioned that it would need to be tuned, so I called your piano tuner yesterday," Jeff said with a smile. "After hearing about how special this piano was for you, he agreed to come today to tune it for you."

Beverly gave a joyous cry and embraced him. "You're the best!"

Jeff had scheduled for the tuner to arrive around one o'clock, but he arrived a little early. He admired the lovely Knight piano and said he'd have it tuned in about an hour. While waiting, Jeff went across the street with her father to play a game of chess with him while Beverly made tea for her friends. Shelley ran to her house to bring over some extra Christmas cookies from the batch she'd made that morning.

Margaret also disappeared, only to come back with a gigantic Christmas gift bag. "For you," she said, giving it to Beverly.

Inside was an artificial wreath, and attached were the shell ornaments that had been on the old wreath. Margaret had decorated the wreath with some gold wire ribbon and small gold ornament balls, but the highlight was the handmade shell ornaments in the shape of musical instruments.

"Oh, Margaret." Beverly's eyes filled with tears as she hugged her friend. "It's so beautiful. Thank you."

"Thank Adelaide," Margaret said. "She did a great job getting the glue off the ornaments, and she also replaced some of the shells that were missing."

"I wonder if these really were my mother's ornaments." Beverly fingered the saxophone ornament. "I had contacted Albert in hopes of finding out, but now I don't think I'll ever know."

"It seemed strange that you happened to find it on the beach," Shelley said. "But after the month we've had, each of us receiving strange Christmas gifts, maybe we shouldn't be surprised."

"I don't think it really matters if it's your mother's wreath or not," Diane said, "because what really matters is that it enabled you to reconnect with your stepcousin."

"And get your grandmother's piano," Margaret said.

Beverly nodded. "I've not only gotten my cousin back, but I feel like my mother and grandmother are closer to me now."

They ate cookies and drank tea in the living room while discussing the living Nativity and how well it had gone, despite everything that had seemed to conspire to prevent it from happening. In the background was the sound of the piano being tuned.

Finally, her tuner came into the dining room. "It's all done, Mrs. Mackenzie," he said to Beverly.

"How much do I owe you?"

"Oh, your husband already paid me in advance," the tuner said. "Gave me a nice tip too. Merry Christmas!"

Beverly sent him home with some of Shelley's cookies, and then the friends gathered around the piano. Beverly smoothed her hand over the cover before lifting it from the white and black keys.

"Let's hear that piano piece you've been talking about all week," Diane said. "I'm curious to know what it is."

Beverly set up the piano book that Albert had given to her, and played Sonatina op. 36, no. 1 by Clementi. The simple, sprightly tune sounded full and rich coming from the teakwood piano, echoing in her living room.

"That's so pretty," Shelley said.

"Now play some Christmas carols," Margaret begged her.

Beverly played one of her grandmother's favorite carols, "Silent Night," and the sound coming from this same piano made tears sting her eyes. Then Beverly played "Hark, the Herald Angels Sing" and finally "Joy to the World" in honor of the living Nativity.

"I have an idea," Beverly said. "Let's walk to the lighthouse."

Her friends agreed, and went to their respective homes to get warmer jackets, mittens, and hats to battle the brisk ocean breezes.

"What's that?" Shelley asked when Beverly met her on the sidewalk, holding a large tote bag.

"It's a last-minute Christmas decoration," Beverly said.

Shelley peeked inside the bag, then grinned. "I think that's perfect."

There weren't many people walking along the beach on Christmas Eve, plus the cold weather kept most dog-walkers closer to home, so the four friends had the boardwalk almost entirely to themselves. As they drew near the lighthouse, Beverly asked, "Do you remember the first time we each saw the light from the lighthouse?"

"I saw it first when I found my dog Rocky," Diane said.

"We all saw the light when we rescued that swimmer," Margaret said.

"It was so mysterious to see a light when the lighthouse was decommissioned," Shelley said, "but we knew that even though it was unexplainable, we were meant to see that light and help that swimmer."

"In many ways, the lighthouse brought us all together," Beverly said. "I was living and working in Augusta and only coming home on weekends, so I didn't know my father's neighbors very well, but our shared experiences bonded us as friends, even though we're all so different."

They had reached the lighthouse and now stood looking up at it. It was situated on a high bluff overlooking the ocean, and the waves roared below them and the wind tugged at the ends of their scarves. A pretty winter sun shone through a break in the clouds, lighting up the site exterior and making the red-tile roof the color of vermillion. Since it was declared a historical landmark, the city of Marble Cove had been keeping it in better shape than it had been when Beverly first saw it—instead of the green moss over the stone base, it was now freshly painted. The bricked-up windows had been restored and strung with tiny Christmas garlands inside. There was a small sign on a hook on the door that gave the hours the little gift shop inside was open.

Beverly opened her tote bag and removed the wreath that Margaret had made for her, as well as a roll of fishing line and a pair of scissors. With Diane's help, she strung the line on the wreath and they hung it on the hook on the lighthouse door. It was a lovely green, gold, and white focal point for any visitor walking on the boardwalk toward the lighthouse.

Beverly touched each of the five shell ornaments on the wreath. *Mother,* she thought, *I've found a good place to call home and good friends to share it with. This is the lighthouse that brought us all together.*

As she stepped back to look at the lighthouse again, Shelley said, "Merry Christmas, everyone!"

"Merry Christmas!" They all formed a four-way group hug.

"Let's head back to my house for hot chocolate," Shelley said.

"Sounds good to me," Margaret said.

"This has been such a memorable Christmas for all of us," Diane said.

However, just as Beverly turned away from the lighthouse, she thought she saw a flash out of the corner of her eye, from the top of the lighthouse. She whirled around.

So did Diane, Shelley, and Margaret.

"Did you see that?" Shelley asked.

"I thought I saw a light," Diane said.

"Me too," Margaret said.

Beverly smiled. "It was as if the lighthouse wanted to participate in the group hug."

Everyone laughed, but somehow it just felt right that the lighthouse would share this moment with the four of them. Beverly knew that none of them could imagine Marble Cove without this lighthouse, and without one another. As they all returned home, she said a silent prayer of thanks for her dear friends and for the miracle of another unforgettable Christmas together.

About the Authors

Award-winning author Sunni Jeffers began writing books when her children grew up and left home. Her first book came out in 2001. She has written many books for Guideposts, including some for the series Miracles of Marble Cove. Sixteen books later, Sunni is on a new adventure as she and her husband explore the United States and Canada in their motor home. As they travel, she continues writing cozy mysteries, romance, suspense, and heartwarming stories of women living out their faith as they face challenges and adventures in everyday life.

Camy Tang has written for Guideposts and Love Inspired Suspense under her own name and has authored Regency romances as *USA Today* best-selling author Camille Elliot. She grew up in Hawaii but now lives in northern California with her engineer-husband and rambunctious dog. She's a staff worker for her church youth group and leads one of the Sunday worship teams. She also loves anime/manga and knitting, and is learning Japanese. Visit camytang.com and camilleelliot.com to read free short stories and subscribe to her quarterly newsletter.

A Note from the Editors

We hope you enjoyed Christmas Miracles of Marble Cove, published by the Books and Inspirational Media Division of Guideposts, a nonprofit organization that touches millions of lives every day through products and services that inspire, encourage, help you grow in your faith, and celebrate God's love.

Thank you for making a difference with your purchase of this book, which helps fund our many outreach programs to military personnel, prisons, hospitals, nursing homes, and educational institutions.

We also create many useful and uplifting online resources. Visit Guideposts.org to read true stories of hope and inspiration, access OurPrayer network, sign up for free newsletters, download free e-books, join our Facebook community, and follow our stimulating blogs.

To learn about other Guideposts publications, including the best-selling devotional *Daily Guideposts*, go to Guideposts.org/Shop, call (800) 932-2145, or write to Guideposts, PO Box 5815, Harlan, Iowa 51593.

Discover More Miracles of Marble Cove!

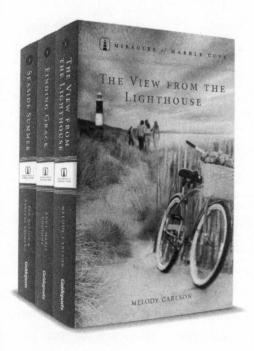

If you enjoyed these delightful Christmas stories, then check out the series *Miracles of Marble Cove*. Return to the quaint seaside town of Marble Cove, Maine, and discover how shared secrets bring four very different women together in an unbreakable bond of friendship.

Join them in their adventures as they delve into the mysteries and miracles of Marble Cove and uncover God's plan for their lives.

Sign up for the Guideposts Fiction Newsletter

and stay up-to-date on the fiction you love!

You'll get sneak peeks of new releases, recommendations from other Guideposts readers, and special offers just for you . . .

And it's FREE!

Just go to Guideposts.org/Newsletters today to sign up.

Guideposts Visit Guideposts.org/Shop
or call (800) 932-2145